THE DAR

Christina Koning was born
Borneo, and spent her early childhood in Venezuela
and Jamaica. She reviews fiction for The Times and
has taught creative writing courses at the University
of Oxford and Birkbeck, University of London. Her
first novel, A Mild Suicide, was published by Lime
Tree in 1992. Her most recent novel is Fabulous Time
(Viking), which won a Society of Authors Traveling
Scholarship; her second novel, Undiscovered
Country (Penguin), won the Encore Award for fiction
and was long-listed for the Orange Prize.

ARBUTHNOT BOOKS

The Dark Tower

CHRISTINA KONING

ARBUTHNOT BOOKS

ARBUTHNOT BOOKS

Published by Arbuthnot Books

ISBN 978-0-9565214-0-8

Cover illustration © Christina Koning
Author photograph © Eamonn Vincent

www.arbuthnot-books.com

For Roger

Burningly it came on me all at once,
This was the place! Those two hills on the right,
Crouched like two bulls locked horn in horn in fight;
While to the left, a tall scalped mountain...

'Childe Roland to the Dark Tower Came' (from *Men and Women*, by Robert Browning, 1855)

Towards morning a strange thing happened. Although there was not a breath of air, the flames of the candles were suddenly deflected, as if some one wished to extinguish them, and I said to him, 'Is it indeed you beside me?'
(Journal entry by the Empress Eugenie, Isandhlwana, March 1880)

'Those guns, man, don't you see those guns? I tell you, the brave fellows will be mowed down like grass...'
(Last words of Archibald Forbes, *Daily News* journalist during the Zulu wars, March 1900).

Rejoice, October 1899: London

Miss Brooke was upset, because Miss Dora had come in late, after having supper with Mr Jack. Miss Brooke said that it couldn't go on, and that Mr Jack wasn't the right kind of man for Miss Dora.

Then Miss Dora flew into a passion and said what did Miss Brooke know of men, and didn't she know that Jack's father was a marquess?

Miss Brooke said nothing to that, but just went on looking at Miss Dora, and then Miss Dora started to cry and ran out of the room, saying that she would never marry, never—because who would want to marry a half-caste?

Then Miss Brooke sighed, and shook her head, and went upstairs to Miss Dora's room. She stood for a time on the landing, calling to Miss Dora to let her in. But Miss Dora only shouted at her to go away.

When she saw that it was no use, Miss Brooke went to bed, telling Rejoice not to forget to lock up, which she did not.

Then as Rejoice was coming back upstairs, she heard Miss Dora call out to her, and so Rejoice went into Miss Dora's room and sat upon the bed.

And then Miss Dora cried and cried, and said she was a horrid beast, but really it was too cruel, to love someone as much as she loved Jack, and then to be told that you were never to see him again. And Rejoice stroked her hair and said, 'Never mind, baby, never mind.'

Because there was nothing more to be said on this or any of it.

In the morning, Miss Brooke was late coming downstairs, and so the boy had already brought the newspaper. And when she unfolded it and saw what was written there, she put her hand up to her throat, as if something choked her.

'Those poor boys,' she said. 'Those poor boys.'

And Rejoice knew that she meant the soldiers who were going to Africa to fight the Boers.

'Have they learned nothing, in twenty years?' said Miss Brooke. It was not the soldiers she meant this time, Rejoice knew, but the government.

Then for a long time Miss Brooke said nothing, but went on turning and turning the diamond ring around on her finger, and staring at the black-and-white columns of type with the words in bolder, blacker type above them.

And it seemed to Rejoice that Miss Brooke had forgotten she was there. Or that maybe her spirit had gone out of her, and was wandering around in another place. Rejoice thought that the place must be Africa.

After a while, Rejoice said should she wake Miss Dora? Because it was getting late, and Alice would be wanting to clear the breakfast things.

And then Miss Brooke gave a little laugh, and said, 'No, let her sleep, poor darling. When I was her age, I could always sleep. It's one of the things you lose, as you get older. Being able to sleep,' she said.

Chapter 1

Laura, July 1879: Oxfordshire

When she heard the cry from the hall, she was, in a sense, prepared—having read the report in the Times the previous day. But nothing could have prepared her for the way she felt then, or was to feel in the hours and days that followed. She had never been struck; but it felt as if she had received a blow to the stomach. She had never been hurt; but it was as if she herself had suffered a mortal wound. Had she been older, or the mother of sons, she might have been familiar with such shocks.

From the moment when she heard the crunch of the gravel under the messenger's foot, to the moment when Mrs Reynolds screamed, can have been no more than a minute. She was already out of her seat, the work fallen from her lap, when the sound came; a confirmation of her own worst fears. She had crossed the room at a run; flung open the door upon the terrible scene. Mrs Reynolds, pale as death, collapsed on the stairs, with the telegram in her hand; Lily raising a tear-streaked face.

'Oh, Miss…'

Even then, knowing the worst had happened, she had done what she had to do; going straight to the fainting woman's side, and sending the servant for sal volatile. The telegram had fallen from Mrs Reynolds' limp fingers. Laura had not permitted herself to read it; although no one would have reproached her, had she done so.

To have seen the words would have been, in any case, superfluous.

So she had averted her eyes from the terrible thing, as she sat there on the stairs, directing her mind instead towards what was most pressing. This was to restore the unconscious woman to her senses—a cruelty, but it had to be done. Seeing the papery closed eyelids flicker, then open; feeling the weight of the older woman's body against hers; smelling the sourish odour arising from beneath the arms of the latter's heavy woollen dress—a smell not quite overlaid by the scent of lavender soap—was more than enough to fill the moment.

And yet all the time she was aware of it—that little slip of buff-coloured paper—lying there on the black-and-white tiles with its freight of despair.

There was a good deal more to do—sending Lily for water; calling for John to come and assist her in getting Mrs Reynolds upstairs; writing a note to the doctor for John to take—before she could think of herself. She picked up the telegram from where it had fallen only after Doctor McKendrick's arrival, and put it on the hall table.

As she did this, she was faced with her image in the looking-glass, and did not known herself for a moment: the fresh colour entirely drained from her face, so that it resembled that of an old woman—or a corpse, she thought. Her hand flew up to touch the locket at her throat, and, for an instant, she felt the choking sensation that was the prelude to tears.

But she did not weep; not then.

Only when she was alone at last—after the doctor had gone, and Mrs Reynolds was asleep—did the realisation of what had happened overwhelm her. Standing there in the now-deserted hall, she felt her legs give way beneath her, so that she was obliged to cling to the banister to keep from falling.

She had climbed the stairs, thinking she would go to her room—although what she would do when she got there she did not know. But when she reached the landing, she turned not in the direction of her room, but towards his. She knew which one it was, even though she had never set foot there.

It did not have the smell of a room left long unused. The bed was made up, and the fire laid, as if in readiness for a homecoming. She stood for a moment on the threshold. To cross it seemed a kind of transgression—yet who, now, would reproach her for entering that place?

It was a plainly furnished apartment: the bed, a chest of drawers, a wardrobe, a chair, a desk, were the only things in it—all of them of the same old-fashioned design as in the rest of the house.

There was a view of the park from the two tall windows, through which a cold light came filtering. So he must once have stood, looking out, as she was looking out, at the wet green lawns and the dripping trees, on which a few blackened leaves still shivered in the icy wind.

Her mind was as blank as the sky. He is dead, was all she could think.

She had never been much of a reader of newspapers; now she cared to read little else. Where it had once been her father who drew her attention to this paragraph in the Times or that, now it was she who read the reports aloud to him: the appalling defeats at Ntombi River and Hlobane Mountain, of which the news had reached them in March, and which threatened to eclipse news of the heroic defence of Rorke's Drift; the victories at Khambula and Gingindlovu, and the relief of Eshowe.

In May, almost five months after that terrible battle, had come reports of the burial of the dead at Isandhlwana: these she had had to force herself to read. The thought of those poor broken bodies being left for so long at the mercy of the elements was hideous; worse was the knowledge that Theo's corpse had been among them.

Now, at least, he and all his dead comrades had been laid to rest: 'embraced by the stony soil of a far-distant land, of which their blood and bone is now evermore a part, and of whose history their noble deeds will remain the chief glory', as the writer of one such article put it. She was grateful to this unknown scribe, identified only as 'S.D.', for the sentiment, however floridly expressed.

Seeing it in black-and-white made what had happened seem both more real and more unreal—as if it were the stuff of fiction, not of life. Unpalatable facts had been omitted, she supposed; discrepancies smoothed out. What remained was a story for reading aloud at the breakfast table; a page to be clipped from the newspaper, and pasted into a scrap-book, with other memorabilia— letters, photographs, a pressed flower.

Theodore Charles Reynolds, who died at Isandhlwana on

22nd January 1879, was the second son of the late Colonel Frederick Charles Reynolds, of Hartwood Manor, Shropshire, by his marriage with Emiline Esther, daughter of the late Sir Henry Thomas Godfrey K.C.B. (Peninsula, Waterloo) of the 3rd regiment (the Buffs). He was born on 12th August 1854, and was educated at Rugby and Oxford. In 1875 he obtained a commission in the Royal Surrey Militia, exchanging into the 2nd battalion of the 24th Foot in 1877. He proceeded with that corps to the Cape, serving throughout the Kaffir war of 1878, before proceeding with the 24th to Natal to join the force being prepared to act against the Zulus in the event of their refusing to comply with the terms of Sir Bartle Frere's ultimatum. He took part with that regiment in the subsequent advance of Colonel Glyn's column into the enemy's country in January 1879; and was present at the storming of Sirayo's stronghold in the Bashee Valley.

On the fatal 22nd January, the day on which he met with his death, Second Lieutenant Reynolds wrote the following in his diary—which, kept up to the very hour of his death, speaks for his cool self-possession: 'At 4pm N.N.C. mounted troops and 4 guns off. Great firing—believed to be by 1/24th. Alarm sounded. Three columns Zulus and mounted men on the hill, E. Turn out! 7,000 men E.N.E., 4,000 of whom go round Lion's Kop. Durnford's Basutos arrive and pursue with rocket battery. Zulus retire everywhere. Men fall out for dinner.'

And while the men fell out for dinner, the right horn of the Zulu army, 7,000 strong, crept around the Kop, and the 'three columns' swarmed down the face of it. Another officer, who escaped the massacre, wrote the following in a private letter to his father: 'The men were laughing and chatting, and thought they were giving the blacks an awful hammering, when suddenly the enemy came down in irresistible numbers from the rear; the left and right flanks came in with a rush, and in a few moments all was over.'

Second Lieutenant Reynolds fell whilst in the thick of the fighting; an assegai entered his breast. He succeeded in pulling it out, but later died of his wound, and lies buried where he fell, along with other gallant officers and men who lost their lives in that fateful encounter.

Second Lieutenant Reynolds was, in the opinion of all who knew him, a most promising young officer. 'He was beloved by all,' wrote one of his comrades; 'and was as gallant an officer as ever fought: in him the regiment has lost one of its brightest hopes.' By others, besides the sadly diminished roll of his comrades, his loss is keenly felt and deeply deplored.

In June, there had been the news of the death of the Prince Imperial—surprised by a war party of Zulus while on reconnaissance. He, too, it was said, had died a hero's death: the spears that had slain him having entered his breast, as he faced the foe...

A message of condolence was sent from the parish to the Empress Eugenie. '*Mon pauvre fils, seulement 23 ans!*' she was said to have exclaimed, on receiving news of the Prince's death. When the body was brought home for burial, enormous crowds waited in silence on the quayside at Woolwich.

Laura was sorry for the poor exiled Empress, now alone in her Chislehurst mansion. She had not wanted her son to go to Africa, it was said—but, with the impetuosity of youth, he had insisted.

When news of the victory at Ulundi came in July, Laura's father ordered the church bells to be rung. 'It was not in vain, the sacrifice,' he said, and she knew she should take comfort from that. Those who had slain Theo and so many of his comrades were now humbled in the dust; their king, Cetshwayo, forced to sue for mercy from his prison cell.

And yet it was a matter of indifference to her: she was as impervious to the nation's rejoicing as to its grief. All that mattered lay buried with her beloved, in a stony field far away. All this talk of honour and glory would not bring him back, nor any of those who had died with him.

She had written, twice, to Mrs Reynolds, in the weeks after Theo's death, but there had been no reply. Hartwood Manor was closed up; its windows shuttered and all but a few of its servants dismissed. When she called by, she had been told that the mistress was gone up to London, to stay with Mr Fred.

Life settled back into what it had been before—or at least, into a simulacrum of that state. No one observing Laura during this time would have known that anything untoward had happened. She was quiet—but then, she had always been quiet.

Bessie was the only one in the family prone to chattering, and even she had grown thoughtful of late, perhaps as a consequence of having turned eighteen. Bob's return from Oxford that summer might also have had something to do with this. For Bob had been accompanied by his friend Harold, a fellow theology student. Harold was handsome, a head taller than Bessie, and his father was a bishop.

Bob's return—and latterly, Teddy's, from school—provided diversions of a different kind for Laura. Bob's library, lately removed from its Balliol home, needed cataloguing and re-shelving. Teddy, who seemed to have had grown several inches since she had last set eyes on him, needed every item of clothing he possessed altered accordingly.

Nor were the demands Laura's father made upon her time diminishing. 'I do not know,' he had fallen into the habit of saying, 'how I would ever have managed without you, my dear...'. Laura knew that it was so; and that it was meant to be some consolation to her for everything that she had lost; yet she could not but wish that he had had less occasion to say it.

Sundays—at least, the hours between Matins and Evensong—were necessarily idle, and therefore offered fewer distractions from darker thoughts. The nights were also bad; then she had nothing to stop her thinking about Theo. The smallest details—a fragment of conversation or a remembered glance—rose up out of nothing to torment her.

That night in the garden. His hands trembling as he'd lit his cigarette. What a beast I am... No, she would not think of it, she would not.

Their conversation in the library, that first Christmas. Yes, that was better...

He had been reading the Idylls, he said.

'So all day long the noise of battle rolled against the mountains, by the shining sea... Like a kettle-drum, do you see? I call

that splendid, don't you?'

'It is certainly very stirring.'

'You are laughing at me, and that is not kind of you, Miss Brooke. I had hoped for much greater enthusiasm.'

'I can see that I must endeavour to improve...'

'No, no. You are perfection itself.'

'Now it is you who is laughing at me,' she said.

'I assure you, I am quite serious,' said Theo, with a look that made her catch her breath.

Yes, that was better, she thought. Since she could not stop thinking about him, she could at least choose what thoughts to have...

In the drawing-room there had been a fall of soot; a bird in the chimney, she guessed. She was reaching for the bell to summon Alice, when her eye fell on the book. Thoughtlessly set down, months ago, it had been put back in the wrong place. She pulled it from the shelf, feeling its familiar weight in her hand. It fell open at once at the place she had left off reading. '*The stars,"she whispers," blindly run; A web is wov'n across the sky: From our waste places comes a cry And murmurs from the dying sun...*'

This had been a present from Theo—'to persuade you of the superiority of the great Lord Alfred,' he had said, when he gave it to her; although she had not needed persuading. Now she could not read a line without wanting to weep.

She was standing with the book open in her hand, when she heard the carriage draw up in the lane. There came the crunch of gravel as the visitor walked up to the house; then the sound of the doorbell, followed by that of hurried footsteps—she must tell Alice not to run—and the murmur of voices.

'Gentleman to see you, Miss,' said Alice.

'Tell him the vicar's not at home. He may wait, if he wishes...'

'He says it's you he wants to speak to particular, Miss,' said Alice, with a stubborn lift of the chin.

'Did the gentleman give his name?'

'Yes, Miss. It's Reynolds, Miss.'

'But that cannot be,' she said; then realized her mistake. 'Yes.

Thank you, Alice. Ask him to come in.'

A moment later, Frederick Reynolds walked into the room.

'Miss Brooke,' he said. 'My apologies.' His tone of voice was anything but apologetic, however. 'I would have written,' he went on. 'But it seemed expedient to come in person.'

A dreadful thought struck her.

'Is it about Mrs Reynolds?'

'Has she written to you?'

'Why, no.'

'Ah,' said Frederick Reynolds.

'Her illness is not worse, I hope?'

He shook his head. 'No. Not worse. Indeed,' he went on, 'my mother's improvement these past few weeks has been remarkable. Remarkable,' he repeated.

'Thank God,' said Laura.

'Aye, thank Him by all means,' said Frederick Reynolds, with what seemed a certain irony. 'My mother speaks of you often, Miss Brooke. Indeed, she speaks of little else. You are quite a favourite, you understand...'

'Oh.' She was at a loss as to how to reply. 'I am very fond of her,' she said.

'I believe you are,' he said. 'Well, you may have a chance to prove it...'

'I don't understand.'

Her visitor sighed. 'I don't suppose you do.'

When she said nothing, he continued:

'My mother has got it into her head that she wishes to go to Africa. Her intention is to visit my brother's grave. It has become an *idée fixe* with her. One might almost call it an obsession, Miss Brooke.'

'I see,' said Laura.

'Do you?' he replied, throwing her a sharp look. 'Perhaps you do. It seems a strange notion to me. Firstly, because my brother is dead; therefore, what earthly difference can it make to him? Secondly, because, to the best of my knowledge, there is no grave to visit.'

She had not thought to ask him to sit down; now she became conscious of this omission.

10

'Please,' she said, gesturing towards a chair.

'Oh, I won't stay long, Miss Brooke. My wife expects me. I will just say what I have come to say...'

She bowed her head.

'I have, as you might imagine, tried my utmost to dissuade my mother from what I feel—from what we both feel, my wife and I—to be a foolish and ill-considered scheme.' Frederick Reynolds gave a short, un-amused laugh. 'But my mother, if you will forgive the expression, will not be 'budged' on this. She will go to Africa. More than this, Miss Brooke,' he said, directing another of his penetrating looks at her, 'she will take you with her. There!' He smiled. 'Did I not tell you that it was a foolish scheme?'

She was silent for so long that, as he later said to his wife, he wondered if she had heard him—standing, still as a marble image, in her dark dress; her face, which until then he had thought unremarkable, quite beautiful in its momentary abstraction.

'When does she wish to go?' said Laura at last.

He gave an impatient shrug. 'I really cannot say. At once, I suppose. Is it of any consequence?'

She said nothing for a moment, but held his gaze. As cool as you like, he said afterwards to Laetitia.

'It is, if I am to accompany her,' she said at last.

He stared at her.

'Miss Brooke, you cannot—surely—be thinking of agreeing to my mother's plan? I have already said that I consider the idea quite out of the question. For a woman in frail health, as my mother is, to make such a journey...'

'She would not be alone,' Laura replied. 'And you said yourself that her health is much improved.'

There was nothing he disliked so much as having his own words flung back in his face.

'I did not say that she is as she was before her illness,' he said coldly. 'She is not a young woman. That is the fact of it. Even for someone half her age, the journey would be arduous. For someone of her years, and in poor health, too, to even consider such a plan is, in my view, little short of madness...'

'It is surely for Mrs Reynolds to decide,' said Laura. There was a steeliness about her of which he had been previously unaware.

11

'Please tell her that I am at her disposal—subject to my father's agreement, of course.'

'I feel sure that your father will think as I do in this matter.'

'You forget,' said Laura calmly. 'My father also knows what it is to lose a loved one.'

She was in the garden, picking peas, when a shadow fell across the path.

'There you are, my dear,' said her father, taking the colander from her hands. For a while they worked in silence, dropping the pods in handfuls into the enamel bowl. It was a job Laura liked: the snap as integument separated from stem was pleasing, as was the scent of peas-blossom—scarlet flowers coming again on the vine where the fruit had been harvested.

It was not unusual for the Reverend Brooke to join her as she worked; although he generally preferred to sit in the shade of the plum-tree and watch her as she went about her tasks, sometimes reading out passages from a sermon he was working on, for her to comment upon.

This was Laura's favourite time: late afternoon in midsummer, with hours still to go before dark. A slight chill was in the air, underlying the warmth of the sunshine. In the long beds, wallflowers blazed like heatless fires. From the plum-tree overhead, a blackbird called, its notes cool and liquid.

Her father drew his thumbnail along the length of the pod he had just picked, revealing the glistening green spheres within. 'I have received a letter from Mr Reynolds,' he said. Absent-mindedly, he began to eat the fresh-picked peas, one by one.

Laura paused a moment, before continuing with what she was doing. Higher up, the plants were heavier-laden, their burden of pods half-concealed by leaves and flowers. She had to stretch in order to reach them; if she did not, the birds would get them.

'He is concerned about his mother,' the Reverend Brooke went on. 'Her state of health is not good, he tells me...'

'Her state of health is no worse than it was before,' said Laura. 'He does not want her to go to Africa, that is all.'

'I was coming to that, my dear,' said her father, with an expression of mild reproof. 'I gather, then, that you already know of this plan?'

'Only from Mr Reynolds,' she said.

'I see.' He allowed a pause to elapse. 'And when was this?'

Laura felt her face grow hot. 'Last Sunday. He called while you were at church.'

The Reverend Brooke was silent once more. When he spoke at last, it was with an air of perplexity. 'I think, my dear, that you might have mentioned it.'

It was as near to a rebuke as he would ever get. She felt the sting of it, and hung her head.

'Mr Reynolds does not wish his mother, whether in good health or not, to go to Africa,' her father continued. 'Nor do I wish you to go. Does that seem so very unreasonable?'

'No, Father.'

'Good.' He smiled at her. 'Well, then...' He turned to go.

'She has lost her son,' said Laura, astonished at her own temerity. 'That is why she feels that she must go.'

'My dear. I really feel...'

She chose her words with care.

'I was a widow, before I was ever a wife. What she has lost, I have also lost. If she asks this of me, how can I refuse her?'

There was a letter, by the morning's post. She knew the hand straight away.

Eaton Square
15th July 1879

My dearest Laura

The swiftness of your answer delights, but does not surprise, me. My darling Theodore always used to say that you were a young woman who knew her own mind. That you intend to join me in this adventure—and it will be an adventure, of that I feel sure—strikes me as entirely appropriate. Dearest Theodore could not have wished for two more devoted mourners to bear witness to his last resting-place.

If you are agreeable, my idea is that we should leave for Africa in six weeks' time, in order to arrive in early September (we shall be three weeks at sea!), when I understand that the weather in the Cape will be better than it is at present, it being their winter, and very wet, by all accounts.

But I will write again when the arrangements have been made. All that remains is for me to add my heartfelt thanks—for as you know, this plan of mine could not be enacted without you.

I am, your devoted Mother (for as such I have long regarded you, dear child),

Emiline E Reynolds

Frederick Reynolds was unceasing in his efforts to point out the folly of his mother's plan. True, the Zulu army had been crushed, its warrior impis scattered—but there remained pockets of resistance. Someone in the know had said something to a chap at his club, who'd passed it on to him, about the conflict being certain to last ten years. Here was a leading article in the Times, in which the South African situation was described as 'contained': 'Contained'—but not completely secure.

'There is a difference, you'll agree,' he said to his mother, with the unfortunate note of triumph he was wont to adopt in arguments of this kind.

To Laura he did not speak. Since their conversation of a few weeks past, he had behaved as if she did not exist. Now, as she stood there, folding clothes into a box, she might have been a piece of the furniture, so resolutely did he seem not to register her presence.

'Contained' seems to me to do very well,' Mrs Reynolds said. 'Better, certainly, than 'uncontained'.'

He did not smile at that.

'It means that things are still unsettled there,' he said. 'Volatile, and far from safe...'

'Dear Fred.' Her drawn features softened into a smile. 'You are anxious, I know. But pray do not be. No one is going to be interested in an old woman like me. I am of no use to anyone. And I will have dear Laura with me, of course...'

Frederick Reynolds frowned.

'I had not thought you a fool, Mother,' he said. 'But you must see that this is a foolish enterprise.'

She bowed her head.

'I have never pretended to be clever,' she said, continuing with her task. 'I leave that to you men.'

Bessie had been furious when she heard.

'But it's so unfair...' Her blue eyes filled with tears that only magnified their blueness. She was looking her prettiest that day, in a new gown of white organdie, with a row of tiny buttons running from throat to waist. The dress was being worn for a reason. Robert was bringing his friend back for tea, after their bicycling expedition. 'You know perfectly well how things stand between me and Harold...'

'I'm afraid I don't,' said Laura.

Her sister glared at her, her face flushing with temper.

'Well, if you don't, then you ought to! He's been here every day for the past fortnight. Who do you think he comes to see?'

'Bob, I suppose,' said Laura.

'Oh, you're quite impossible!' Bessie's face took on the sulky look it always wore when she failed to get her way. 'I'll be nineteen next birthday,' she said. 'If I lose this chance, who knows when another will come along?'

There was no denying the truth of this.

'I'm sorry.'

Bessie's reply was a wordless shrug.

'It's only for a few months,' said Laura. 'Perhaps a year...'

'A year!' Bessie's tone was one of bitterest scorn. 'I'll be an old maid by then...'

Laura's wardrobe was not extensive, and yet it filled a steamer trunk; Mrs Reynolds's, as befitted a Colonel's widow, required two, and several suitcases besides. In addition, there were the clothes belonging to Mrs Reynolds's Scotch maid, Elspeth, who was to travel with them as far as Durban, where the young man she was to marry was stationed with the 90th. After that, the plan was to engage a local girl.

It was with some amazement that Laura regarded their assembled luggage. However were they to transport so much stuff? It seemed enough for an army. One trunk—the smaller—held her things, which was everything she owned: two woollen dresses and four summer frocks; one tweed skirt and one linen—and four blouses.

Added to this were six petticoats—two flannel and four cotton—four pairs of stays and a dozen pairs of drawers. A dozen pairs of stockings, four cotton chemises, four nightgowns and two shawls made up the sum total of her undergarments. A warm cloak, two pairs of boots, two pairs of shoes, six pairs of gloves and two bonnets—one straw and one silk—were her outerwear.

There were also two sashes—one of which was a parting gift from Bessie ('I don't suppose I shall want it,' she had said. 'So you might as well have it.'); a travelling canteen in polished walnut, complete with cutlery, plates, glasses and corkscrew, had been a present from her brothers.

Her father's gift was a miniature writing desk. This last, with its glass phials of ink, its steel-tipped pens, its stock of smooth white paper and envelopes, had taken up the most space of any of the things in her trunk.

'You know my feelings on this subject, my dear,' he had said. 'On that matter, we will say no more. But even if we are divided in this, we need not be so in other things. Write to me as often as you can, dear child, and our separation will seem the shorter.'

She would miss her brothers of course; although the boys had been often away these past few years, and so the bond had necessarily weakened. Bessie, she was sure, would not miss her; nor she Bessie, if the truth were told, which it could never be. It was little Violet she would miss: a year without her would seem long indeed. To be away from her father, too, would be hard to bear.

A smaller box contained other essentials. Books: a Bible, the Idylls of the King; Keats's Poems; Men and Women. This last had been another of Theo's gifts. A new edition of the Woodlanders, its pages uncut, was also to be found; as were the Sonnets of Mrs Browning, the Letters of Mr Macaulay and a Guide to the Flora and Fauna of Southern Africa (with illustrations).

Last of all was a volume bound in red morocco, whose pages were blank. This had been Mrs Reynolds's gift. 'I don't know if you keep a journal, my dear,' she had said. 'But this will at least enable you to do so.' She had been reading Theodore's journal—returned with his things by the War Office—and it had given her the idea. 'It is so full of interesting observations about all sorts of things,' she said. 'I never knew until now how hard it must be to be a soldier.'

An entire box was given over to Mrs Reynolds's medicines, since these would be hard to come by in the place that they were going. Laura herself had packed only the usual remedies: sal volatile for headaches and tincture of laudanum, for menstrual cramps. Other necessities were contained in her travelling bag: documents necessary for travel; a pocket knife, a hairbrush, and a toothbrush.

A silver propelling-pencil and a magnifying glass were also to be found; so, too, was a handkerchief—one of the two dozen she had packed; and two bundles of letters, tied with black ribbon.

Chapter 2

Theo, July 1878: Cape Town

His letters had come—one from his mother, one from his tailor (confound it. There was still that outstanding bill) and one in Laura's hand. He slipped this last inside his tunic, to read later. First there was Chapel to sit through, with a thousand voices roaring out 'Old Hundredth', followed by one of the Chaplain's more robust sermons (the men liked it when there was a good dose of hellfire) and then the serving out of the tobacco ration.

There'd be time for Laura after that.

He recalled the first time he had seen her: how timid she had been, and how pretty he had thought her. He had been standing at the window as she had walked up to the house. The dogs had been kicking up a row, and he saw from her face that she was afraid of them. If he had not opened the door at that very moment, she would have run away, of that he was sure. As it was, she had no choice but to remain; he had invited her in, telling her his mother would be down directly.

All of it was just an excuse to keep her there.

He could not remember what they had talked about; he would have been spouting some nonsense or other, as he always did when he met a girl he liked. She had said little, avoiding his gaze and smiling at the floor in that way she had. He remembers how shy she was—positively shaking with nerves, he remembers noticing. Although whether that was on account of his presence of that of the dogs he couldn't be sure.

He had seen her again at church the following Sunday. She was sitting a few rows in front of him; he could just see the back of her head over the top of the pew, next to that of a girl he assumed to be her sister. All through the service, he kept his eyes fixed on the white nape of her neck, beneath the smooth coils of light brown hair.

Afterwards, he had gone up to speak to her. She had shown more composure than before—perhaps because she was surer of her ground. Throughout their brief conversation, she had the little girl, Violet, by the hand. The child was twisting about impatiently, the way children do, and Laura told her to be still. She did not introduce her other sister; although the girl was making sheep's eyes at him.

It was she who had let him in, when he called at the vicarage that evening. He had only meant to leave a note, to say he was going away; but the girl had insisted he should come in and wait.

'She's only gone out for a walk,' she said, with a sidelong look from under long dark lashes.

Then, with an artlessness as studied as it was beguiling: 'I saw you at church. How do you do? I'm Elizabeth—but you can call me Bessie.'

He was aware of how it must have looked to Laura, coming in a few moments later, with a bright colour in her face from the wind, to find them alone together. He had stammered his apologies. He had not meant to disturb her. Her sister had kindly asked him to wait. He would take up no more of her time—except to say that he would like her permission to call again, next time he was at Stonesfield.

For the next six weeks, he could not get her out of his mind. The way she moved, and her eyes and hair, and her soft voice, which sometimes said the most surprising things.

He recalled a particular occasion, some weeks after their first encounter. He had returned home on a furlough. The following week, he was to be sent to Woolwich. It was a wet afternoon, and they had had tea sent into the library. His mother had—tactfully, he realised now—gone up for her rest, and he was alone with Laura.

Her face was a perfect oval, he thought—like that of a Fra Lippo Lippi Virgin and Child he had seen in Florence, the year before he went up to Oxford. Beautiful seen with eyes downcast, as she was when she was thinking or reading; more beautiful still when she looked up...

'Don't stare.'

'I can't help it.'

She sighed—with amusement or exasperation he could not be sure—then carried on with the book she was reading.

'What's so much more interesting than I am?'

By way of answer, she held up the volume. It was one of his own favourites. But, he was inclined to feel, hardly suitable for a clergyman's daughter...

'I'm surprised your father lets you read such things.'

'My father has never stopped me from reading anything. Don't look so shocked.' She threw him a mischievous look. 'It is not so very dreadful, is it? I am sure there are much wickeder books.'

'As to that, I couldn't say...' Then he saw that she was laughing at him.

'Man's love is of man's life a thing apart,' she read. ''Tis woman's whole existence...' Do you think that can be true? It seems awfully hard on us poor women.'

'I think the noble Lord was writing about himself,' said Theo, recalling the passage from which the quotation came. The thought of his chaste Madonna reading such frankly carnal stuff was curiously stirring. Suddenly he wanted very much to kiss her.

He did so. When at last they drew apart, her pale face was flushed, and her breath uneven.

'Wait until we are married,' he said. 'Then I will show you what a man's love is like.'

It was not long after that visit home that he had received news of the South African posting: it had been a disappointment at first, because he had hoped for India. But he had soon reconciled himself to it: the chances for promotion were as good there as anywhere, after all. When he returned in a year or so, he would be in a better position to marry, if she chose to wait. But two years was a long time, and so he would not hold her to their engagement, if she wished to break it...

The words had scarcely been out of his mouth when she told him she would not do it.

If, after a year, he had almost forgotten her face, still she existed for him through her letters: in these, if not in the photograph, it was possible to discern the real Laura. It was, as she put it, a re-markably drawn-out conversation they were having, given the delay between committing a thought to paper and its eventual receipt by the one for whom it was intended.

Your commendation of Stones of Venice made me take up Sesame and Lilies again, which as you know I could not get on with the first time. On this occasion I made better progress; although Mr Ruskin and I are still 'out' on the question of women's education, which he believes to be important only in as much as it may 'enable her to sympa-thise with her husband's pleasures, and those of his best friends'; in other words, so that she may not appear a per-fect fool at her own dinner table.

Now, whilst I cannot disagree that the sphere of men and women is different, that—to cite Mr Ruskin again— 'the man is eminently the doer, the creator, the discoverer, the defender, whose intellect is for speculation and inven-tion and whose energy for adventure and for war' etc etc, it does seem hard to me that the woman's role, as he con-ceives it, should be so entirely passive.

It is not that—like 'sweet Polly Oliver' in the old song—I have any particular wish to 'list for a soldier and follow my love', nor that I feel that I should be anything but an indifferent 'doer' of great deeds. My aspirations are indeed modest enough: to construe a certain tricky pas-sage of Virgil without recourse to the dictionary; and to reach the end of *Childe Harold's Pilgrimage* without ei-ther Cook's shouting up the stairs to me that the butcher's boy has brought the wrong order, or Violet's running in (as she did just now) with a face all over tears on account of a bee-sting.

It is not, you understand, that I am in any way disin-clined to the ordering of beefsteaks or the soothing of bee-stings; it is just that I do not see why these activities should disqualify one from a life of the mind.

Oh my dearest, I cannot 'follow' you—see what you see, do what you do—except in imagination. There, at

21

least, there are no limits. Tell me at once, by the by, what you thought of The Hand of Ethelberta. I did not like it so much as his last—but then I cannot get on with Mr Hardy's women, either. They seem to me insipid creatures, when they are not foolishly headstrong.

Oh, what a cross mood I am in! And here it is four o'-clock and tea still not ordered. Poor Father will be wondering what has become of it...

Theo put the letter aside. The thoughts it aroused were not comfortable ones. It was as if he had been cut in two, with one half remaining behind in England, as the companion of Laura's walks and the confidant of her thoughts, whilst the other measured out its dull existence in this God-forsaken place.

'I cannot follow you—see what you see, do what you do...'

It was as well, he thought.

They'd been garrisoned at Cape Town for six months before he'd heard a shot fired in anger—and even that was only one of the men letting loose at a native policeman in the course of a drunken brawl. The men were bored and restless; one could hardly blame them—stuck here in this filthy hole month after blistering month, with nothing to do but polish the buttons on their scarlet coats.

Small wonder that tempers were short, and quarrels flared up out of nowhere. A gambling debt unpaid; a woman's smile, meant for one man, intercepted by another; a casual insult, muttered out of the side of the mouth, which must at once be avenged if not retracted.

Some of the men had already seen action—in India, or Afghanistan. Others—the raw recruits—were coiled springs, ready to fly off at the slightest pressure. Racked with impatience to be gone—to be 'in for it' at last. These were the ones you had to watch, for signs of despair; the madness that comes with waiting.

The older, more experienced, men tended to be steadier. But the younger ones—boys, some of them—were harder to get the measure of. Hot-bloods, flushed with drink and loud with argument, who'd crumple into tears if one invoked their mothers. Callow virgins, who turned—overnight it seemed—into voluptuaries, squabbling over the Cape Malay whores as if burning to prove themselves the equal of their seniors.

Theo was uncomfortably aware that he himself fell into the latter category only by virtue of his superior rank. He was twenty-four. There were men his age and younger in the ranks who had seen action in India and Afghanistan, yet who—never having had the benefit of his three years at Oxford and his year at Sandhurst—were obliged to defer to him. It seemed to him that the respect in which they appeared to hold him and his fellow officers could only be a matter of form.

When he had expressed the thought to Hallam, his friend had laughed.

'My dear fellow. The army is entirely a matter of form. It couldn't function otherwise...'

When Theo had looked doubtful, Hallam continued, 'You mustn't think that experience has anything to do with it. Any fool can gain experience...' Hallam himself had been at Kandahar. 'It's how one applies that experience that makes the difference between a good officer and a bad one. The men know that, of course...'

'Do you mean that they hold us in contempt?'

Hallam laughed.

'Not they. My dear chap, they revere us. We epitomise everything they are fighting for. Queen and Country, Hearth and Home. The Englishman's inalienable right to seek out 'fresh fields and pastures new'—that is, fresh lands for conquest. We are all that to them, and more, don't you see?'

'A heavy responsibility, if true...' He had caught Hallam's freakish mood. 'To be the standard-bearers of Empire.'

'Precisely. That is why we must strive to live up to it. We are the flower of Europe, my dear Reynolds—come to bring civilisation to this dark continent...'

'You make it sound a noble cause indeed.'

'Oh it is,' drawled the other with his enigmatic smile. 'The noblest, noblest cause of all.'

Of the group of fellow officers it had fallen to his lot to share a room with, Hallam was the only one whose opinion he cared a straw for. His people were army people, too.

'You could say the army's in our blood. We've certainly spilt enough of the stuff, in one war or another,' Hallam said.

Hallam's elder brother had served under General Gordon in the Sudan. An uncle had been aide-de-camp to Lord Raglan in the Crimea. That had been a shocking mess. It was to be hoped that Thesiger would make a better job of commanding the troops in Africa.

'Not that one expects him to be another Wellington,' Hallam said. Hallam's great-grandfather had served with the Iron Duke. 'But it would be reassuring to know that the government haven't kept all their best generals in Afghanistan.'

Hallam was popular with the men—a reputation for coolness under fire having preceded him to Africa. 'He's a good sort, the Captain,' was a view Theo had heard expressed on more than one occasion. 'No 'side' to him. If he gives you an order, you know there's a reason for it. Not like some of these jackanapeses...'

Theo wished the same could have been said about him. He supposed it would be better once he had the benefit of the campaign behind him; as it was, he felt himself to be there under false pretences—not quite a novice, but certainly not experienced enough to merit a position of responsibility.

It was evident that some of those under his command shared this view.

'Cut himself shaving, ah look!' a big bruiser named Quinn had sung out, as Theo was passing. It had been a week ago—but the memory still stung. He had broken step for a minute; then continued. He would not let them see that he had heard.

'Don't s'pose he shaves very orften,' had been the rejoinder. He didn't know the man who'd spoken. 'Gawd. The babes they send us. Wet be'ind the ears ain't in it...'

Now, as he lay stretched out on his camp-bed in the room he shared with Hallam and Marlowe and the others, as he had been for the past hour or so, with nothing to do but polish his already immaculate kit or clean a gun that had yet to require cleaning, he wondered how much longer he would have to wait before he got the chance to prove himself.

Sighing, he reached for his pen. Laura's letter could wait for a reply; he had still to write to his mother. Although what he was to say that would possibly be of interest he could not imagine. Certainly his letters could convey little of the truth: the heat, the dust, the sheer monotony of his existence—to say nothing of its coarser realities—could be mentioned only in passing, if they could be mentioned at all.

He amused himself for a moment with what he might have said in his letter, had these restrictions not applied:

> Dearest Mama
>
> Well, it has been a week like any other. O'Leary was arrested for brawling—again! He is such a contentious fellow. Of course he was drunk, as many of the men are, much of the time. He was lucky not to have been made an example of, for calling his commanding officer a 'fucking Nancy-boy'; but then I am of a forgiving nature.
>
> I was less lenient, you will be pleased to know, with young Frobisher, when I visited him in the sick-bay, where he is presently recovering from a dose of the 'clap' (as we call it in our rough way). Frobisher was very sorry for himself indeed, and kept asking, was 'it' going to drop off (referring, you understand, to his manly part). I was very stern with him, you may be sure—pointing out that he had only himself to blame for the sorry state in which he found himself. Oh, he looked very sheepish at that, I can tell you!
>
> All in all, it has been a quiet week. I had to reprimand Holyoake for smoking on duty, and Noakes because his buttons were dirty. The food is as vile as ever: half the men are afflicted with diarrhoea (or 'the shits', as we call it) and the barracks stinks like a midden. Thank you for the socks, and tobacco...

No, it wasn't the kind of stuff which could be read out at the tea-table for the edification of Mother's friends. Nor, for that matter, was it suitable for a love-letter.

The weather. One could always talk about the weather; although since it was almost always fine, variation on this theme was limited. An excursion to the theatre to see Miss Kitty Malloy, newly arrived in the colonies with her troupe of Goodtime Girls, was more promising—if one excised the bawdy turn the evening had taken—with the ladies of the chorus flaunting their lace-clad posteriors for the delectation of the baying crowd.

> *O, I long to take you*
> *Up the Khyber Pass (whoops!)*
> *Up the Khyber Pass (whoops!)*
> *Up the Khyber Pass...*

A picnic 'got up' by the Colonel's wife, and a few Cape Town ladies with marriageable daughters, was another topic from which he'd managed to wring the utmost, without giving away any of its less palatable details. Such as the fact that Major Dawlish and Mrs Van Den Bergh were within a hair's breadth of becoming an open scandal. Or that young Winslow—emboldened by fruit cup and too much sun—had made a lunge at one of the Misses Plunkett-Green, and had had to be sent to the lock-up to cool down.

Then there was the Cape Town itself—oh, the landscape was fine enough, granted, but what of the city? A meaner, more squalid place would have been hard to imagine, with its streets that were little more than dirt tracks, so that the passage of any vehicle threw up a shower of dust. As for the stench—it was that of an open latrine. On hot days—and they mostly were hot—the stink was enough to make one heave.

Perhaps the worst thing was the desperate poverty one saw everywhere. Not that one didn't occasionally run across something of the sort at home. But this was of a different order altogether. He recalled with a shudder the dead child he had seen in the first week after his arrival. He had thought at first that it was a bundle of sticks, wrapped up in an old rag, until he had caught sight of its face... Its mother, with another starveling at her breast, sat beside it in the dirt. The wheels of the cab had nearly run over them. 'Damn' Hott'nots,' said the driver, a Malay.

Theo had called to the man to stop; had fumbled—too late—

for his purse. But when he'd looked back, the woman and her pathetic bundle had vanished as if they had never existed. The driver in his cone-shaped hat had flicked his reins to move the horse along, and then spat an oyster-sized globule of phlegm into the dust.

When he'd told Hallam about it that night the latter had sighed. 'What is there to be done?' he'd said. 'They will go on breeding, poor devils.'

No, it wasn't the sort of thing one could put in a letter. Nor indeed, were the beggars, holding out hands that were mere lumps of flesh, fingerless and gnarled. 'Leprosy,' said Hallam. 'Cured, of course, or they'd be driven away.'

Or the street girls, clustering like bright birds at every corner.

'Riddled with disease,' was Hallam's dry remark, on seeing his friend's eyes go to them. 'Not that the men care, either way. If we stay here much longer, there won't be a soldier in the regiment who hasn't taken the mercury cure.'

Hurrying down Long Street, earlier that day, Theo had almost run slap-bang into one such girl. Shiny black hair down to her waist, and the light gold skin that showed she was of Malay extraction. When she'd smiled, there'd been a flash of gold, too. Her breath smelled of cinnamon.

While he was still stammering out an apology, she'd seized him by the wrist. Pressed his hand against her breast, so that he could feel its hard tip through the thin cotton. 'Feels good, *ja*?' she said.

When he'd pulled away, her face had clouded, momentarily; then she'd smiled. 'Don't be frighten'. I don't bite...' Her laughter had pursued him along the street, so that it was as much as he could do not to break into a run.

Reaching the bottom of the street, he'd almost slipped and fallen on his arse.

There was blood all over the pavement, and a terrible stench rose from the piles of rotting entrails and discarded skins that lay about him. For here, where the street ran up against the harbour, was the city's abattoir, where the carcasses of newly-slaughtered beasts hung from tall iron posts. The guts were thrown into the bay, where they turned the water bloody.

27

This is in many ways a primitive country, he'd observed, in one of his letters to Laura.

> You would, I think, be surprised by some of their ways. How it makes me long for home, dearest girl, where everything is certain to happen at the same time and in the same way—from the delivery of the post in the morning to the lighting of the lamps at night. Here, nothing is certain...

It was a country of extremes. If the poverty one saw in the streets exceeded that of even the worst London slums, so the wealth seemed no less excessive, in its fashion. Some of the mansions one saw on the Constantia Road seemed fit for English lords, rather than for the fat Dutch merchants who had built them; whilst the womenfolk of such types, in their Paris gowns and ostrich-plumed hats, might have graced the Court of St James—at least until they opened their mouths.

Everything was larger-than-life: brighter, louder, more intense—from the brilliant colours of birds and flowers, to the sudden violence of rainstorms, which appeared out of a clear blue sky and flattened everything in seconds. It felt, at times, as if he had strayed into some febrile dream—or an hallucination, such as one experienced under opium (or so he had read, having tasted the stuff but once, when he'd had the toothache).

He'd never seen such darkness; nor such stars. One night he'd walked up Signal Hill for a breath of air, and found himself utterly alone—the scattered lights of the city below paling into insignificance beneath the glittering canopy of the heavens. From where he stood, shivering a little in the night breeze, he could see the winking harbour lights, where the land's edge gave way to the dark mass of the sea.

Rising up from this plateau was another darkness, shaping itself as rock. The immense curved wall of Table Mountain seeming a kind of fortress; a rampart holding back what lay behind, which was all of Africa. On either side lay what seemed to his restless fancy the forms of recumbent beasts: the horned monster of the Devil's Peak; the sphinx-like bulk of the Lion's Head, silhouetted against the stars.

And what stars they were! Great golden lamps, hung in a black velvet sky. Their beauty seemed to him in that moment a manifestation, not of grace, but of divine indifference. A world which contained such splendour might also contain the dead infant and the bleeding carcasses he had stumbled over in the street.

If God was present in this landscape, it was in a less comfortable and benign form than He was wont to manifest Himself at home. Here, He was so altered as almost to have constituted a different god altogether: a dark and terrible being...

'Writing to that popsy of yours again?' Coleman said, having exhausted the fun that was to be had from trimming his moustache, and flicking the clippings at Parr.

'What's it to you?'

Coleman had never been known to write to anyone, although it was rumoured he'd left a wife behind. 'Glad to see the back of him, no doubt,' had been Hallam's uncharacteristically sharp observation.

'It's nothing to me,' said Coleman. 'Although I suppose she must be worth it. Scribble, scribble, scribble.' He mimed a lewd act. 'It's a wonder your hand doesn't fall off, the amount of scribbling you do...'

Lying on his back, his gaze on the hot blue square of sky which was all that could be seen through the bars of the barrack-room window, Theo could hear the hoarse staccato shouts of the drill sergeant from outside; the clatter of boots in the corridor; a burst of rude laughter, instantly quelled. Pervading the atmosphere at this, the dinner hour, was an unappetising smell of broiling meat.

On the wall by the bed were brownish smears of blood, where his predecessor had whiled away an afternoon, killing lice. A dull, persistent headache—the legacy of last night's beer—throbbed behind his eyes.

An image of the coloured girl with the gold teeth flashed across his mind. Feels good, ja? Her hard little breast in his hand...

Angrily, he brushed away the thought; drew the photograph of Laura from inside his journal. It wasn't a good likeness, conveying nothing of what he thought of as the essential Laura. This was a catalogue of attributes, merely. A faintly smiling mouth;

fairish hair; a smooth brow. Eyes that returned the camera's gaze with a quizzical air.

She'd handed it to him, half-apologetically, at their last-but-one meeting. 'To remind you of today...'

They'd taken a picnic up into the hills—returning, sun-burned and a little tipsy from the cider they'd had with their bread and cheese, after a day spent rambling about in the fresh air. As he'd helped her down from the trap, he'd clasped her in his arms, and she hadn't pulled away. He could taste the cider on her lips, smell the faint scent of dried grass that clung to her hair, from where they had lain, sprawled flat on their backs, on Badbury Hill.

He had thanked her for the gift: 'I will treasure it always. It is not as pretty as the original, however...'

Now it was the photograph he saw, and not the face. That had been obscured—its pale tints and girlish contours fading in the vivid light cast by a darker countenance.

He had been again to Long Street, hoping to catch sight of the girl. In the low sun of late afternoon, its drifting crowds had seemed a celestial throng, each figure as it came towards him haloed with gold, the lineaments in darkness. And yet these were not angels, but businessmen from the commercial area, in their top-hats and frock-coats.

Less angelic still was the group of soldiers, in all probability from his own regiment, emerging from a pot-house across the street. He should have taken their names for disorderly conduct; instead, he pretended not to see them. If his own brother had walked up to him at that moment, he would not have known him.

He walked in a daze, in a dream of longing. Her face. Her tumbling hair.

When a woman spoke to him, he almost jumped out of his skin.

'Where you going, darling?'

He blinked. It was not in his nature to speak roughly to any woman, and so he smiled as he shook his head to signify his lack of inclination for what she had to offer.

Still she persisted. 'Lonely, are you, darling? *Ag*, shame. A handsome boy like you...'

Although she wasn't much more than a girl herself. Pretty enough, too—if your mind were not filled with thoughts of another: one paler golden in colour and with eyes of a blacker hue.

Once more, he shook his head. 'I am not lonely,' he said.

'Shame,' she cried again, her rueful laughter following him down the street. 'Well, if you change your mind, soldier, ask for Hennie.'

This last brought him up short. He didn't even know her name, his dark and golden beauty. He had no idea where in the city she might be living.

The thought that his enterprise might be doomed to failure gave him the courage to call after the girl. 'Hi, there! Wait. There is something you can do for me, if you will...'

She turned, an ironic expression on her face. 'Change your mind, soldier?' When he explained, her face grew sullen. 'Can I help you find a girl? Depends which girl. What's her name, this girl?'

He confessed that he didn't know.

'What's she got that I don't?' she retorted with a pout. 'She pretty, eh?'

He stumbled through a description, staying within the bounds of propriety as he did so. He could hardly tell this other one— versed in the ways of the world as she undoubtedly was—how that breast had felt under his hand.

While he was listing the remaining attributes—dark hair, dark eyes; height a little above the middling—the face of his inquisitor never lost its look of faint boredom.

'*Ja, ja.* Dark hair. All hairs is dark. All eyes, too—except yours...' She twinkled roguishly at him, evidently hoping that he might relent of his earlier rejection of her favours.

Only when he mentioned the shawl—green silk, with a pattern of red parrots—did her face clear. 'Oh, you mean Pretty. Why didn't you say so? *Ja*, she live round here. I'll take you to her...'

So it was that he found himself on the stoep outside a low white building, in a street of identical houses whose inhabitants, to judge from those he glimpsed going in and out during that quarter-hour sojourn, were largely Malays; although the occasional coloured dandy in spats and frock-coat, or pig-tailed

Chinese, was also to be seen.

He was the only white man; but his presence seemed to cause no undue consternation amongst the rest of the populace: the groups of children who stood watching him from a safe distance, or, growing bolder, vied with each other to chase after the coins he tossed for them in the dust; the old men in long white robes who sat smoking their hubble-bubbles in the doorways, and who returned Theo's polite gaze with seeming indifference.

When his guide, the loquacious Hennie, left him it was with the instruction to wait, and the promise that 'She not be long.'

Even so, he was startled by the summons when it eventually came: a smooth bare arm, its owner otherwise concealed by a half-drawn curtain, beckoned from an upstairs window. He stared, transfixed, until the arm vanished from view, uncertain whether or not the signal was meant for him.

Then it was that he heard again the sound of her laughter, calling him to her as it had done at their first meeting.

Climbing the steps, he was suddenly bathed in sweat. What if he failed, at the important moment? He hoped she would know what to do. His knowledge of the proceedings was crude, to say the least—being derived, for the most part, from the filthy jokes he'd heard around the mess-hall, and imperfectly understood. For a panicked moment, he thought about running away...

But then the thought of that laughter, following him along the road as he made his ignominious escape, stiffened his resolve. That, and the remembered jolt of pleasure he'd felt at the touch of that firm, brown flesh.

He found himself in a dark hallway, with arched doorways leading off it and the sound of a fountain playing in an unseen courtyard. A short flight of stairs led to the room where she was waiting for him, where the harsh light of day was diffused through rose-coloured silk into a pleasant dimness. An aromatic smell—sandalwood, he guessed—hung heavy on the air.

Pretty was on the bed, sprawled at her ease in a dressing-gown of figured satin. 'So,' she said at last. 'You come back.' She yawned and stretched her thin brown arms above her head, with a soft clashing of golden bracelets.

'What's the matter?' she said, when he made no move towards

her. 'You never seen a girl before?' She held out her hand. 'Come here.'

When he was lying beside her, it grew easier. The rose-pink room with its spiralling curls of smoke was a world of its own, far from everything that lay outside it. She drew his hand to her breast, to feel once more its solid form, the breathing warmth of skin and flesh. But when he tried to kiss her lips, she pushed him away, laughing.

She helped him out of his clothes with a practised ease; and made his passage into her almost as effortless. When he cried out, she stroked his hair, and murmured soft words in a language he did not understand.

In a transport of relief and pleasure, he would have fallen asleep in her arms, but she shook him awake. 'Time you go. Come back another day...' She took the money without awkwardness, and placed it in a little painted jar on the table.

Outside, he walked like a man possessed, uncertain of where he was or where he was going. It seemed inconceivable that the world could continue just the same. Everything seemed transfigured. The beauty of the world, the paragon of animals, he murmured under his breath.

In front of the slaughterhouse, men were washing the blood from the pavement with soapy water—each bubble a rainbow pleasure-dome, a miniature universe of light.

After the trembling delight of the first time—the smell of her body, her hair; her slender brown limbs entwined about him— he knew that he had to return. Her room, with its pink-shaded lamp and its smell of incense, was a haven, in whose pleasures he could lose himself, if only for a few hours. Here, the brutish realities of the barrack-room and the braying humour of the officers' mess were no more.

In Pretty's arms was to be found a kind of oblivion—the kind war-weary Odysseus found with Circe, he thought. Of his faithful Penelope he tried not to think.

On his third, or perhaps fourth, visit, he met a man—a soldier—upon the stair. The fellow was whistling through his teeth, with what seemed an odious self-satisfaction. As he passed by

Theo, who was coming up as he was coming down, he made a lewd gesture with his tongue. Theo felt a powerful impulse to hit him. Under any circumstances but these, he might have done so—or at the very least, taken the man's name.

As it was, he stared stonily ahead, as if he had not seen. A rude burst of laughter followed him up the stairs.

'Who was that man?' Theo demanded, with an anger he had not known until that moment he was capable of feeling.

'What man?' said Pretty, who was admiring herself in the mirror. She was naked, except for a rose-coloured silk scarf, which she was winding around her throat. 'Do you like this one?' she said. 'Or that one?' Holding up another, in peacock blue.

'You know very well which man I mean.'

'Oh. That man. He's just a man. Like you.' She yawned extravagantly. 'Maybe I don't like either of them,' she said, throwing down the coloured silks with a petulant frown. 'Maybe you have to buy me something new.'

'I don't want you to see him again, do you hear?'

In the heat of the moment, it was easy to overlook the fact that he had no right to her exclusive attention.

'Are you listening to me? A man like that is nothing but a scoundrel...'

How hard it was to stay angry with her! She was so pretty.

Seeing her advantage, she pouted. 'Why are you so unkind to me?' Winding her arms about his neck and drawing him close to her.

'I mean it,' he said, as, with deft little fingers, she began to unbutton his tunic. 'I want you to be mine alone—and nobody else's...'

As he was dressing, she lay on the bed, smoking one of the cigarettes she favoured. He had tried one, once. It was filthy stuff. Dagga, or some such. It had made his head swim most unpleasantly.

'I want to go out,' she said suddenly. 'Will you take me?'

He had been going to spend the evening playing billiards with Hallam at the Club.

'Where do you want to go?'

'I want to go driving,' said Pretty. 'In a fine carriage. I want to wave to all the fine, fine ladies and gentlemen in Adderley Street. I want to go to the George Hotel, and have a nice dinner, with lobsters and champagne.'

'Well...' said Theo.

Pretty burst out laughing, exhaling a cloud of aromatic smoke. 'You see?' she said. 'You are not the only one to want what you can't have.'

Chapter 3

Laura, September 1879: Cape Town

When they reached Table Bay, it was blowing a South-Easter and the famous mountain was half-obscured by a bank of cloud. Of Cape Town itself, they could see but little. A squalling rain drove hard against the sea, whisking its surface into a froth. Most of the passengers who had ventured on deck, finding themselves drenched by this flying spume, chose to retreat behind the glazed-in porch of the hurricane deck.

Laura was not among them. For her, there was a charm in the very unsettledness of the weather. This, then, was the 'Cape of Storms', of which Theo had written. Not a smiling vision of fairy-land, but a sterner landscape altogether. Changeable. And indeed by the time they weighed anchor, the storm had subsided and the clouds had blown away. Before her, in the sparkling air, rose the great cliff of Table Mountain, in the face of whose unsmiling eminence she felt herself to be of no more significance than a fly.

On the quayside a howling mass engulfed them. All classes of humanity were represented, it appeared. Englishmen in white ducks and solar topees mingled with Chinamen in blue jackets and pig-tails; Malays in high-crowned straw hats rubbed shoulders with half-naked Africans; while Dutchmen in khakis, their faces burnt a deep red, strode up and down. Everyone was talking at the tops of their voices: a veritable Babel of sound, of which only a few words were intelligible to Laura above the guttural exhortations of what she took to be Cape Dutch; the more mellifluous clicks and whistles of the various African tongues.

Setting foot for the first time in two weeks upon solid ground was less steadying than might have been expected. Perhaps it was merely that the gentle rocking underfoot to which they had become accustomed had now been replaced by a different kind of momentum: a whirling of shapes and colours. As they stood, dumbfounded at the sight of the maelstrom into which they were about to cast themselves, a stinging cloud of red dust flung itself in their faces.

As Laura wiped her streaming eyes, she heard a voice; 'Mrs Reynolds and Miss Brooke, I take it?' Looking up through a blur of tears to see a smiling visage, above a dark blue coat. 'Captain Linley?' she heard her companion say. 'How very kind of you to meet us.'

Elspeth was to follow with the luggage, and so the two ladies seated themselves in Captain Linley's dogcart. The journey to the hotel was not long, he said; a few minutes should do it. He hoped they would find it convenient. There was no room at Government House just at present, on account of the French delegation, but he hoped the accommodation would suit for the time being...

As they drove along the sea-front towards the city centre, he pointed out sights of interest. There was the Castle, a very historical building, now the army's headquarters. Here was the City Hall, completed only last year, and quite as fine, in his opinion, as anything one might find in Whitehall. That tall mountain with the round bald top was the Lion's Head; this flat-topped eminence was Table Mountain, of which they might have heard...

In Greenmarket Square, they came to a stop in front of a broad façade, surmounted by a sign that read: Imperial Hotel. An establishment for commercial gentlemen, was Mrs Reynolds's impression, conveyed sotto voce to her young friend. 'Not the worst hotel in town,' remarked Captain Linley with an awkward laugh. 'I hope you will be comfortable.'

Both hastened to reassure him. After the glare and dust of the streets, it was a relief to have somewhere to lay their heads at last. But it would not do. Indeed, it would not do.

Even as the grinning boy in his stained white jacket was depositing their bags in the room, with its broken-backed beds and its smell of bad drains, it was apparent to both ladies that a mistake must have been made. Neither had the energy to rectify it, though.

After taking off her hat and casting around for somewhere to put it, Mrs Reynolds sat down in one of the sagging armchairs with which the room was provided and fell at once into a light doze.

From the balcony, Laura gazed out at the strange new city. The blazing light of noon illuminated everything with extraordinary clarity: the bright glitter of the waves; the astonishing height of the mountains; the colour of the sky—a dazzling azure, deeper even than the skies over Tenerife. The diversity of the people was another marvel: was there anywhere else on earth where so many races co-existed in such apparent harmony?

In the street below, a child raised its hands in supplication. Lady, lady... Smiling, Laura unclasped her purse, took out some coins and dropped them into the little girl's open palms. The small black face blossomed into a smile that was quite beautiful. Thank you, lady. Then the child ran off, shouting with glee. It was impossible not to feel an answering emotion.

A moment later the door opened and Elspeth put her head around. 'Oh, Miss,' she said. 'The bags have arrived.'

Laura frowned at her, indicating that she should lower her voice; but it was too late. Mrs Reynolds opened her eyes. For a moment, their expression was vacant, and her lips moved soundlessly, as if trying to form a word.

'You were asleep,' said Laura. 'Wouldn't you be more comfortable lying down?'

But Mrs Reynolds shook her head. 'I am quite rested. Truly.'

She wanted nothing, she said. Some tea; that was all. Against Laura's protests, she urged her to go out. They had no engagements until later that evening, when Captain Linley was to call for them. 'I shall be quite content, my dear. I have letters to write—you would not believe how many!'

Laura hesitated no more. 'I will not be long,' she promised. She took her hat—the heat was appalling—and stepped out into the brilliant African noon.

'After so many weeks at sea, the sense of freedom was delicious,' she wrote later in her journal.

Smells, sounds, colours, offer a riot of sensation to one long starved of such variety. The stalls are piled high with fruits of every description: oranges, pears, mangoes, pineapples and others whose names are unknown to me. Prickly-skinned and star-shaped; waxen looking and warty. The smell, at once sweet and faintly rotten, assails the nostrils to intoxicating effect. The colours are astonishing: the scarlet and green of the peppers, the yellow of grapefruit, the purple of aubergine.

But it is the faces which fascinate one most; although one has to refrain as far as possible from staring. Some seem carved out of polished wood, or beaten from bronze: hieratic masks, of ancient lineage. Many are of remarkable beauty, with curves of lips and eyelids that seem to belong to classical antiquity. The women, in particular, are extraordinary, in their colourful print wrappers and turbans. Their eyes, meeting mine for an instant, held no hint of a smile, but gazed with a level look, in which curiosity was mingled with wariness. The babies hid their faces in their mothers' bosoms; or, foolishly goggling at the apparition, had their eyes shielded by a mother's hand. As if the very sight of a white woman were unlucky...

With no real sense of where she was going, she turned into a broad street that rose from the harbour towards the distant crag. Here, the crowd was less dense, and the strolling groups included those of her own kind: the gentlemen in light-coloured suits that were ubiquitous in the tropics; the ladies in white, or pale shades of blue, lilac and rose. A few curious glances came her way: a woman on her own; but she ignored them. It would not do to stray too far, but the sensation of freedom was delicious...

She drew a deep breath of the sweet, salt-smelling air that blew from the bay.

'Why, Miss Brooke! Of all people! This is the strangest chance! I was just speaking of you—was I not, Gertrude? And now here you are, wandering around in the dust...' Cora De Villiers's penetrating tones did not conceal a faint disdain.

If Laura had intended to make herself an object, Mrs De Villiers's look implied, she had succeeded.

They had met on the boat—that is, she and Mrs De Villiers had met; for the latter and Mrs Reynolds, it had been a renewal of acquaintance. Mrs Reynolds and Mrs De Villiers's sister had been schoolmates. 'Dear Eliza!' said Mrs De Villiers of her sibling. 'She is grown quite stout, after all those great girls of hers. How glad I am to have had only my dear little Daisy...'

Now here she was again, only an hour after they had parted.

'But where is poor dear Emiline?' she demanded of Laura. 'Surely you have not lost her?'

When Laura had explained, a look of consternation furrowed Mrs De Villiers's pretty brow. 'But how appalling! The old Imperial Hotel, Gertrude. Can you believe they are staying at that dreadful place? I simply cannot allow it.' She turned to Laura. 'You must remove from there immediately, and come to me.'

There had been three weeks, on the S S Isis, of circular walks around the deck in the company of Mrs De Villiers and her companion, Miss Leibbrandt, and three weeks of playing piquet in the evenings. Time enough, in Laura's view, for both parties to have wearied of each another. But no. Mrs De Villiers was adamant that they should be her guests for the duration of their stay in Cape Town. 'De Villiers is away at his mines in Kimberley,' she said with a yawn. 'I shall be very dull, with nobody to speak to but Gertrude.'

They remained at Mrs De Villiers's for a month; Mrs Reynolds being prostrated by the rigours of the journey. It was out of the question for her to attempt to go another step further while she was in so fragile a state, declared their hostess. Durban was an unhealthy spot at the best of times. And besides, Spring was the loveliest time to see the Cape. When poor dear Emiline was well again, they would have all sorts of lovely drives along the coast. Sea air was the thing for invalids. Why, when she herself had been so ill after dear little Daisy was born, the doctors had insisted on fresh air, and sea-bathing. As for moving to Government House—which, the French Legation having departed, had now become a possibility—they were not to think of it. Such a grand, chilly sort of place! They would be much cosier with her. No, they must not say another word about putting her out; having them as her guests was too delightful. She would arrange such nice parties—nothing too taxing; just the simplest little suppers and tea-parties.

Why, it would be just as if they were at home! Quite informal. That was what she liked best. And if a few friends—close friends—should choose to drop by—why, they, too, should be regarded as members of the family. Dear Julia Van Kleef—that was Lady Van Kleef- well, one never saw dear Julia standing on ceremony. And dear Colonel Schermbrucker—rather hard-of-hearing these days; and that charming young fellow—what was his name? Mr Blythe—who had written such a clever play. And Marie Koopmans. Dear Marie. They must certainly ask to see Marie's wonderful picture collection. Her latest protégé was Marcus Roxborough. Such a brilliant young sculptor! Exactly like Donatello, they said. Not that she herself knew much about Art; music was really her passion. Which reminded her that Madame Lucille was singing tomorrow night at the Opera House. They must certainly go. They would have a light supper afterwards, to which the wonderful Madame L. would be invited. They said she was the new Jenny Lind. Oh, is would be too delightful!

It was settled that there would be an evening party. Nothing elaborate, said Mrs De Villiers. There would be just themselves, and a few others. Lady Julia, and dear Cornelia Perry, and Major Fitzpatrick, and Mrs Wessels. No more than twenty. Thirty, at most. It would be quite intime. They were going up to dress, when Mrs De Villiers laid a hand on Laura's arm.

'Do let me send Polly to you. My black maid. She is nimble-fingered, though I say it myself. I trained her, you know. Now she is quite the equal of any Parisian femme de chambre.'

'You are very kind...' Laura began, trying to think how best to frame her refusal.

'Oh, do not think that it will put me out,' said her hostess. 'I can certainly spare her.'

'Thank you. But I have always managed for myself.'

'As to frocks,' Mrs De Villiers went on, quite as if Laura had not spoken. 'I am sure that Daisy has one or two she no longer wears. You and she are much the same size, are you not?'

This was certainly the case—Daisy De Villiers having turned out to be a well-grown young woman of twenty-two, rather than the prattling infant of her mother's conversational asides. To have refused the dresses on top of the maid would have given offence, Laura saw, and so she accepted, with as good a grace as she could manage.

When she was ready, she knocked on Mrs Reynolds's door. That lady was sitting at her dressing-table, while Elspeth finished doing her hair. 'Why my dear,' she said, catching sight of Laura in the dressing-table mirror. 'That colour becomes you very well. I do not think I have seen that dress before.'

Laura explained. A certain hesitation in her manner must have expressed more than she meant, for before she had finished speaking, Mrs Reynolds began to laugh.

'Oh dear,' she said. 'That is Cora all over. She was always high-handed, even as a little girl. She was Cora Stubbs, you know, before her marriage. Such a spoilt little thing. And quite plain—although you would not think it now. I remember her the year I came out—she must have been fourteen—such a cross-patch! She was too young to attend any of the parties that year, you see, and she thought it terribly unfair... Oh, don't look so surprised, my dear. We are almost of an age, Cora and I. She must be forty-five, at least. Although she does not admit to being more than thirty-nine.'

She caught Laura's eye in the glass. 'Of course, she has improved with age, whereas I have grown quite withered and old.'

'That is not so.'

'Oh, but it is, my dear.' With an abstracted air, she fingered the necklace of jet beads that lay upon her bosom. 'I became old the day I heard that he was gone.' She was silent a moment. 'Come, she said, with a return of her usual cheerfulness. 'Let us go down. We must not keep poor Cora waiting.'

When she walked into the room, it took an effort of will not to run straight out again. She had never seen so many people got together in a single room in her entire life. It seemed a sea of faces, all turned—so it seemed to her nervous fancy—in her direction. She could not go in. She could not. And yet it had to be faced...

Fragments of talk came at her:

'...boxed her ears for her, you may be sure...'

'...looks bad for Barnato. But you never can tell...'

'...too killing...'

'...these Jews stick together...'

'...lilac crepe de Chine. The sweetest thing you ever saw...'

Over it all, a solo instrument to this cacophonous orchestra, came Miss Leibbrandt's tremulous fluting.

'Why, Miss Brooke! And Mrs Reynolds, too! Such an age since we were all together on the dear old Isis. Such happy times—I quite pine for them—do not you?'

Miss Leibbrandt, it transpired, had been staying for the past fortnight with her brother and her brother's wife in Simon's Town. 'Poor Evangeline had a difficult time with her last one,' she confided. 'Now she does nothing at all except lie on the sofa. They quite depend on me, when I am there. The poor, dear thing has no strength left in her at all. 'What I would do without your help with all these boys'—they have five, you know—'I cannot imagine' says she. Poor thing. She gets so very low at times...'

A maid appeared with a tray of glasses. 'Fruit cup,' said Miss Leibbrandt, with a satisfied air. 'I made it myself, with my own hands. Cora insists on it for all her At-Homes. 'Gertrude,' she says. 'A party isn't a party without your fruit cup.' Good, is it not? Though I say so myself...'

'Thank you, Gertrude,' said Cora De Villiers.

Miss Leibbrandt excused herself, with a nervous laugh.

Their hostess was resplendent that evening in crimson silk, cut low to display the jewels that sparkled at her throat. Beside her was a white-haired foreign-looking gentleman wearing the sash of some order-of-merit across his chest.

'Allow me to present Senor Sarramago, the Portuguese Ambassador,' Mrs De Villiers said.

Senor Sarramago made his bow. 'Charmed,' he said, placing the emphasis on the second syllable.

'And this is Mr Doyle.'

This was a gentleman of about thirty, whose evening clothes were worn with a negligent air.

'Delighted,' he said, holding out his hand to Laura.

There was something she could not place about his manner of speaking. A certain freedom of expression, perhaps.

'Mr Doyle writes for the New York Times,' said Mrs De Villiers.

'Wrote,' he corrected her.

A look passed between them, so swiftly that Laura was not sure if she had imagined it or not.

'Wrote, then. He's an Irishman...'

'American. My parents were Irish.'

'O, you are determined to be difficult!' said Mrs De Villiers with a pretty pout. 'Is he not being difficult, Senor Sarramago?'

'Indubitably,' agreed that gentleman, frowning ferociously at the difficult Mr Doyle from under his black brows. 'In Portugal, duels have been fought for less...'

'Then I am glad we are not in Portugal,' said Mr Doyle with a bow.

'Mr Doyle has just returned from India...' said Mrs De Villiers.

'London,' muttered the American.

'...where he has been writing about the war.'

'The Afghan war?' said Laura.

'The Afghan war. The Zulu war. Any war you care to name,' was Mr Doyle's reply.

'Now, you are not to mention the war to the Governor,' Mrs De Villiers admonished him. 'He has heard quite enough about it, I am sure. The Governor said he might look in,' she explained to the two English ladies. 'Unfortunately he has another engagement which he simply cannot get out of.'

'Never fear,' said Mr Doyle. 'I wouldn't shake old Frere's hand if you paid me to. Not after the mess he made in Natal...'

'Of course, you are quite the expert, after having visited the place once,' interjected Mrs De Villiers with a sarcastic laugh.

'You have been in Natal?' Laura asked him. At last—here was someone who knew the country at first hand.

'Why, sure. I was there not five months ago, covering the campaign for the Illustrated London News.' He smiled, with becoming modesty. 'Perhaps you have read my despatches from the battlefield?'

'But how wonderful!' She could not restrain her delight. 'Of course I have read them. Why, we have talked of little else, these past few months, have we not?'

It was Mrs Reynolds she addressed, but that lady was not paying attention, having been drawn into conversation with someone else. This was a Mrs Bain—a pleasant-faced lady of middle years, whose family were from England, it transpired. Mrs Bain's husband was an engineer.

'Such a clever man,' Mrs De Villiers was saying. 'He has built ever so many roads all over the Cape. It is quite a marvel.'

As soon as she could do so without impoliteness, Laura looked around for her new acquaintance. But he was nowhere to be seen. Instead, a large lady in purple satin, whose manner was one of profound condescension, bore down upon them.

This was Lady Julia. She pronounced herself charmed by the floral arrangements—'Although I never would have put Strelitzia with lilies. Such a novel idea!' Did they not find the heat exhausting? The wind was worse. Quite insupportable—although of course she was used to it. It was better than the fogs and damps of London, did they not find?

A gentleman with luxuriant dark whiskers then appeared, and bowed very low over Cora De Villiers's outstretched hand. This was Mr Blythe, a famous playwright. They were not to say a word in front of Mr Blythe, Mrs De Villiers said. He was such a terrible satirist. Anything they said that was at all clever would be written down that very night, and might re-appear in the mouths of one of Mr Blythe's characters.

Mr Blythe looked Laura up and down with a supercilious air. He did not think, he said, that the ladies had anything to fear from him. He had never yet made a lady cry. He preferred to make them laugh, if anything—and for that, he would admit to a not inconsiderable talent.

Further introductions followed. A Mr Wolhuter, who held the record for the most animals shot in a single day. A Mr Van Der Byl, who was a great friend of the Prince of Wales. A Mrs Melck, whose family was one of the oldest in the Cape. Laura herself was not obliged to say very much. A few phrases sufficed: How interesting; how delightful, or (on occasion) how unfortunate.

Even so, it was with some relief that she heard the summons indicating the start of the entertainment.

This was to consist of two or three pieces, played on the pianoforte by Miss Daisy; followed by the piece de resistance: a selection of Schubert's Lieder, sung by the famous Miss Lucille.

Just then, a small commotion near the door heralded the arrival of the guest-of-honour. This, then, thought Laura, was the man who had taken them to war.

She saw a tall, thin gentleman with white hair and a neat moustache. His upright carriage belied his years; although she knew him to have served for a long time in India. She had read of his mission to Zanzibar to persuade the Sultan to put an end to slavery: that, at any rate, had been a noble thing. Her father had preached a sermon about it.

Now he was here, in the room with her, taking his seat near the front with many protestations of apology. As he sat down, she caught his eye: a cold blue orb, singularly guarded in its expression. She dropped her gaze. Because of him, young men had fought and died. Sir Bartle Frere is on the warpath, Theo had written. He will not rest until the Zulus have been smashed, and we can all go home again.

Madame Lucille finished singing of roses and love, and began a song in a more melancholy key. Laura let her gaze drift around the room, with its crowd of elegant ladies and fine gentlemen. Suddenly, the thought of shaking the Governor's hand—a hand that had signed a death-warrant, in effect—and of meeting that cold gaze was unbearable to her.

She looked around for a means of escape, and saw Mr Doyle, standing at the back of the room. What was it he had said? I wouldn't shake old Frere's hand if you paid me to... She could not help but agree with him on that score.

Afterwards, when the applause had died down and supper had been announced, she saw him talking to Cora De Villiers. A reluctance to find herself once more in that lady's orbit made her hang back; that, and a suggestion of something more than casual about their colloquy.

It was nothing very much. A bejewelled hand laid, for an instant longer than might be thought proper, on the gentleman's sleeve. A smiling mouth placed rather too close to his ear.

She caught up with him at last in the hall. He had his hat in his hand, and was evidently on the point of leaving. But she could not let the opportunity slip.

'Mr Doyle...'

He turned towards her, his expression one of polite enquiry.

'You are not going yet, I hope?'

He smiled. 'I was. Now I have a reason to remain.'

She was not sure how to respond to this piece of gallantry, and so paid it no attention. 'I had hoped you would tell me about your experiences...'

He seemed taken aback. 'My...?'

'I meant of course in Natal.' She was suddenly conscious of the awkwardness of their situation—standing as they were in the general thoroughfare, with people coming and going all around and the door being opened to allow those that were leaving to go out. 'Is there nowhere quieter we could go?' she said.

Again, a look of slight surprise, mingled with something else—amusement, perhaps—crossed his features.

'I don't think you'll find much quiet here tonight,' he murmured, as a burst of laughter came from the room behind. 'Say, why don't we step outside for a minute? I've a Hansom waiting, but he can wait a while longer... unless you think you might be cold,' he added, with a glance at her bare arms.

She reassured him.

'So—what exactly do you want to know?' he asked, giving her his arm as they walked out on to the veranda and descended the steps to the dark garden. 'I put most of what I saw in my despatches, you know. It's a hard country—that much I can tell you.' He threw her another look. 'Where is it that you're from, in England?' he said.

'Stonesfield. It's in Oxfordshire.'

'Pretty little place, is it? Peaceful and so forth?'

'Very.'

'Well then,' he said, pausing to light a cigar. 'Let's just say that Natal is as different from Stonesfield as it's possible to get.'

'So I gathered from your articles.'

'Oh, sure. My articles.' Around them the night was suddenly loud with the croaking of frogs. 'I shouldn't set too much store by those...'

'You are too modest. How else did those of us at home learn the truth about the war?'

'Ah, the truth,' said the journalist, drawing on his cheroot with a reflective air. 'Well, I guess you could say we do our best by it.'

'I don't follow you.'

'No.' he sighed, exhaling a cloud of aromatic smoke. 'Forgive me. One gets awfully cynical in my profession. Of course you're right. What you read in the newspapers is as near to the truth as my esteemed colleagues and I can make it. You want the truth about Natal? It is a desolate place, Miss Brooke. The Cape is a paradise beside it. The nearest thing in my own country is the Wild West—though we at least have tamed all our native Indians. Those that we haven't slaughtered, that is. The Zulus have yet to be thoroughly broken...'

'You talk as if you admired them.'

His white teeth gleamed in the darkness.

'Oh, but I do! That such a bunch of unlettered savages armed with spears and sticks should have taken on the might of the British Army and won... Why, don't you see? It's nothing short of astounding...'

She was silent.

'You must excuse me,' he said, after a moment. 'I had forgotten to whom I was speaking. As an American, you understand, I take a somewhat less partisan view...'

'It is of no consequence,' she said. 'I too believe the Zulus to have been a more formidable enemy than might at first have been supposed. How else to explain such a defeat?'

'There have been many explanations. My own view is...'

But whatever it was, Laura was not to hear it that night—for at that moment, the voice of Miss Leibbrandt was heard calling from the veranda.

'Miss Brooke! Coo-ee! Are you there, Miss Brooke?'

'I guess you're wanted,' said Mr Doyle. He tipped his hat to her with an ironic air. 'Goodnight, Miss Brooke.'

'Goodnight.'

'Why, here you are!' said Miss Leibbrandt, a little out of breath. 'Is that you, Mr Doyle? I thought I saw you slipping away into the dark. Cora was just wondering where you'd got to...'

'I told her I was leaving,' said the young man.

'And yet here you are still,' was Miss Leibbrandt's reply. 'I hope you have not caught a chill, Miss Brooke. The night air is so very damp.'

'Thank you, but I do not feel the cold,' said Laura.

'How fortunate you are! Why, when I was your age, I suffered dreadfully from chills. 'Gertrude,' my poor dear mother used to say, 'you are not to venture out without a shawl, on pain of death!' Those were her very words. 'On pain of death'...' A coughing fit overwhelmed Miss Leibbrandt. 'Oh, are you going after all, Mr Doyle?' she said, as that gentleman began to walk away. 'I am sure Cora will be quite vexed. She told me particularly to put out the brandy-wine for your nightcap, as usual...'

'Please apologize to Mrs De Villiers for me. Tell her I'll call to-morrow, if that's convenient.'

'O, I am sure you need not stand on ceremony,' replied Miss Leibbrandt. 'You never did before. Mr Doyle makes himself quite at home in our house,' she said to Laura. 'Do you not, Mr Doyle? But I will tell Cora to expect you... Come, Miss Brooke. Mrs Reynolds has been asking for you. You will find her in her room—quite tired out, poor thing. The evening's excitements will have been too much for her.'

Chapter 4

Septimus, September 1879: Cape Town

He'd had no intention of falling in love with Laura Brooke. It had happened, that's all. Being thrown together with her at Cora De Villiers's; and then finding her so very much out of reach. If she'd been a widow, it might have been easier; or even a woman un-happily married—he'd met a few of those. But to have fallen for someone who barely knew he was there, because her thoughts were fixed on the man she loved—a man, moreover, who happened to be dead—was the kind of darned bad luck he'd never run into till then.

She had intrigued him from the start. She was reserved—but then most Englishwomen were. This was more than just maidenly bashfulness. He'd never had the slightest trouble overcoming that. A remark about the brightness of someone's eyes, or the whiteness of someone's hand, usually sufficed in such cases, he'd found.

Septimus was not unduly prone to vanity, but he knew that he generally passed muster with the female sex. Women liked him; they noticed him.

Only this woman failed to notice him.

He'd called the morning after Cora De Villiers's party, hoping to see her once more, but had found only the mistress of the house, looking sallow and greasy-faced after a late night and too much champagne.

'Oh, it's you,' she said, as he walked into the room. 'I thought it was that old bore Schermbrucker. He's got it into his head that he's in love with me...'

'The way you looked last night in that pretty red dress, I can't say I blame him at all.'

Cora raised an eyebrow at this. 'Flatterer. I know it's not my charms which draw you here.'

He was startled. What had she guessed? Then he saw that she was laughing.

'Confess it,' she said. 'You've fallen in love with Laura Brooke. Don't think I didn't see you, whispering away in the corner together...'

It was easy to parry absurdity with further absurdity.

'I can tell you straight out—she isn't my type. I like a woman with a bit more 'go'...'

Miss Leibbrandt, who was mending a stocking in an obscure part of the room, gave a small cough.

'You Americans and your barbarous expressions,' said Mrs De Villiers lightly. But he could tell he had pleased her, by the amorous look she threw him. 'You'll be joining us for luncheon, I suppose?'

He'd opened his mouth to refuse when the sound of voices drifting through the open veranda doors alerted him to the return of the two English ladies. 'Why, that'd be swell,' he said, and was rewarded with another soft look from his mistress.

When Laura Brooke walked in, he was struck again by the graceful way she held herself; she had none of Cora De Villiers's imperious style, and yet she drew the eye. He thought she seemed glad to see him, although she threw him only a brief smile. But maybe that was on account of Cora being there, with a face like a cat watching a mouse. There wasn't much love lost between those two—that much was plain to see.

'Ah, there you are, Miss Brooke!' said Cora. 'So thoughtful of you to join us at last! And dear Emiline, too,' she added, as that lady came in. 'You are looking very pale, my dear. I hope you are not tired out from all your rambling about the garden...'

'Not in the least,' said Mrs Reynolds. 'The air has done me good.'

'Miss Brooke does so insist on her walks—do you not, Miss Brooke?' went on Mrs De Villiers. 'I have never met such a one for walking. Only the other day I had to send the boy to find her, because she had got lost in the woods at Newlands...'

Laura smiled. 'I was not lost. I had forgotten the time.'

'I have warned her and warned her of the dangers of snakes

51

and scorpions,' said Cora De Villiers. 'But do you think she will listen?'

'I always have a good stick with me,' said Laura. 'And my boots are quite stout.'

'Indeed,' said her hostess, barely suppressing a shudder.

'If you like walking, you must certainly climb the Lion's Head,' said Septimus, aware as he spoke that his intervention could only add fuel to the fires of his mistress's jealousy. 'There's a remarkably fine view to be had from the top of it. I could take you, if you like...'

It was worth any amount of sulking on Cora's part to see the look that Laura Brooke gave him. As if he had offered her the dearest wish of her heart.

'Would you?' At once her expression clouded. 'But it would be an imposition...'

'Not a bit,' he replied, amused by the furious looks that Cora was directing at him. 'We could go tomorrow, if you like. The climb itself takes little more than two hours. Early morning is the best time—to avoid the worst of the heat, you know.'

'I should like that very much,' said Laura. 'That is—if you can spare me,' she added to Mrs Reynolds.

'Oh, my dear, of course you must go,' said that lady. 'Since Mr Doyle is so kind as to offer to accompany you...'

'Why don't we all go?' interjected Mrs De Villiers, with a triumphant glance at her lover. 'Emiline will enjoy the drive—will you not, dear? There is a pleasant enough view from Signal Hill. And Gertrude likes a walk—do you not, Gertrude? She can go with you on your climb, whilst Emiline and I have a nice long gossip. We can take a picnic!' she cried, her good humour quite restored, it seemed, by her annexation of the plan. 'Cold chicken—I am sure there is some cold chicken left over from last night—and potted shrimps, and all kinds of good things. Such a charming idea. I am glad I thought of it.'

In the event, it was late afternoon before they were ready to go, since—as Septimus knew from intimate experience—Mrs De Villiers was seldom visible before noon, her mornings being consumed by complicated rituals of bathing and dressing. By that time, the heat was intense and there was no option but to wait it out—sunstroke being so very disagreeable, Mrs De Villiers said, with her tinkling laugh.

It was still hot when they set out, although the sun was low in the sky, striking off the white walls of buildings in the city's bowl, as the carriage ascended the lower slopes of Signal Hill. For those, like himself, who were familiar with the climate, it was possible to differentiate between this relative coolness—comparable to that of an English summer or a New York fall—and the fiery temperatures often reached in December.

Not that he was overly troubled by the heat, but he felt some concern for the fair skins of the English ladies. Both wore hats, it was true, but Miss Brooke had soon discarded hers, preferring, she said, to feel the sun on her face; even Mrs Reynolds had thrown back her veil.

'For it is such a treat,' she said. 'not to be cold all the time—is it not, Laura dear?'

Cora De Villiers took no such chances. To the protective screen of hat and veil she had added a silk parasol. 'Otherwise one burns as black as the natives,' she said. She seemed in high spirits—shouting at the driver to go slowly over the ruts, so as not to shake up the champagne too much. 'We will all be as merry as crickets by the time we have finished our walk.' Quite forgetting she was not of the walking party.

When the driver had been thoroughly scolded, she turned her attention to Septimus. His clothes were quite frightful, she said.

'I am quite ashamed to be seen with you,' she cried. 'You look as if you are dressed for a day's shooting, instead of for an afternoon's picnicking with ladies.'

Of Miss Brooke's appearance she said nothing, only nudging Septimus's foot with her own, to direct his attention to the younger woman's footwear—a pair of unremarkable brown boots.

'Like a housemaid's,' was Cora's whispered verdict.

Privately, he thought Miss Brooke's boots perfectly fine, and quite the thing for walking. They were certainly more suitable than the dainty kid slippers Cora was wearing. As if by accident, she let her foot rest against his for the remainder of the journey. A month ago, that slight but insistent pressure would have thrilled him, with its promise of carnal pleasures to come; now, her touch seemed merely annoying.

The fact of it was, he was more excited by the glimpse he got of Laura Brooke's slender ankles, briefly visible above the clumsy boots as she jumped down from the carriage, than by all Cora's studied charms.

'Don't be too long,' that lady called from her seat in the landeau. 'Or the champagne will be getting warm...'

Whether it was this last injunction, or simply a desire to be free of the constraints of the past few days which determined the smart pace at which his young companion set out, Septimus could not be sure; any doubts he might have had as to whether Miss Brooke would be 'up to' the climb, vanished in an instant. The path was steep, with tumbled rocks here and there forming a kind of staircase; these she ascended in a twinkling, with no more effort than if she were running upstairs at home to fetch something she had forgotten.

At the top of this first 'flight' she stood waiting for him to catch up with her. Both waited as Gertrude Leibbrandt toiled up behind them. From here, the view was of wooded slopes, thick with flowering shrubs. Protea of some sort; he did not know the names. Birches and silver trees. In the distance, rose the mountains: the Twelve Apostles to one side; the Devil's Peak to the other, with the great span of Table Mountain between it and where they were standing.

At this distance, the city seemed no bigger than a toy, built out of a child's wooden blocks. Beyond, was the curve of the bay, a deep azure at this hour.

'How wonderful,' she said.

She was as he had never yet seen her: her eyes bright with pleasure, a warm colour in her cheeks from her exertions. A transformed creature, he thought, allowing himself to speculate as to which was her truer nature: the shy girl of the night before, or this Maenad, with flushed face and tumbled locks. He knew which of the two he preferred.

'Shall we go on?' he said.

'O, surely we have only just started?' she replied, as—Miss Leibbrandt having got her breath back—they set off once more.

'I believe you're going to Natal?' he said. He did not say from whom he had heard it, since this was obvious enough.

'Yes.'

'You didn't mention it last night.'

'There was not an opportunity to do so.'

'I'm sorry. I do tend to run on...'

'I meant that we were interrupted. By our friend,' she added sotto voce, since Miss Leibbrandt was within earshot. She smiled. 'You see now why I was so intent on quizzing you about it.'

'I guess so. It's a dangerous place for a woman, you know...'

'So people keep telling me. I'm not afraid, however.'

'I'm sure you're not. You don't strike me as the type that's easily scared.'

She laughed. 'You seem very sure of my character, for someone who has known me a mere matter of days.'

In another woman, he would have called her tone flirtatious. But when he glanced at her sideways, her expression gave nothing away.

'I find I can generally form a pretty good opinion of a person's character from a few moments' acquaintance,' he said. 'It goes with my profession...'

'Of course. What an interesting profession that must be.'

Again, he had the feeling that she was laughing at him.

'I find it so, most of the time. But we were talking of your trip to Natal...'

'Were we? I didn't think that there was much more to say. Beyond the fact that it is generally considered to be a dangerous place, and quite unsuitable for ladies.'

'I didn't say that.'

'Not in so many words.'

They had reached the point where the sandy track up which they had been climbing with increasingly difficulty gave way to a steep rock-face. A chain was attached to the rock, by means of iron rivets, hammered in at intervals. It was with the aid of this that they were intending to reach the summit. Now, as they waited for Miss Leibbrandt to join them, he felt an impulse to confess all that he knew. It was with a flicker of shame that he recalled how it was that he had come to know it.

He'd been in bed with Cora De Villiers at the time. Earlier that evening, she'd thrown a tantrum, about the attentions he'd—allegedly—been paying to Miss Brooke. It had taken a good deal of placatory—and amorous—activity on his part to disabuse her of the notion. Afterwards, she was like a cat that had got the cream—stretching her long white arms above her head in an exaggerated yawn of satisfied desire.

'Anyway,' she had said, continuing the conversation interrupted by these transports, 'even if you were thinking of amusing yourself with our Miss Brooke, she's not for the taking.'

'Why? Is she engaged to be married?'

Cora De Villiers laughed. Her handsome head, with its coils of dark hair, turned towards him on the pillow. 'In a manner of speaking. The man she was going to marry was killed a year ago, out in Natal. At Isandula, or some such...'

'Isandhlwana.'

He was silent a moment, recalling his visit to the place, five months before. Even now, he could not suppress a shiver of disgust at the memory. The piles of desiccated corpses. The pervasive stench... He had never seen anything more disgusting, nor more pitiful.

There had been a great black crow at work upon something—a human skull, he saw, when he drew nearer. He'd shouted to scare it off, but it had merely flapped its wings and settled a short distance away, awaiting its chance to return.

'Did I not tell you?' Cora was saying. 'It was Emiline Reynolds's son she was engaged to. The two of them—she and Emiline, that is, not the son, you know—are making a pilgrimage to the place where he was killed. It is all quite romantic. Although what they hope to find there, I can't imagine...'

Now he turned to Laura Brooke.

'I'm very sorry for your loss,' he said.

She did not reply at once.

'I'm also sorry if I offended you. My remarks the other night were ill-judged...'

'I was not offended.'

It was at this moment that Miss Leibbrandt joined them, red in the face and out of sorts. 'I am finished,' she said. 'I cannot go another step. The view is very nice indeed, but at my age, one can have enough of views.'

From here the view was of the broad sweep of the Atlantic coast, dotted here and there along the edge of it by the elegant villas of Sea Point. A bench had been placed at the spot. Onto this Miss Leibbrandt subsided, with a grateful sigh.

'I will sit here, and wait for you,' she said. 'I have done my best. I am sure Cora would not expect me to do more.'

Laura's hands were already grasping the heavy chain. As Septimus watched, she swung herself up to the first rocky ledge, as light as a fairy, he thought, setting off after her.

But even with the chain for a handhold it was harder going than before. More than once he heard her exclaim under her breath at a slip or stumble.

Of course it was harder for her; she was, after all, of the weaker sex; although he for one had never cared for the term. He had known several young ladies in his time who could ride a horse or draw a bow as well as any man, and he had once heard Mrs Stanton speak at a rally in New York City. A handsome woman, and most persuasive on the suffrage question, he'd thought. If there were any justice in the world, she'd have a seat in Congress by now.

'Oh...' This time she had almost fallen. 'These wretched skirts,' she said. 'They do so get in the way.'

'Here. Take my hand.'

She hesitated no more than a moment. It was simple expediency, was it not? And they were now out of sight of censorious eyes.

'Thank you.'

Her hand felt warm, and a little gritty, after her recent tumble. But had it been as cool and smooth as marble, it could have produced no more powerful a sensation in him. He was not unacquainted with the sensation, of course; still, it was disconcerting when it happened in the presence of a lady.

When they reached the top, she disengaged herself briskly.

'I'm sure I shall manage from now on.'

A rough path climbed up the side of the crag, between tumbled rocks. Out of a cleft, a tree grew—at what seemed an impossible angle. She wondered at it.

'How does it sustain itself? There is barely enough soil for a blade of grass.'

'Things seem to grow here in the most inhospitable conditions,' he said. 'In Namaqualand, it rains but once a year. When it does, the desert is filled with flowers.'

'How I should like to see that!'

It was on the tip of his tongue to say that he would take her; if she had been an American girl he would not have hesitated. But his years in England had taught him that one did not express oneself with such freedom to English girls.

So he merely said, 'Come. You'll like the view from up here. We'll have all of Cape Town at our feet.'

When they got to the summit, the sun was low in the sky, and the whole scene was bathed in a golden light: mountains, rocks and far below, the intricate grid of streets which was the city. The sea was a deep blue. The sheer rock face of Table Mountain, cleft with deep shadows in the evening light, seemed, to his fancy, to be half alive—a breathing presence. How insignificant he felt in the face of it...

He was about to make some such observation—to remark on how one's sense of self was diminished in such a landscape— when he saw she was no longer beside him.

'Say—take care, won't you?'

For she had stepped without hesitation over the narrow space which lay between the cliff's edge and a shelf of rock which jutted out from it, so that she stood suspended directly over the frightful drop—it must have been a thousand feet. More.

From where he stood, dry-mouthed at the sight, it appeared as if there were nothing between her and the sea below. If she fell she would be dashed to pieces.

'Step back,' he called. Thinking, if I try and grab hold of her, she might lose her balance...

But she did not hear him—or pretended not to—the wind whipping her skirts around her, so that it seemed for an instant as if she might be tugged over the precipice whether she wished it or no.

Then she turned to face him, a smile of such delight on her

face that he felt his heart turn over. She spread her arms wide, to encompass everything beyond: sea, sky, and shining city.

'Is it not the most beautiful sight you ever saw?' she cried.

Only then did he venture closer. 'I'd like it a lot better if you were to admire it from a safer distance.'

'You are afraid I will fall and kill myself,' she said. 'But don't worry. I am quite sure-footed.'

A moment later, she leapt nimbly across the gap and stood beside him. He breathed again.

'I am sorry if I frightened you,' she said, with a mischievous look.

It was true that he'd been frightened. But he wasn't going to admit it.

'You are not dressed for climbing,' was all he said. 'You said so yourself.'

'When are we women ever dressed for anything—except sitting with our hands folded in our laps?' she replied.

He was not sure how to answer her.

'Please do not think me ungrateful,' she went on. 'I could not have seen this'—again, her arms were spread wide to embrace the broad sweep of the landscape—'without you to bring me.'

He started to say that he was glad to have been of service, but she cut across him.

'I have wanted to see this view more than I can say. To see it for myself, that is—for I feel that I have seen it before, in another's account of it.'

She broke off; then drew a breath and continued: 'Lieutenant Reynolds came here, you know, and stood where we are standing. It was he who told me about the rocks which hang out over the bay.'

She said nothing more, but stood as if lost in thought, looking back at the spot where she had stood so precariously balanced between heaven and earth.

Septimus could not repress a pang of envy towards the other man, if only for the fact that it was of him that she was certainly thinking—although it was ridiculous, surely, to be envious of the dead?

He'd been working as a stringer for the New York Times—writing occasional pieces on up-and-coming politicians, and reports on which of the aforementioned was in attendance on such and such an evening at the salon of this or that fashionable Manhattan hostess—when the call had come. The Queen had been proclaimed Empress of India (a clever piece of work on the part of Disraeli) and they needed someone in London, to cover the ensuing celebrations.

Webster was to have gone; but Webster's wife was sick—and so he, Doyle, would take Webster's place, said his editor, the formidable Ormerod.

He had expected to find London a backward city, full of mouldering mansions and gimcrack palaces, and stuffed with duchesses and bishops; it turned out to be as modern as he could have wished. Duchesses were certainly to be found, but not in unreasonable numbers; as for the palaces, there were much grander buildings on the Upper East Side, in his opinion.

What impressed him more than the crumbling glories of Westminster and St James's was the City, with its towering marble banks and offices. Here, at the heart of the Old World, was a modern metropolis. The Fleet Street office where he spent his days was as up-to-date as anything in Manhattan, with its constant chatter of telegraph and rattle of type-writing machines, and its uniformed messenger-boys running in and out.

At the end of three months, when he found himself recalled to New York, he had made up his mind to stay on. A job had presented itself, fortuitously, at the Illustrated London News. The remuneration, if not exactly princely, was adequate and the brief—to cover the recent disturbances in Kabul—one he could not resist.

It amazed him, looking back, to think that he had ever thought London parochial. It was the hub of everything that was going on, not only in the (quaintly-named) British Isles, but all over: India, China, Africa. Could his native land claim as much? He thought not. America—although undoubtedly progressive—was also sadly inward-looking. Even its wars were internal affairs. What sort of country was it, after all, that would have allowed its citizens to turn upon each other, as his countrymen had done in '61?

The British ordered these things better: for them, war was a branch of foreign policy.

He had been fortunate enough to observe this at close quarters, during his time in Afghanistan. He had remained there for six weeks, stationed with the Yorkshire regiment, who were on a tour of duty in the border region. His account of the conflict, A Plain Man's View of the Afghan War—accompanied by sketches that were later 'got up' by one of the paper's resident artists—proved a great success.

It was on the strength of this that he was given Africa.

The news had come in on the wire on the morning of the 12th February. Septimus had been cooling his heels in McClintock's outer office, in the hope that something of interest might be put his way. The glory of his Kabul article had begun to fade a little, and pickings, of late, had been small. A Prime Ministerial speech on the Suez canal. A state visit by the Tsar and Tsarina.

What he longed for, shifting uncomfortably from one buttock to the other on one of McClintock's hard chairs, was for a return to Afghanistan. The situation had cooled in recent weeks, it was true; but there was always a chance that it might grow hotter again.

So it was with some alacrity that he got to his feet, as the door of the inner office burst open, and the editor's red-bearded face appeared.

'Something's happened,' McClintock said. 'Not good. Not good at all, from the sound of it. There's been a battle. Great loss of life. Ours, it would seem...'

Then, as Septimus—his heart already leaping at the prospect of what must surely follow: India; the North West Frontier—got to his feet, McClintock went on,

'We'll need a man out there of course. You'll do. But it might take time. The government'll be sending reinforcements, I imagine. Or they might not. One thing's certain—there's going to be an almighty row about this. I mean,' said McClintock, permitting himself a wintry smile, 'to lose a whole regiment looks like carelessness, doesn't it? Dizzy's going to be hopping mad. Given that he'd practically washed his hands of Africa...'

'Africa?' Septimus had been unable to keep the dismay from his voice. He had not been thinking of Africa.

'Why, yes. Didn't I say? They've gone and started a war. In Zululand, I believe. Very embarrassing all round—to be soundly beaten by a lot of savages. But that's the English for you,' said McClintock, who was Scottish. 'Always underestimating the enemy.'

In the event, it was the end of March before Septimus reached Natal—in time for the first despatches from Khambula: a victory, at last. 'The tide is turning in our favour,' he wrote in his report. 'In the space of a mere six weeks, the Zulu army has been utterly routed, and the rule of law imposed on these uncivilised lands.'

Privately, he wondered whether this was true. There was still a war to win, against an enemy which could not always be found, and which all too frequently refused to obey the rules of civilised warfare. Not that the Zulus were the only ones capable of barbarism, that was a fact—although like a lot of other facts, it could not be published.

After Rorke's Drift, any Zulus found hiding in the fields around the camp, had been rounded up and strung up on a makeshift gallows. Others, too badly injured to be worth the bother of hanging, had been clubbed to death with rifle butts, or flung into the burial pit still alive. At Khambula, too, native prisoners had been slaughtered—again, nobody could say how many. Fifty, a hundred—or perhaps five hundred?

These things could not be spoken of; far less written about in the pages of eminent journals, such as his own. To have done so, would have been to incur the wrath, not only of the officer corps, but of the British public as a whole. The heroes of Isandhlwana and Rorke's Drift could not be associated with any kind of improper conduct—least of all cold-blooded murder.

What the public wanted was tales of heroism and sacrifice, not beastliness. 'The Saving of the Colours' or the 'Defence of the Mission Station'—those were tales of which people could not get enough, it seemed. He himself had contributed his share...

'It was a very pitiful sight,' he wrote in his first despatch from the battlefield, 'to be walking there, under the blue heavens, and to stumble, amongst the long grass, on the bleached bones of some poor fellow who had breathed his last upon that alien soil.'

Here lay the remains of one such—speared through the heart with such force that the corpse was pinioned to the ground. There, another lay sprawled as if in sleep, the remnants of his scarlet coat fluttering in the light wind that stirred the grass, like the petals of a poppy in a cornfield...

That was coming it a bit, he knew; but the public liked a touch of poesy with its morning eggs and bacon.

See, further up the hill (that terrible hill!), where the flight of those last survivors can be traced in the line of bodies, strung out like beads upon a string—or, dare one say, like bullets upon a bandolier—all the way along the ridge. Here they fought; here they fell; here they died, these noble men. For theirs, make no mistake, is the stuff of nobility. Englishmen everywhere...

Septimus's pen held fire for a moment, then wrote on, an English pen for the duration.

Englishmen around the globe, wherever they might be in the service of this greatest of nations, will raise a cheer, or bow a head, or wipe away a silent tear, to think of the deeds that were accomplished on that day: January 22nd, Anno Domini 1879. Let it be written in letters of fire...

Again, he hesitated a moment; remembered the eaters of bacon and eggs, and continued.

...in letters of fire, I say—a date to be spoken of with awe and remembered for as long as men have brains to think or hearts to feel...

It was strong stuff—but the readers of the *Illustrated London News*, the *Daily News*, the *Telegraph* (for Septimus was syndicated now) could not get enough of it, evidently. And his was the pen, English or not, to give it to them—whether it was tales of

63

courage under fire, of Captain Younghusband, on his rocky eminence, holding the savage foe at bay; or of self-sacrifice. Lieutenant Smith-Dorrien risking death to help a wounded man; Lieutenant Pope firing his revolver to cover the escape of his comrades, until stopped by an assegai thrust in the heart. Cavaye, Coghill, Melvill, Mostyn, Shepstone, Smith, Wardell: names that would live for all Eternity, if he, Septimus Doyle, had anything to do with it.

As well as the stories of bravery and dash, there were those that touched the heart: Younghusband (again) shaking hands with his surviving men before turning to face the foe for the last time; Private Wassall bearing his comrade Private Westwood to safety on his own horse; Colonel Durnford, in his red bandana, making his last stand upon the kopje—all these were real enough, if perhaps a little 'touched up' for the benefit of the sentimental public.

The reality had been very different, of course: there had been nothing poetic or inspiring about his first visit to Isandhlwana. Even now, he could not recall it without a shiver of disgust. He had seen men killed by the score in Afghanistan—their bodies blown to bits by heavy artillery fire—and considered himself inured to such horrors.

But he was unprepared for what he found here. The sheer scale of the carnage was something he had not met with before—that, and the fact that, four months on, the battlefield was now a charnel-house. Four months of heat and flies had done their work on these poor unburied corpses. What was left was both horrible and pathetic.

The stench was the first thing that alerted them to what they had come to. As he and his confreres—Forbes of the Daily News, and his colleague Prior—rode up, the burial party, consisting of General Marshall's cavalry and some native auxiliaries, was already at work. Some of the men had tied handkerchiefs over their mouths and noses to block the smell, but this must have made little difference.

'My God,' said Prior, who had turned pale under his sunburn. 'What a fearful mess.'

What became all too apparent, as they slowly circumnavigated the ruined camp—stumbling over the remains of its erstwhile defenders as they did so—was that this had been, not a battle, but a rout.

All across the broad plain, the skeletons of men and animals lay scattered. In the ravine, the dead lay thickest—tumbled over one another, in ghastly intimacy: their bodies, that had once moved, breathed, and felt the sun, now reduced to grisly cadavers, with skin toughened to the colour and consistency of leather, the flesh having wasted away.

Some—dismembered heaps of yellow bones, at which wild animals had evidently been at work—were scarcely recognisable as human. Others retained the semblance of men, petrified in attitudes of desperate flight and final agony. In their blackened and contorted features could be discerned traces of human expression, and the emotions written there were terrible.

'Christ damn it all,' said Forbes, into the silence. 'I cannot show this.'

For the past hour, he had been making notes and sketches—as they all had—to record the principal features of the scene. Now he threw down his notebook. Septimus had come to the same conclusion: the horror of this could not be told at home.

He took out his cigarette-case and passed it to Forbes, after taking one for himself. The taste of the thing was foul, but it helped to kill the stink of corruption that rose all around them.

Prior had dismounted and now wandered distractedly around the field, pausing from time to time to examine objects that caught his eye. Amongst the bare bones and half-rotted remnants of a once proud uniform, were memorabilia of a different kind. One such fragment he handed to Septimus, without comment. It was a photograph of a young woman, of no particular beauty, with a child aged about two years old on her lap. On the back was an inscription: To dear darling Dadda.

Septimus looked at it for a while, then made to give it back, but Prior waved the thing away with a pained grimace.

'Perhaps the General will have a use for it...'

And indeed the commanding officer had given orders that such items, where possible, were to be collected up, for distribution to the families.

Septimus nodded, and slipped the sun-faded image inside his

notebook for safe-keeping—realising, as he did so, that he might have another use for it. The photograph was in fact still in his possession. The story he had written about the unknown infant pictured there and his 'darling Dadda' had been one of his more successful, he felt, with the faint stirring of self-disgust such occasional lapses of scruple aroused in him.

Chapter 5

Theo, October 1878: Cape Town

So they were mobilizing at last. After all the months of waiting, they were to be off, on the first stage of the journey which would bring them closer to their goal—although what that was, precisely, not even those commanding the operation seemed entirely certain. There was the question of the Zulus, of course; and there was the question of the Boers. Both presented varying degrees of threat, which would have to be confronted. Each might—and this was where strategy came in—be set against the other, thus rendering the threat in each case ineffectual. For the time being, at least, it suited the British government to regard the Boers as allies.

Once the Zulu question had been conclusively settled, there would be time enough to deal with the remaining problem.

In the meantime, there was the small matter of moving an army. The distance involved was not great, in African terms—barely two thousand miles; and a good deal of it, from Cape Town to Durban, would be managed by sea. This, at least, would be the route by which the guns would travel, in company with those battalions not in charge of supplies.

For the latter, the overland route—by rail, where it existed, by foot and by ox-cart—was the more practical. Provisions for sixteen thousand men and nine hundred horses—two thousand tons of them, contained in nine hundred wagons drawn by ten thousand oxen, and in sixty mule carts drawn by five hundred mules—presented a not inconsiderable problem of transportation.

Amongst this mass of stuff were boxes of rifle ammunition calculated at two hundred and seventy rounds per soldier—seventy rounds to be carried by each man and two hundred for his especial use to be carried in clearly identifiable wagons. Sufficient tentage had to be transported for all the officers' and troops' mess rooms, mobile bakeries and field hospitals; medical supplies had of course to be carried, as did spare uniforms and footwear (marching over stony ground being hard on the boots); cooking utensils and blankets, axes and waterproof sheets, lanterns and lifting-jacks, ropes and shovels, stretchers and engineering equipment.

Then there was the matter of foodstuffs: tins of bully beef and sardines, bags of hardtack biscuits, corn and tea. Beef cattle had to be transported: a mighty host, to feed another. Each fighting man consumed one pound of fresh meat a day, as well as one-and-a-half pounds of bread or biscuit. Fresh vegetables supplemented this diet when they could be got; bottled beer and tobacco augmented it.

For the officers, there was daintier fare: broiling fowl, rabbits and whatever game could be found along the way relieved the monotony of roast beef; as did cured hams and pâté de fois gras. Bath Oliver biscuits were required for the General's table, to accompany the fine old Stilton to which he was partial. Smoked kippers were another delicacy not available to the lower ranks; neither was the patum peperium which added savour to the General's hot buttered toast offered to them. Tins of pepper for the General's soup and mustard for his beef needed also to be carried. Fresh fish was freely available, thank G-d, and fresh vegetables, too.

Indeed, there was no need for the General and his officers to go hungry—nor thirsty, either. Madeira and hock and burgundy and champagne were to be found on the General's table; as were brandy and whisky and gin and fine old port. Cigars were another necessity—designed for more sensitive palettes than the rough 'shag' smoked by the men. Bottled Vichy water was no less essential, to ease the aching head, on those mornings when the General and his companions had sat up late at cards.

At East London, they put in for supplies, and to collect the guns which had been brought up by ox-cart from Port Elizabeth. These included a Gatling gun, six twelve-pounder field-pieces, and two twenty-four pounder rockets. Coleman was to have supervised the loading of these, but Coleman was sick: 'a dose picked up from some filthy Kaffir tart,' was his explanation.

So it fell to Theo to go ashore, which he minded not a bit, after two days cooped-up in the noise and stench produced by two hundred men, and exacerbated by close quarters. How any of these naval types stood it for more than a week was beyond him; he said as much to Hamilton, the ship's medical officer, and the latter had replied that there had been times when he felt the same. 'But you know, one can get used to anything,' he said, with a rueful smile.

After Durban, Hamilton was to proceed to the mouth of the Tugela River, where five companies of the Buffs were stationed, under Colonel Pearson's command. There had been heavy rains for a month and most of the men had diarrhoea. Sleeping sickness was rife, too. The mosquitoes were particularly bad in that part of the country. For his own part, he was eager to see some real action at last, after months of ferrying other chaps up and down this barren coast.

He was reading Heine.

'Do you like the Germans?' he said to Theo.

Theo confessed that he did not read German.

'Oh, but you must!' cried Hamilton. He read aloud a line or two: "*Ich weiss nicht, was soll es bedeuten, dass ich so traurig bin...*" A soulful language, is it not?'

Landing at East London, Theo found Captain Essex, who was in charge of Transport, striding up and down the quayside in a filthy temper. 'There you are!' he said. 'About bloody time, if I might say so. I've been kicking my heels here for the best part of a day, waiting for you people to arrive. At this rate the Zulus will have given up and gone home...'

Getting the guns on board the Active proved to be quite a business. The silting up of the river's mouth being as bad as it was, they were obliged to anchor a quarter of a mile off, beyond the bar, and to ferry the guns out by lighter. It was late afternoon by the time they set sail, and a haze lay over the green wooded coastline, so that it seemed to float upon the waters, its massive stone cliffs seeming no more substantial than clouds.

'*The hills are shadows, and they flow from form to form,*

69

and nothing stands,' murmured Theo.

'Very apposite,' said Hamilton, who stood beside him. 'But I still say you ought to try the Germans.' He drew the pouch from his coat pocket and began to roll a cigarette. 'Oh, I'm sorry, old man, I was forgetting...Would you care for a smoke?'

Theo shook his head.

'After a day spent in the company of fifty men, all puking their guts up, I find nothing but a good strong whiff of the fragrant nicotinia will do.'

But Theo was not listening.

'The hills are shadows,' he repeated softly. He was a shadow, too; they all were. Soon, they too would melt like mist in the sun, and it would be as if they had never been.

By mid-morning of the next day, they were running in close to the Natal coast. The rocky heights of Pondoland had been left behind and all was lushness and profusion. Here and there amongst the trees was a patch of vivid green that Hamilton said was a sugar plantation, with low thatched huts resembling beehives. Mangoes and bananas grew in abundance, as did clumps of tall bamboo, and the ubiquitous palm. Theo remarked that it seemed a veritable Eden, and Hamilton laughed.

'Indeed! But there are serpents in your Garden of Eden, believe me. And mosquitoes—with a bite like the very Devil...'

'Dearest Mother,' wrote Theo.

> Well, as you see from the above, we are in Durban, which is very hot and very damp and full of biting insects. This much having been said, it is a fairly pleasant spot— and the food, after a week of salt pork and hard 'tack', is greatly improved. Last night the officers' mess sat down to a cold lobster bisque, followed by saddle of mutton and all kinds of cold jellies and sweets. At this rate, I shall return quite fat!
>
> You would hardly recognise me as it is, I have grown so brown—like a native, I am told! My swimming has come on immensely: on the voyage here, I swam every day from the quarter-deck. There is no swimming here, though, on

account of the crocodiles, which infest all the rivers.

Thank you for the tobacco and the ink—both in short supply. Some of the fellows have been reduced to using gunpowder mixed with water—I mean of course to write with, not to smoke! Please send my thanks to Miss Brooke for the books, especially 'Vanity Fair'.

It is hard to find anything decent to read here. All the newspapers are a fortnight old by the time they reach us, so we are by no means 'in the swim' with regard to developments. Most of the news seems to be of Afghanistan— which seems hard, when we are intent on fighting a different war. Some fellows are saying that Dizzy would funk it if he could. The government does not care a rap for Africa—that is the truth of it.

Well, on to happier things: how is the dear old homestead, with all its dear, familiar faces? I trust you are well, dearest Mama, and that the trouble you mentioned in your last has now eased. How are the dogs? I was sorry to hear about poor Rags. It sounds as though she will not last long, from what you say.

Alas, I am at the end of my allocation of paper. If you could see your way to sending me a quire or two, I would put it to good use, you may be sure. Whilst it is by no means as dull here as it was in Cape Town, we are thrown very much upon our own devices, in the way of entertainment. Reading and writing letters is our only solace—you never saw such a crew for scribbling!

Write soon, dearest Mama, with as much news as you can muster. Remember me to anyone who knows me, and reserve my fondest love for yourself, my sweetest Ma. By the way, did you like the photograph? I had it done in Cape Town. It is not a good likeness, but it will serve to remind you of

Your affect. son,
Theodore Charles Reynolds

On the bed next to his, Marlowe was laying out a game of Patience. It would not come right, and he clicked his tongue, as the cards refused to fall. Young Parr was reading a letter from his girl. Coleman, passing by at that moment, snatched it out of his hand.

'O my darling,' he read in a shrill falsetto, 'How I long to see you...'

'Give it here,' said Parr, his face flushing scarlet.

But Coleman was enjoying the joke too much to stop. His remarks grew lewder. Parr was on the verge of tears.

'Let him have it,' said Hallam, without raising his eyes from his book.

'What's it to you, old boy?' said Coleman, smiling unpleasantly.

'I said let him have it.'

With a show of magnanimity, Coleman surrendered the letter.

'Have your simpering little schoolgirl back, then. I'm off to find a real woman to fuck...'

'There's a good chap,' murmured Hallam. 'Don't hurry back, will you?'

He glanced up, and his eyes met Theo's. Theo was the first to look away. He regretted, now, having been so frank with his friend about his own troubles. But Hallam had been there, that last day in Cape Town, and knew the truth of the affair. 'I say, old man, you are in a scrape,' he had said. 'But I shouldn't let it worry you unduly. In another six weeks, when we facing up to the enemy, all this will seem very small beer indeed...'

Since that conversation, it seemed to Theo that a certain constraint, which had not been there before, had affected his relations with Hallam. The easy friendship of their first few months had gone, replaced by a wary politeness. It was almost, Theo felt, as if Hallam despised him for his weakness. Hallam was not a man to tolerate weakness—especially over a woman. If he himself had ever resorted to such temptations, he kept it very dark.

In Durban there was a Miss Morel. Her father was a lawyer, and she had just turned eighteen. At a party in one of the grand houses on the Berea, Theo had danced with her several times; and had fetched her an ice between dances. In the garden afterwards, he had held her hand.

Next morning, he received a visit from Morel: a red-faced little man with a truculent manner. 'Now, look here,' was his opening sally. 'What exactly is it you intend towards Maisie?' Theo had blustered at first: Miss Morel was a charming young lady. Naturally, his feelings for her, though entirely respectful, could only be of the most superficial. Given the briefness of their acquaintance... etc etc

Old Morel brushed these remarks aside with a gesture of weary disdain. 'Let me make myself plain,' he said. 'Mrs Morel and I have a future in mind for our daughter. And anything less than a Brevet-Major ain't it.'

After Maisie Morel, he steered clear of young girls with irascible relations. A Mrs Swinburne, whose husband often had business that took him to Johannesburg, proved more accommodating. Enjoying her ample charms in her capacious bed offered a distraction from thoughts of one he had left behind.

If Mrs Swinburne noticed his abstracted moods, she made no mention of them. 'I've a son your age,' she told him, at their last parting. 'Stationed with the Royal Artillery in Kabul. Lovely lad. You remind me of him, a bit. Of course, I was married out of the schoolroom.' She was a good-looking woman; although she must have been close to forty.

Durban had given them a good send-off. Dances and dinners every night, and no end of invitations to luncheon parties from the matrons of the Berea. Here, the talk was all of the coming war—for it was all much closer at hand than it had been in Cape Town, where Zululand might as well have been on the moon, for all the interest most Capetonians took in what was happening there. In Durban, there was a sense of urgency, and of barely contained excitement. War fever, one might have called it, had one been so inclined.

At the theatre one evening with Hallam, a fat man had come onstage wearing a leather apron and feathered headdress, his face blackened with burnt cork. During the burst of laughter and clapping which greeted this apparition, Hallam told him that it was meant for Cetshwayo, the Zulu king—although, he added, sotto voce, he was, by all accounts, far from being the buffoon represented here.

'Quite a cool customer, by all accounts. An absolute monarch, of course. If one of his followers displeases him, he has the fellow executed on the spot. I do not think one would risk making fun of him to his face, do you?'

King Cetshwayo's comic 'turn' was followed by a musical number, performed by a choir of young ladies dressed in white, with pasteboard helmets and tridents, suggestive of the Britannic goddess. It was a song which was all the rage in London, it was said. He remembered nothing but the chorus: '*We don't want to fight, but by jingo, if we do...*'

When the house-lights came up, and it was perceived that there were officers of Her Majesty's 24th regiment in the audience, a cheer went up, and several of the young ladies in white threw roses plucked from their bouquets towards the box where Theo and his companions sat.

'They love us now,' murmured Hallam in Theo's ear. 'But they'll have forgotten all about us in a month's time, when we'll be up to our necks in it...'

At Pietermaritzburg, there was no leisure for theatre-going, or any other recreation, apart from shooting—which, in any case, was necessary, if the officers' mess was to enjoy anything other than salt beef for its dinner. Here, the citizenry were outnumbered two to one by the military, and the streets were awash with scarlet. As well as those from his own regiment, the 24th, Theo recognised men from the 9th Lancers, the Dragoon Guards, the 80th and the 90th Foot, together with some from the 5th Company of the Royal Engineers, whose job was bridge-building and road-laying—although they would all have a taste of that, by all accounts.

If they had thought the roads bad up till now, Colonel Glyn informed them one night over dinner, they were in for a nasty surprise. 'For there are no bloody roads worth the name, in this godforsaken country!' he roared out, to general laughter.

They would need decent roads if they were to move the wagons. Even on foot, the going would be hard. Each man had a rifle and bayonet, two pouches, an ammunition bag, a haversack, water-bottle, mess-tin and two days' rations to carry—the whole weighing fifty-seven pounds. Thank God they no longer had to carry their bedding, which could be thrown on the wagon with all the rest.

The new issue Martini-Henry rifles were a lot lighter than the old Snider-Enfields, too; although there was nothing light about the charge they delivered: they could knock a man back in his tracks, and stop a charging buffalo, it was said.

Theo had never seen the latter claim put to the test, but he had seen what the gun could do to those less experienced in handling it. When it got overheated, its barrel tended to foul, so that it kicked like a mule when it went off. Nosebleeds and bruised shoulders were a regular result amongst the novices, at target-practice.

More serious was the Martini-Henry's tendency to jam when sand got into its breech mechanism. It was to be hoped that there would not be too much sand about, where they were going.

Chapter 6

Laura, October 1879: Cape Town

So it was that with many protestations of regret on the one hand, and of gratitude on the other, they took their leave of Cora De Villiers and boarded the train for Simon's Town, from whence they were to take ship for Durban. It was a fine day, with no prospect of storms: a perfect day for a sea voyage, said Captain Linley.

As she watched the low white houses along the bay grow gradually more distant, until they slipped out of sight around the headland, Laura felt anew the pleasure of solitary reflection. Although it was true she was not quite alone: Mrs Reynolds, wrapped in shawls, was ensconced on the upper deck with Elspeth; Captain Linley, as ever, hovered close at hand. But this freedom—this freedom from noise and bustle, and the banalities of Cape Town drawing rooms...

It felt as if a weight had fallen from her neck.

In the crisp bright air of the Spring morning the rocky peaks were as distinct as if they had been etched on glass. It was a treacherous coast, Captain Linley said, where many ships had been lost; to Laura, it seemed quite beautiful.

By the evening of the following day, they had reached Port Elizabeth, where they were to pick up the mails, and a fresh load of passengers. Teutons, for the most part, said Captain Linley. They would find the place thoroughly overrun. Not that he minded the Germans: their hotels were a good deal cleaner than most. If the ladies liked, he could take them to a beer-garden not too far from the centre where they might dine very well indeed.

Were the running of this country to be left to Englishmen and that of the hotels to Germans it would be to everyone's advantage, in his view.

From the ship's deck next morning Laura watched the busy scene in the bay. Of the ships anchored there, four were steamers, like their own, bound for distant ports. Smaller sailing vessels could also be seen, discharging cargo, and the shore was alive with black men, wading out into the water towards the lighters, to bring in the goods with which they were loaded.

It seemed a picture from an earlier time, she thought. The tumbling surf, swarming with half-naked bodies; the rhythmic motion with which the bales were passed from hand to hand. Quite picturesque. Although doubtless less so, to the labourers themselves...

A figure loomed at her side. She suppressed a sigh.

Had they time, Captain Linley said, they might have travelled by rail to Grahamstown, which was well worth a visit; or even as far as Graaff Reinet, in the Karoo. A charming town.

But alas, they must push on—East London was their next port-of-call. They would like East London; he himself thought it a 'go-ahead' place. There was no doubt that the war had been good for these little 'dorps'. Why, even a few years ago, it had been nothing but a fishing village; now it was quite the metropolis.

After East London, the coast grew wild, and the signs of human habitation fewer. Great cliffs rose up from the sea, which, even on a day as calm as this, grew savage as it struck the rocks. A hundred years ago, the Grosvenor had been lost here, with its fabulous cargo of Persian gold, said Captain Linley. They had never found it—although many had perished in the attempt.

Descending to the tiny cabin, she found Mrs Reynolds still sitting up. She was terribly pale—although the voyage had been calm so far—but seemed in fine spirits. She had given Elspeth a present of a hundred pounds, she said. She had hoped it would cheer her, but the silly goose had not left off crying since. The sooner she was married to her sergeant the better.

It was not until midday the next day that they rounded the Bluff, and saw Durban spread out before them, its harbour buildings almost obscured by a forest of masts. Above the town, rose the wooded eminence of the Berea: it was here they were to pass the next few days, with a sister of Colonel Philips. This was Mrs Tremayne; it was to her house that they were presently conveyed. Here, on the heights overlooking the bay, the air was cooler. In the city, the air had a close, damp heat, which was quite intolerable after the Cape breezes.

'And this is Major Hallam. He was with the twenty-fourth, you know,' said Mrs Tremayne.

'How do you do?' said Laura. It was difficult, at first, to look at his face. One side of it was all right, but the other was dreadfully scarred. 'I believe you knew Lieutenant Reynolds?'

From the start he gave, she knew it must have been so.

'He spoke of you often in his letters,' she said.

'You must be Miss Brooke...'

She smiled.

'Forgive me. I had no idea that you were here.'

'We have only just arrived.' She saw the enquiry in his eyes. 'Mrs Reynolds and myself.'

'Mrs Reynolds...' An expression passed across his features which she could not decipher. 'You mean his mother? Is she here then?'

'Yes. Let me take you to her. She will be so glad...'

Again, the strange expression: as if there were something he could say, but would not.

'I was not there, you know,' he said in a low voice. 'I mean, at the last. Our companies were separated. His remained in the camp. Mine had already been ordered out, before the fighting began...'

'We read the account in the Times,' she said.

Now it was his turn to smile. 'As to that,' he began; and checked himself. 'All I have to say is that I saw as little of what happened as the journalist who wrote that article. I am afraid that I can tell you nothing.'

'You were his friend,' she said.

Throughout their conversation, he had kept his scarred cheek averted, as if to spare her the sight of it; now he looked her full in the face.

'It is hard for us... for those of us who remained at home,' she persisted, when he said nothing. 'To imagine what it must have been like...'

On his ruined face, the smile had a sardonic twist.

'I am afraid that fighting a war is a great deal less exciting than you ladies suppose. Most of the time it is very dull indeed, with precious little opportunity for heroics.'

'I must confess that I was a little stung by his remark,' she wrote in her journal that evening.

I replied with some asperity that I was well aware from Theo's letters of the tedium he and his comrades had often had to endure, and that it was not heroics I meant, when I asked the man I knew to be his fellow officer and friend to describe what their last days together had been.

'But perhaps,' I could not prevent myself from adding, 'You and Lieutenant Reynolds did not part on good terms...'

It was a cruel thing to say, and I reproached myself for it as I saw its effect on the poor Major. His face flushed a deep red beneath the scar, and he said, in a voice that trembled slightly, 'Never say that! Lieutenant Reynolds and I were always the best of friends. Indeed...' Here, his smile was of a sadness to touch the heart. 'One might have said he was my only friend.'

He was silent a moment, his thoughts evidently preoccupied with the one who was dear to both of us. Then he said—Oh with what strength of feeling in his look and voice! 'It was only that, seeing you... and knowing of his deep attachment to you... well, it brought home to me that I shall never see the dear fellow again. Forgive me if I spoke harshly, but...' Here his voice faltered, and he looked away, so that I should not see how moved he was.

In a low voice (for we were surrounded by others) I begged him not to reproach himself—feeling quite wretched as I did so, for the pain I must have caused him. But in truth, he had already told me everything I wanted to know. That Theo was beloved—by himself, and no doubt, by others—was enough. I needed no tales of heroism.

We were joined at that moment by Mrs Tremayne, and a lady all in black she introduced as Mrs Hitchcock, whose late husband had been with the 24th. She had not long recovered from lying-in, she confided to me in a low voice, when the news of her husband's death was brought. It had been hard, but she had her sweet babe to console her, she said. Poor soul! She put a brave face on it, but I could see that her heart was breaking.

Perhaps made uncomfortable by such woman's talk, Major Hallam made his adieux soon afterwards, promising that he would call upon myself and Mrs Reynolds before we left Durban.

If I live to be a hundred, I shall never forget the sadness in his eyes as he spoke of Theo. It was as if he had lost the dearest friend of his heart—no woman mourning a sweetheart could have looked or sounded more grief-stricken.

O my beloved, if you could only know how much you are missed! To have lived, as you lived, a mere twenty-five short years, and yet to have inspired such profound emotions... My heart is too full to write more, and the candle is burning low. Tomorrow we begin our preparations for what may prove to be the hardest part of our journey. We have engaged a maid, to replace the inestimable Elspeth (who parted from us with many tears and protestations of affection). Her name is Rejoice, which I take to be a good omen for our endeavour...

Pietermaritzburg was a pleasant place, set on a mountainous ridge, and surrounded by groves of blue-gum trees. After the stifling heat of Durban, it was a relief to breathe its cooler air, and to be free from the ever-present mosquito. The military element was more in evidence—this being a garrison town.

Here they engaged a guide, a dour Dutchman named De Kuiper. He had served with Piet Uys's Irregulars, under Colonel Wood, and knew the country well, Captain Linley said.

'There is no one more reliable, in my opinion.'

'That is recommendation enough,' said Laura.

'I am glad you think so,' he said.

Since their brief interview the previous day, there had been an awkwardness between them. She was sorry for it, because she liked him; but there was nothing to be done.

They had been talking of her imminent departure for the interior.

'If you were my sister,' he had said, 'I would not want you to expose yourself to such danger...'

'But I am not your sister,' she had replied, perhaps too sharply.

'No.'

After this, he had lapsed into his habitual silence.

Now he stood avoiding her gaze. 'Well,' he said. 'I must wish you a safe journey.'

'Thank you.' She regretted her earlier abruptness. 'You have been very kind.'

'As to that...' But whatever he had intended to say was cut short by the appearance of Mrs Reynolds, followed by a man who could only have been their prospective guide.

'Ah,' said Captain Linley. 'There you are, De Kuiper. I hope that you will take good care of these ladies.'

De Kuiper said nothing to this, but looked Laura up and down with a directness she might have found disconcerting, if it had not been so very much a part of his general demeanour.

'Mr De Kuiper has arranged a most beautiful cart for us,' said Mrs Reynolds. 'I have been admiring it. It is fitted out with cushions, and hampers for our food, in the most convenient way.'

'Anyone would think we were going on a picnic,' said Laura. Only Mrs Reynolds smiled.

'How long do you suppose it will take you to reach Grey Town?' said Captain Linley to the guide.

De Kuiper considered a moment. 'Five days, if the weather holds.'

Captain Linley nodded. 'Good man.' He turned to the ladies with a smile. 'It seems that you will be in Grey Town for Christmas. I quite envy you. It is a pleasant spot.'

Laura held out her hand. 'Goodbye,' she said. 'I hope we meet again.'

'Nothing would give me greater happiness,' he said.

For the first few miles the road, although no more than a broad dirt track, was good. No rain had fallen in that part of the country for a month, their guide said, and so conditions were better than might have been expected. The wagon—which proved to be equipped with rather more than cushions and hampers, having in addition two months' worth of provisions, cooking pots and kettle, a pick and spade, tents and a wagon-jack—rolled along steadily, at a rate no faster than that of walking.

The driver, Lucky, whom Laura guessed to be about fourteen years old, managed the span of six oxen with the insouciance of one born to the job. Constant, the elder of the two youths De Kuiper had engaged, rode beside the cart on a rough-coated little pony. De Kuiper rode ahead on his own red mare, pausing at the brow of each hill to allow the heavy cart and its occupants to catch up.

'Oh, this is delightful,' said Mrs Reynolds, as they reached the top of one such hill, and began to roll slowly down, to the accompaniment of the oxen's gentle lowing, and the private language of shouts and clicks with which Lucky communicated his intentions to them. 'It reminds me of my girlhood in Shropshire. Riding on the hay-wain, you know. Such a treat for us girls!'

'You have three sisters, do you not?' asked Laura.

'Four. Three still living. And three brothers. Oh, those were happy times!' cried Emiline Reynolds. 'What I would not give to live them over again.'

They had set out before it was light; it was now mid-morning, and they had gone barely ten miles. De Kuiper seemed satisfied with their progress, however, and said that they might stop for breakfast. If they continued at this rate, they would reach the Umgeni bridge by nightfall.

The laborious business of unyoking the oxen—'out-spanning', De Kuiper called it—and watering the horses having been done, the boys were dispatched to gather sticks for the fire. The girl, Rejoice, with a look of disdain on her face, followed at a distance.

When the fire was built, Laura set herself to making tea—to the evident disapproval of their guide. 'It is for them to do these things,' he said, indicating the Basutos. 'This kind of work is not for ladies.'

'I am familiar with work,' she said. 'I grew up in the country.'

Something resembling a smile briefly animated De Kuiper's

severe features. 'The country,' he said. 'I think that must be a very different kind of country from this one, ja?'

'He is a strange "type", our guide,' she wrote in her journal, as they sat out the heat of midday, in the shade of the canvas awning Constant had rigged for them.

I am not sure what to make of him. For whilst his appearance—hair falling to shoulder-length; beard almost as long; yellow corduroys tucked into leather boots and broadbrimmed hat—suggest the frontiersman, his demeanour is that of a respectable Dutch burgher. Smiles seldom cross his face, his conversation is terse to the point of rudeness, and yet his manner is not un-amiable. Of his personal circumstances he has divulged little; although he confessed to Mrs Reynolds that he had never met an Englishman he could trust until he met Colonel Wood. The latter he holds in high regard. 'A brave man,' he says (a fulsome testimonial by his standards). He served with the Transvaal Rangers under Col W. at Hlobane Mountain. Mrs Reynolds got the story out of him. He says nothing to me, beyond the briefest remarks...

The red dusty road was full of stones; the wheels of the cart jolted over them, so that its passengers were flung from side to side. Mrs Reynolds did not complain, but her face was very white; from time to time she was unable to restrain a small cry, which was instantly stifled.

'It cannot be much further before we reach our stopping place, can it?' she said.

'Are you feeling unwell?' said Laura.

'No, no. Only a little tired,' was the reply.

Laura pressed her companion's hand. In the travelling-case was the tincture they had brought from England, which, mixed with water, would bring relief—for a while at least. They were already onto the second bottle, although its strength was such that one needed no more than a few drops of the mixture to make a draught. Laura fervently hoped there would be enough to last the journey.

They reached an incline, and the oxen began to labour, stumbling with every other step, it seemed. With each jolt she felt Mrs Reynolds flinch, although she made no further sound. At the next halt, Rejoice took Laura's place, supporting the older woman's body with her own. Though she said little, she seemed to know what was required without being told. If her employer had been a sick child, she could not have treated her with greater tenderness.

Laura got down, saying that she would walk for a while.

De Kuiper shook his head. 'Better not. There are snakes.'

When she insisted, he dismounted from his horse with an ill grace, and broke a dead branch from a nearby tree, paring it with his knife until it was free from twigs. 'Here. You must take this.'

Certainly the stick made it easier over the rough ground. If there were snakes, she did not see them; but the going was hard enough, even so. The sharp thorns of the bushes that grew on either side of the narrow track tore at her skirt, and her boots were soon caked with dust, but still she went on. After the jolting motion of the cart, walking was a positive pleasure.

The grass was almost as tall as she was: its bleached stalks turned to gold in the late-afternoon light. For as far as the eye could see stretched the veldt, with its tangle of grasses, grey thorn-trees, and the strange earthern mounds De Kuiper had said were termites' nests. Once, she was startled to find herself observed: a long white face looked sideways at her through the grass. Then the creature bounded away.

'Gemsbok,' said De Kuiper, with some regret, for he had raised his gun too late. He was more successful with the little Springbok that crossed their path some minutes later, and the carcass was slung on the back of the ox-cart, in readiness for dinner.

As the sun sank lower in the sky, the hills towards which they journeyed intensified in blueness. To reach these uplands, they had first to cross a deep ravine, through which a river ran. Reaching its edge brought them within sight of a tumbling mass of waters, two hundred feet high, which fell into a rocky basin at the cliff's foot, sending up a dense mist, like steam. In the faint afterglow of the sunset, the river alone reflected what light there was, until it seemed a broad vein of silver, its undulations resembling a life-line on the palm of a hand.

The sky was soon as black as pitch—night having fallen with the suddenness it always did in that country—rent by flickers of lightning along the distant ridge.

'Best we get under cover,' muttered De Kuiper.

And indeed their progress was increasingly hampered by gusts of wind, which shook the canvas awning of the cart so fiercely, that it seemed as if it must tear loose from its fastenings. The thunder was closer now—each resounding drum-roll followed, a heartbeat later, by a burst of violet-coloured, unearthly light. The effect of this on the oxen was all too apparent: their eyes showed white in the gloom, and they tossed their heads nervously from side to side.

At a command from De Kuiper, the little procession halted, and Lucky made haste to unyoke his charges from their burden. The rain had started in earnest now, and both men and beasts were soon drenched by the downpour, which fell with a hissing sound upon the parched earth. Shouting above the noise of the rising wind, De Kuiper ordered the women to quit the cart. The iron hoops with which it was roofed were a draw for the lightning, he said. They must take shelter beneath the cart, where it was safer.

Safer it might have been; but it was also more exposed to the elements.

'I never thought to find myself so cold in Africa,' said Mrs Reynolds, with a laugh. Laura took her hand, and found it like ice.

'Take my shawl,' she said, wrapping it around Mrs Reynolds's slight form.

Rejoice was shivering, too; her eyes very large in her round dark face. Whether it was fear or the unaccustomed cold which so affected her was impossible to say.

From that vantage-point, the women were afforded only partial glimpses of the tempest raging overhead: black-and-white images of tossing grass-stalks and bare thorn-twigs, appearing, with each momentary flash, like successive impressions from an inked steel plate.

After an interval, De Kuiper's face appeared. 'There is a cave, not far from here. When the rain lets up, we will go there.'

The cave had a dry, sandy floor and, although no larger than a fair-sized room, offered a welcome refuge from the elements. Once a fire had been lit, it grew warmer; quite cosy, said Emiline Reynolds. What sensible people these cave-dwellers must have been.

On the walls were strange daubs and scratchings, which, on closer inspection, proved to be figures of running men and beasts—gazelles, zebra, buffalo and others less easy to identify. They had been there a long time, De Kuiper said—how long he could not say. A hundred years—perhaps a thousand. Who had made them he did not know.

'Why, look,' said Laura. 'That is surely a horse. His rider lies there, upon the ground. But how can that be?'

For the sprawled figure was wearing a red coat. A spear was stuck fast in his breast.

'That picture is not, perhaps, so old as the others,' said De Kuiper.

'I wish I had not seen it,' she said.

Outside, the storm had receded to a distant rumbling note, as if a hand beat softly on a kettle-drum. Soon, all that could be heard was the sound of the invisible waterfall, whose sonorous music drew the cave's exhausted inhabitants along in its wake, and propelled them over the precipice of sleep.

They woke to an altered world: everything seemed new-made; fresh; entire. The air was crystalline. From the mouth of the cave, Laura watched a bird pecking at a bunch of seeds, which hung in tassel from the top of a large, spiky plant. How greedily it tore at the thing! It seemed to have no fear of her at all. In size and shape it resembled a blackbird, she thought—except for the vivid scarlet breast.

But then everything here had a strangeness to it; and yet seemed, at the same time, to be oddly familiar. The roaring of the waterfall seemed thus to her to resemble nothing so much as that of a distant railway train—although she knew the analogy to be absurd. They were hundreds of miles from the nearest railway; as indeed, they were from anything that might have been called civilisation.

Mrs Reynolds was now awake, and none the worse, she said,

for having passed the night on the floor of a cave—indeed, it had been at least as comfortable as the Great Eastern Hotel. Although it seemed to Laura that her friend was growing weaker. Every step she took seemed an effort for her, and when Rejoice was doing her hair, she flinched, as if even that light touch were too painful to bear.

When Laura herself had finished dressing, she wandered a little way along the track that followed the edge of the ravine. This, a great cleft in the rock some five miles long, cut across a landscape of rolling hills, bare of any sign of human habitation. Here and there, between clumps of trees, could be discerned moving shapes—vast herds of beasts she thought at first must be cattle.

'Wildebeest,' De Kuiper said, coming to stand beside her. 'And those are eland. Look.' He indicated a cluster of deer-like creatures near the river.

But she had seen something else: a tawny shape, in the thicket at the water's edge. 'I believe that must be a lion,' she said, directing his attention to it.

He agreed that it was. 'But do not be afraid,' he said. 'It cares more for the eland than for us. Also,' he added, patting the stock of the rifle which was slung across his shoulder. 'I do not often miss.'

'That is a consolation,' she said.

At Grey Town, there were letters waiting—one was from Laura's father. It was two days before Christmas, and she sat under the blue gum trees in the shady courtyard of the little inn and read it through again. The date was six weeks before; it had been forwarded from the Cape.

St Michael's Vicarage
12th September 1879

My dearest child

I do not know when—or indeed, if—you will receive this, but can safely assume, the mails being what they are, that by the time you do so, it will be many weeks from hence, and your sister Elizabeth will be married.

I will not conceal from you the distress which this

news has caused in all quarters: they are both so young, and she has, as you know, no money, except for the small legacy she had from your late mother. The young man's— that is, Harold's—family were not, I believe, any better pleased by the announcement than I; but it seems that there are matters which make the match imperative.

They are to be married from Uppingham—that is Harold's family home. I believe the local man is to officiate (a Revd. Chase; I do not know him). Your brother Robert is to attend on my behalf. As you know, my health does not permit me to travel far these days.

Well, my dear, you can imagine how sad I am to have lost two of my girls in one year—although I know that you, at least, will be home before long. My dear child, you cannot know how much your presence has been missed in these past months; nor how earnestly I have prayed for your safe return...

She folded up the letter. How typical of Bessie to insist on bending everything to her will—she did not care whom she hurt. Not that she cared for herself, but their father was getting old. He should not have to suffer the slights and malicious whisperings the affair would bring down upon them all.

There would be nobody at home now except their father and Violet. The Rectory was quiet at the best of times; how cheerless it must be now, at this, the coldest time of the year. Here, it was difficult to imagine being cold...

Only Mrs Reynolds seemed impervious to the heat. She had caught a bad chill, and could not seem to throw it off. 'What a tiresome old woman I am,' she had said, her eyes bright with fever. 'I am sorry, my dear. You did not come halfway across the world to tend to an invalid.'

On Christmas morning, she could not even muster the strength to go to church; although she insisted on getting up for luncheon. It was roast guinea fowl, and quite delicious—if rather a change from goose, she said. But she had no appetite for more than a mouthful or two.

Afterwards they exchanged presents: Laura gave Mrs Reynolds

some handkerchiefs she had embroidered during the long, weary afternoons at Mrs De Villiers's; in return, she received a pearl necklace that had belonged to Mrs Reynolds's mother.

'They say that pearls are for tears,' she said. 'But I think that you have already had your share of those.'

As well as her father's letter, there was another, written in an unfamiliar hand. Its dashing style told her the writer's identity before she had read a line.

Dear Miss Brooke

You will, I guess, be surprised to receive this—although not, I hope, too surprised. Our talks were so very pleasant to me, that I dare to hope they might have been so to you. It's a rare enough thing in this world when two people 'hit it off' the way you and I did, if you'll excuse the vulgarism. At any rate, here I am; if nothing else, this poor scrawl might amuse you for an hour, as you recall that very odd American fellow you met in Cape Town!

Picture, then, if you will, the scene at Beaufort West—to which pleasant town on the edge of the Great Karoo (a name meaning 'dryness' or 'thirsty land') your humble servant has been conveyed by rail. It is around 4 a m on a freezing morning and the coach—prop. Messrs Freeman-Cobb—has just come around the corner, with a frightful blaring of bugles, and twelve bony-looking nags clattering up at a gallop. On we get, the poor bleary-eyed passengers—ten of us, crammed into a space barely large enough for half that number.

Inside this wretched hutch, we are tumbled about for the next five days and nights, with only the briefest stops for sustenance. Nothing to see on either side but mile upon mile of red desert. Nothing to hear but the groans of our fellow passengers, as they are tossed and buffeted; and the uncouth shouts of the Cape Dutch drivers; and the crack of the whip, wielded by the Hottentot guard...

Then there are the passengers themselves: a queerer crew it would be hard to imagine. For here is Overseer Van

Donk—and a flintier-faced, colder-eyed individual you'd hope never to meet. One trembles to think what life must be like for the poor wretches under his iron command.

It is men like Van Donk who have made the diamond fields what they are today, I am assured by my neighbour, Mr Leitch, who travels in tin... that is to say, tin saucepans, teapots, and other 'sundries' of use to the housewife. Mr Leitch ventures the muttered opinion that Van Donk is a 'hard man, but a fair one'—thought fair in regards to what he does not say.

Mrs Colquhoun—a female of indefinite age and dubious mien—is another member of our travelling community. She is lately returned from her daughter's wedding in Oudtshoorn, she informs me, although I have expressed not the least curiosity. Mrs Colquhoun runs a 'grog shop' on the edge of the diamond fields—where, one supposes, she dispenses conversation along with bokbier...

In another two days we will arrive in Kimberley, which I am told (Mr Leitch again) is one of the most remarkable places in all South Africa. Although to call it a 'place' when it is no more than a very large hole in the ground seems absurd—if one were not already inured to absurdity in this topsy-turvy land, where winter is summer, and water runs the wrong way down the plughole of the bath in one's hotel (that is, when there is any bath at all, which is not often).

But I suppose you must have reached Natal—which, though a green and pleasant land in the rainy season, must be very hot and dusty just now. Knowing the country a little, as I do, I can only admire you for undertaking what seems to me a very bold adventure. I guess you won't take it amiss if I say that there are many men with not half your 'pluck'. How is Mrs Reynolds, by the way? Well, I trust. Please send her my sincerest regards—and keep some for yourself, my dear Miss Brooke.

Well, we have arrived in Hope Town (a good omen, don't you think?) and I must send this back with the coach to catch the Durban mails. If all goes according to plan—

and in journalism, as in life, nothing is certain—I shall be back in Cape Town for Christmas. Do let me know when you return. I shall be very 'blue' without your company to cheer me...

I am, dear Miss Brooke, your very devoted friend,

P. Septimus Doyle

Chapter 7

Septimus, November 1879: Kimberley

The beetle, which was black and shiny, and so large that its armoured carapace seemed too heavy for its puny wings, crashed itself against the glass—evidently under the impression, Septimus thought, that that transparent substance was the sky. This proving not to be the case, the beetle fell and lay supine for a while, apparently gathering its strength to right itself, in order to begin the whole doomed enterprise again.

It was less out of pity for its plight, and more because the sounds it made as it crashed and fell were disagreeable to him, that he rose at last from where he had been lying sprawled on the bed in his hotel room, and went to open the window. The room, he observed with gloomy satisfaction, although not the worst he had ever stayed in, was still a pretty bad room. Its walls were so thin that one could hear every snore and fart and hiccup of one's neighbour on either side. Its bed was so full of lumps that one spent the night tossing and turning, and so narrow that one ran a very real risk, in doing so, of ending up upon the floor.

Nor was it especially cheap. For this was Kimberley, and hotels could charge what they liked and still remain full, the year round. Everybody—from the smallest dreamer-of-dreams investing his life-savings in what might turn out to be a worthless 'claim', to the greatest-of-great Panjandrums—wanted to go to Kimberley, it seemed. Not since the days of 'Forty-Nine, when his own countrymen had succumbed to the collective madness of 'Gold Fever', had the wilderness been so colonised by desperate men.

And women, too... Like its counterparts in the 'Old West', Kimberley over-flowed with whores. In their purple feathers and high-laced boots, they lingered in the doorways of the drinking-shops along the main street, and haunted the lobbies of the seedier hotels, in search of likely prey. If he had been so inclined, picking out a girl he liked from the gaudy throng and bringing her back here for the afternoon might have struck him as a good idea.

But he was not so inclined—not any more.

He succeeded at last in getting the window open (for it had stuck fast, as gimcrack constructions are wont to) and let the beetle out. Its surprise at being airborne at last made him smile for the first time that day. For in truth since his arrival, he had met with nothing but frustration. Not that he was unused to waiting—it was all part of the journalist's lot. But to have to kick his heels in such a one-horse town, with nowhere to go and nothing to see, was enough to put a fellow's nose seriously out of joint...

Well, there was no help for it. Pouring himself a finger of whisky—bought at an outrageously inflated price from one of the dirty little grog-shops across the street—and doing his best to ignore the drunken strains of 'Rosie O'Grady' emanating from the wall behind his head, Septimus reflected on the circumstances which had brought him to this unprepossessing spot, and which had—accidentally or fatefully, depending on how you saw these things—led to his first meeting with Laura Brooke.

For after that—to him—fateful day, when they had walked up the Lion's Head, and he had known himself no longer heart-free, he had done everything in his power to elicit an answering emotion in her. But—although he had called every day, contriving to do so at a time when she was setting out for her morning walk, so that nothing could seem more natural than that he should accompany her—he had got no further with her, where affairs of the heart were concerned, than he had before.

In a word she was already promised to another fellow. The fact that the fellow was no longer of this world appeared to make not a jot of difference.

But Septimus was not a man to give up hope easily. Nor was he a man who threw up his hands at a challenge, especially when the prize was a lady... So, for the duration of her stay in Cape Town—which had not been long—he had continued to turn up, as regular as clockwork, to go walking with Miss Brooke in the woods at Newlands. That the time for such excursions was the early morning—hours before Mrs De Villiers was accustomed to rise—made deceiving his mistress easier. That he no longer felt the slightest attraction to the latter also helped to make things clearer. One could not be unfaithful to a woman one had never loved.

Among Newlands' pretty groves of pine and silver trees, one could wander for hours, without meeting another living soul. Here, if anywhere, a girl might come to her senses at last, in the company of a young man who adored her...

Laura Brooke was almost as silent as during these untrammelled ramblings as she was in Mrs de Villiers's drawing-room; although it was, he saw, a different kind of silence. There—beside the dash and sparkle of a Cora de Villiers—she could only appear subdued. Here, she was silent because there was no need to talk.

That he now infinitely preferred her stillness to his mistress's animation, was something of which he had been aware for some time. It pleased him to think that he had, at last, acquired discernment. Whether the object of his interest was aware of his feelings, he could not be sure. On the whole he thought not. All her thoughts were of the man she had lost; all their conversations tended towards that topic.

Once, during one of their walks, she had asked him, apropos of nothing, whether he believed in the transmigration of souls. As a confirmed rationalist, he took no account of such things, of course. The world was all one could see, hear, taste, touch, smell; no more.

But he understood her question as a plea for reassurance. She had lost the one who was dear to her—intolerable to think that nothing of that loved being could have survived. So he chose his words carefully:

'I have no idea what becomes of us after death. It's the last mystery, isn't it? But I reckon that any Creator worthy of the name would have considered the question carefully. If we survive in some form...'

'I did not mean table-turning, or anything of that ilk,' she said.

'I didn't suppose it for a moment.'

'It is just that, the more I think about it, the harder it is for me to accept that the mind, and the will, and the passions—all that makes us human, in fact—simply disappears...'

'I'm sure that it does not,' he said.

'You have said what I hoped you would say. But it is not what you believe.'

'As to that,' said Septimus lightly. 'I'm a man of few beliefs. Many opinions, but few beliefs. That's a journalist for you...'

She had smiled, but afterwards he wondered if she had thought the remark trivial.

The day before he was due to leave for Kimberley, he had called to say goodbye. He had waited, out of sight at the end of the driveway, as Mrs De Villiers's carriage drove past. All he hoped was that Laura Brooke was not inside it; from what he had divined of the relationship between the women, he thought it unlikely.

His intuition had proved correct.

Laura was on the veranda, a book open upon her lap. She did not appear to be reading it, for her gaze was directed out at the garden, where a flock of green and red parakeets were squabbling in one of the umbrella pines.

When he walked out through the doors that led from the parlour, she gave a small start.

'I guess I'm disturbing you...'

'Not at all. As you see, I'm entirely idle.'

They discussed the novel she was reading. Meredith's latest. She could not get on with it. 'But then,' she said, with a smile, 'I'm hard to please...' Other inconsequential topics followed. A concert both had attended. A planned excursion to Cape Point.

All the while he was thinking how best to approach the only subject which interested him, and on which, so far, he had been obliged to remain silent.

'I've come to say goodbye,' he said at last. 'I leave for the diamond fields first thing tomorrow.'

'Oh. That is a pity.' A look of faint embarrassment crossed her features. 'You have just missed Mrs De Villiers. She will be vexed not to have seen you...'

'As a matter of fact...' he began, when there was a footfall behind him.

'Well, well,' said Cora De Villiers. 'You're very cosy here together. I left my gloves. Otherwise I should have missed you altogether.'

'I was just leaving,' he said.

'So soon? Poor Miss Brooke will be quite bereft without your company.'

Cora was smiling, but her eyes were hard as jet.

'I'll wait for you in the carriage,' she said, and it sounded like a command.

'Well, goodbye,' said Laura, when they were alone once more.

Her smile betrayed no awareness of what that parting meant to him; nor of the humiliation under which he was smarting. Damn Cora. No man should be spoken to as she had spoken to him. As if he were a whipped dog. He'd stand for no more of it.

'I hoped to have had more time to talk,' he said. 'But I see it's not to be. May I write to you, at least?'

The surprise on her face was another blow. Surely she must have had some inkling of his feelings?

'We leave for Natal within the week,' she said. 'But I'm sure that Mrs De Villiers will forward any letters we might receive.'

He was far from sure about that—especially if the letters came from him.

He took her hand. 'Goodbye, Miss Brooke.'

She pressed his hand by way of reply. How long he would have to endure, with just that gentle pressure to console him!

In the carriage, Cora De Villiers threw him a sardonic look.

'I always said you were a dark horse. But don't you think it in poor taste, to keep a woman waiting, while you make love to her rival?'

He did not even bother to contradict her.

Now he had come to Kimberley. And a drearier spot, in which to reflect on his hopes—or lack of them—would have been hard to find. That this was also the centre of the universe—his universe—was another unfathomable fact. That such a hole could be the fulcrum around which everything revolved was hard to believe; and yet it was so.

For although the war was over, the war had only just begun. That was the fact of the matter. Zululand had been annexed and

Cetshwayo humbled; the next prize was the Transvaal. The Kimberley mines, to be exact. For more than ten years, the place had been spewing out diamonds by the bushel, with four 'pipes' in Kimberley alone. Since the installation of steam-engines to haul up the precious loads, production had increased a hundred-fold.

Not that there wasn't the demand to match it. Diamonds were what everyone wanted, these days, it seemed. Diamonds to adorn the bosoms of fashionable ladies in London, Paris and Rome, and to ornament the crowned heads of Europe. Diamonds whose fortuitous discovery, here in the barren wastes of Africa, offered a fresh source of revenue for an Empire already hard-pressed by the demands of an ever-increasing population, and a series of costly little wars.

Of course, the mines themselves were already under British control—Rhodes being the major shareholder in the largest of them. There was talk that he would not rest until he had succeeded in buying out Barnato, his chief rival; but so far it was only talk.

It was to see Rhodes that Septimus had come. The man was a phenomenon. Tales of the fabulous wealth pouring out of his mines had been circulating in London for months. The granting of unprecedented powers to the De Beers Mining Company—of which Rhodes owned the controlling stock—was the big story in the City. Under its terms, De Beers could not only mine diamonds, but build railways, lay telegraph wires, raise armies and install governments—do everything, in fact, except declare war.

Not since the early days of the East India Company, had a business operation been given such unlimited capacity for expansion.

Even Septimus, who had no interest in financial affairs, never having had more than two cents to his name, could see the story's potential.

'You're a man who knows a bit about Africa,' McClintock had said. 'Go and see for yourself what this cove Rhodes is up to. And bring the missus back a wee diamond or two, would you? I'm no' exactly in her good books at the moment.'

So here he was, stuck in the middle of nowhere, killing time until the great man would condescend to see him. Mr Rhodes was very busy just now, his chief clerk, a man by the name of Warburton, had said, with a shrug. He might be free tomorrow or he might be free next week. Impossible to say for certain. If Mr Doyle had nothing better to do that afternoon, a tour of the mine might be arranged. Or, if he felt so inclined, there was a billiards room at the Club; and even a fairly decent lending library...

His glass was, unaccountably, empty. He tipped the last drops from the bottle and threw the 'dead man' in the trash, where it clinked against another, jettisoned by a previous incumbent. Next door, the drunken singing had subsided. A faint breeze, warm as an exhaled breath, stirred the strip of grimy lace that hung across the window.

If the truth were told, he cared nothing for diamonds—or for the men who pursued them. It was a craving, he saw—like that for gold, or drink, or whores—which could never be satisfied. What foolish creatures men were! Eternally chasing after what they could not have. In his case, he supposed, what drove him was the desire for a good story. Although, of late, even that obsession had been displaced, in his mind, by another...

With a sigh, he reached for his journal, which lay on the rickety night-stand. The last entry had been written two days before, during one of the stops on that infernal stage-coach journey. He had put some of the observations recorded there in a letter to Laura Brooke, which he had written, on a whim, late one night. He had no idea whether she would reply, or even if she would ever receive it. But it had seemed important at the time that she should know that he was thinking of her.

'She has bewitched my thoughts,' he wrote. 'Waking or sleeping, hers is the only face I see...'

Where was she now, at this moment? She'd have left Durban, he guessed. In his imagination, he followed her on the successive stages of that perilous journey, which he himself had made not so very long before. Would to God that he could have gone with her, to keep her safe from harm! If it had not been for this cursed assignment, he might have contrived it. Well, it was no use thinking about that... If he could just see her, talk to her, he thought, in an agony of frustrated desire. He guessed that she liked him a little—hadn't he made her laugh, once or twice, with some foolishness or other?

The crazy thing was, he'd never intended to fall in love. Love and war correspondents didn't mix, it was well known. Married woman, up to now, had been his preference; they had a vested interest in discretion. Now all that had changed. He was properly 'dished'.

'Dished, and done for,' he said aloud, into the silence of the room.

Chapter 8

Theo, November 1878: Grey Town

It had been raining for two weeks without a break when they reached Grey Town. He could not remember ever having been more wretched in his life. The ground was sodden; pitching the tents proved a nightmare, with the waterlogged canvas too heavy for the poles, and the men slipping and sliding as they struggled to gain a footing on the greasy mud. When the tents were up, it proved no better. Leaks had sprung in the fabric of many, rotted through as it was by the incessant downpour, and parts of the campsite were little more than standing pools of filthy water, where men shivered in damp blankets and mosquitoes swarmed for a blood-feast of captive flesh. Several of the men in 'C' Company were sick with fever, and diarrhoea was rife throughout the camp.

Getting the ox-carts unloaded proved another nightmare, with half the supplies ending up in the mud, and one cart overturned completely, dragging a number of the poor yoked beasts down after it, and breaking their legs. A pestilential day. If anyone had told him a month ago that it could rain so hard in Africa, he would not have believed them—although it had rained often enough at the Cape—but in squalls, followed at once by sunshine. This black, unremitting deluge was something new. A month ago, the very touch of wool against the skin had seemed a torment. Now, he could not get warm; dry stockings, and blankets untainted by mould, seemed unimaginable luxuries.

On Christmas Day, the fog lifted, allowing a glimmer of sunshine to illuminate the blue hills towards which they were to proceed. There were extra rations of rum and tobacco for the men, and roast suckling pig for the officers' mess. Hallam had a bottle of brandy, and together they toasted their loved ones, growing quite melancholy. Hallam's widowed mother and sisters were in

Lincolnshire: 'the quietest spot in all the world,' he said. The village churchyard was full of Hallams. 'I daresay I shall be there myself one day.' He was the last of the line—an elder brother having died some years before. After him, there were only girls.

'You might marry,' Theo reminded him, but he dismissed this notion with a wave of his hand.

'O no, my dear fellow. Married life is not for me.' His smile had wry twist to it. 'I am wedded to the Army, you know. No, when I am gone, there will be only the girls left. How they will manage I do not know...'

His youngest sister was his favourite, he said.

'If you were not already an engaged man, I should have liked to introduce you to Clara.' His expression grew fond. 'She is not as handsome as your Miss Brooke, but she is a dear girl, is Clara. Yes, I should have liked to introduce you to Clara,' said Hallam, his voice no longer perfectly steady.

War—and this war in particular—Theo was beginning to understand, was as much to do with transport, of men, munitions and supplies, as it was to do with actual fighting. Everything—with the exception of fresh meat—had to be brought up from the coast. It was like one of those arithmetical problems he had detested so much at school: If an ox-wagon, travelling fifteen miles a day, carries six thousand pounds of biscuit, or six days' biscuit ration for one thousand men, who are lying one hundred and fifty miles from the sea-coast, whence the biscuit has to come, how many days before the rations for the aforesaid men run out?

Nor was the slowness of the transportation the only problem with which he, and those of his fellow officers also charged with the task of ensuring the delivery of supplies had to contend. For the road from Durban was far from being a straight and level thoroughfare, such as one might expect to find in England and, indeed, in most of the rest of Europe.

No. It was two hundred miles of steep and stony track between bare rock walls, where a man might stumble and break a leg in an instant; of barren plains covered with scrubby thornbushes which shredded clothes and skin alike; of dried river-beds which turned, after a night's rain, into raging torrents in which a wagon might be swept away as easily as a toy. Added to which quotidian hazards were other factors. He had thought nothing could be as bad as the misery of damp sheets and festering mosquito bites they had endured at Pietermaritzburg; now he saw that there were physical torments to rival even these.

Hauling a loaded wagon over stony ground for hour after hour in the blazing sun, until every nerve in the body pleaded for respite—only to have the vehicle topple into a ditch, its axle broken and its cargo spoilt, was gruelling enough. Haranguing the men from dawn till dusk to keep in step and to keep up with the rest also took its toll—not least on the men, burdened like pack animals as they were, poor devils. But to add to this the constant danger of sunstroke, together with the minor annoyances of prickly heat, ticks and blisters, was almost more than flesh and blood could stand.

He had not known until now how much hard labour was involved in soldiering. The actual fighting was a small part of it.

Then there was the water. The rivers were generally safe to drink from; but the waterholes could not be trusted. He had told the men time and again; yet still some fool like little Robbins chose to ignore the danger—only to spend the next two days doubled up in agony in his own filth. Already, he had lost a man to blood-poisoning: Willcock, who had stuck a pick-axe through his foot and lay screaming for a day and a night. It had created a bad feeling in the camp, but what was he to do? He had lectured them all until he was black in the face about the proper use of tools, and the correct way to clean a gun. He had warned them of the dangers of snakes, scorpions and of eating contaminated meat. Still they reported to him with guts-ache, with torn fingers and with purulent blisters. They seemed not to have grasped the fact that a wound, however small, had to be kept clean.

At least, far from anywhere, there were no more fights over whores, and no new cases of the clap. There had been fewer floggings for drunkenness, too. This last was, in Theo's view, a barbaric practice, but he kept such opinions to himself. To acquire the reputation for being soft on discipline was tantamount to suicide in this profession.

He thought of Bingham, whom he had known in his first year

at Sandhurst. A mild and pious creature with little aptitude for soldiering, Bingham had once opined, in the hearing of certain members of the officers' training corps, that they, as a body, were merely being prepared for a career of licensed murder. He himself was not afraid to die, but he would prefer to do so in a state of grace, rather than of mortal sin.

'Grace'—or 'Your Holiness'—had thereafter become his nickname. In six weeks, he had been transformed into a shivering wreck, afraid of his shadow. 'I could bear it, Reynolds, if it were just me,' he had confided the night before he hung himself from a water-pipe in the latrine-block. 'But they say they're going to do vile things to Sally'—Sally being his invalid sister.

The affair had been hushed up; at least one of Bingham's tormentors had gone on to a glittering career in the War Office; another, a Duke's son, had been mentioned in dispatches from Kabul. Evidently, none of them had been troubled by thoughts of murder, licensed or otherwise. As for himself, he was not as brave as poor Bingham. He, at least, had had the courage to speak out.

There were other afflictions to be confronted apart from those of the body. Witchcraft—or the fear of witchcraft—was not merely the stuff of children's fairytales in this country. Theo's first encounter with such things had been in Cape Town. One of the men—not an African, but a white man, and something of a rogue, by the name of Campbell—had become convinced that he was bewitched. A confirmed womanizer, he had been stricken with impotence—the result of a curse placed upon him by a local woman, he said. When questioned, Campbell admitted that he had knocked her around a little—'No more than she deserved, the dirty whore.'

Despite Theo's best efforts to reassure the man that the problem was likely to be of a temporary nature, Campbell was adamant that he would not recover. 'She's done for me, sir,' he said. So it turned out. Unable to bear the diminution of his manly powers, Campbell had shot himself through the roof of the mouth and had died two days later.

Now, far from the temptations of the capital city, it was happening again. One of the Native Auxiliaries, who answered to the name of Blessing, seemed to have fallen victim to such a curse. 'Drinking foul water, more like,' said Rowlands, the camp doctor. Whatever the reason, the consequences for poor Blessing were terrible: his belly swelled to the size of a football, and his groans could be heard all over the camp.

'Christ, I wish the fucker would die, and leave off his blasted moaning,' said one of the men, in Theo's hearing.

'Shut up, Clancy. Don't you know it's ill-luck to wish a man dead?' said his comrade. 'You'll see. It'll be one of us next.'

Things grew worse after Blessing died.

'The men are in an uproar,' Theo complained to Hallam. 'It is impossible to get a good day's work out of them. All their talk is of the evil eye...'

'Bad for discipline,' said Hallam.

In vain did Theo lecture and threaten; nothing he said would convince the men that they were not all doomed to an early grave. Over the next few days, a series of misfortunes—some minor, some more serious—only served to confirm the superstitious in their folly. One man was badly scalded when a pot of soup was overturned in the camp kitchens. Another lost an eye during firing practise, when the breech mechanism on his gun became fouled with sand and exploded in his face.

'It's all the fault of that damned witch,' one man was heard to mutter to another whilst the company was drawn up on parade.

'Any more talk of that sort and tobacco privileges will be withdrawn for a week,' said Theo.

The 'witch', it emerged, was one of the Basuto drivers—a small brown man of inoffensive appearance named Mlamvu. It was he who had put the evil eye on poor Blessing, allegedly— Blessing having cast aspersions upon the chastity of Mlamvu's mother, it was said.

'It seems that Mlamvu is an important man in his native village,' Theo informed Hallam, with a grin. 'He calls himself *sangoma*—which means witch doctor, you know.'

Hallam did not appear to find this funny.

'A *sangoma* has a great deal of power,' was all he said. 'It's as well to remember that.'

But Theo had other matters to distract him. Crossing the

Tugela Drift proved to be a great deal more troublesome that he had expected. The river's broad flat surface looked, from the river-bank, to be shallow enough to wade across. Faced with the prospect of shifting forty twenty-foot wagons, each drawn by sixteen oxen, across by pontoon—a far slower and more laborious method—Theo decided to take the risk. He accordingly gave the order, and the first two carts rolled slowly down the bank.

For the first fifty yards or so, things went smoothly enough; another fifty yards, and the wagons stuck fast, unable to go forwards or back. The water in mid-stream, it became apparent, was much deeper than anticipated—added to which was a nasty current, which threatened to carry the whole turn-out downstream. Panicked by the shouts of the men, and by the increasingly desperate exhortations of the drivers, the oxen began to plunge about in the water, straining their necks upwards to keep their heads above the oily brown surface.

With all his energies concentrated on dealing with this emergency, Theo did not see what happened next until it was too late. There was a crash; a muffled scream; then silence.

One of the wagons, making the slippery descent to the river-bank, had overbalanced, it seemed—tipping its load of crates onto the ground. Beneath this lay the figure of a man. Dead, or nearly so. His rib-cage was quite stoved in. He could not last an hour.

Theo swore under his breath. This was all he needed. Half the stores about to be swept away downriver; the rest flung down in the mud. Colonel Glyn, waiting for supplies at Helpmekaar, was not going to be amused. More unpleasant still was the prospect of having to make a report on the matter to Captain Essex, his immediate superior. Essex was not renowned for his patience at the best of times. He had already given Smith-Dorrien a dressing-down for that business with the ponts.

It wasn't until the smashed crates and their contents—what else but tins of bully-beef?—had been cleared, that he realised the identity of the injured man.

He swore again. 'All right. Which of you saw what happened?'

Nobody had seen anything, it seemed.

All one could surmise was that Mlamvu—for it was Mlamvu, wretched man, who had been standing in the way when the boxes fell—had got down from his perch on top of the wagon to make some adjustment to a wheel. At any rate, he had been stooping when the strap holding the load had broken. If it had broken...

Theo knelt down beside the limp body, from which the worst of the debris had been lifted. He cleared his throat. 'Well, then,' he said. 'How are you bearing up?' It was a foolish question.

Blood had seeped into the earth around the man, who lay spread-eagled, a figure outlined in red. The dying eyes fixed on his, a cloudiness already coming over them. 'You'll be all right, man,' Theo was going on to say, but the words died upon his lips. The man was not all right. He was far from all right. Mlamvu, too, seemed to recognise this.

As Theo watched, frozen into inactivity (for what was there to do? What help could he muster?) the witch seemed to gather his strength for a moment. The clouded eyes glowed, with a residue of heat. The lips moved—so faintly, that Theo had to bend closer to hear. My curse upon you all. So softly articulated that it seemed like no more than a breath. Then the light went out from the eyes. The lips went slack. What had been alive before, was not.

'How did they manage it, I wonder?' Theo said to Hallam later that day, the rest of the wagons having been got across the river without further incident, and the remains of the unfortunate Mlamvu disposed of.

Hallam looked at him. 'There are ways and ways.'

'But... cold-blooded murder...'

'It would not be the first. What do you intend to do?'

'I do not know. I have questioned the men that were nearest, of course—but none of them admit to having seen a thing. Even if I did discover the culprit, what am I to do with him? Shoot him?'

'I should save your bullets,' said Hallam. 'You might need 'em soon enough...'

At least there was no more talk of witchcraft. In the camp, the mood was calm, even light-hearted, as if a crisis had passed.

'I find it hard to believe that supposedly rational beings should allow themselves to be swayed by superstition,' said Theo. 'And yet I have seen the evidence with my own eyes.'

'It does strange things to people, this country,' said Hallam. 'India was as bad, you know. Why, I've seen a man walk on burning coals, and another raised up from the dead. One can believe anything after that.'

At Helpmekaar, the first person he had seen was Hamilton, the medical officer he had met on board ship.

'My dear fellow. You look all in,' Hamilton said.

'It has not been the easiest weather for travelling.'

'Don't I know it! I took the railway as far as Pine Town—but that is only ten miles, you know. The remaining hundred and fifty was most uncomfortable. The road was washed away in places. I really thought we should have to swim.'

He insisted on giving Theo a tour of the field hospital, which had been set up in a corrugated zinc shed to one side of the camp. This had once held stores. Now, decomposing bags of maize, which had been got at by the damp during the past few weeks of heavy rain, were piled along the outside of the building, giving off a sour, farmyard smell. Inside, long flat boxes containing biscuits were arranged along the walls. These had been covered with sacks, in lieu of blankets.

'Of course we shall have beds in due course,' said Hamilton, with a shrug.

'It does seem a little Spartan...'

'That is nothing, I assure you. All I have at my disposal in the way of medical supplies is a case of pills whose purpose is obscure, some powders for treating diarrhoea, some bandages and a tourniquet. They have allowed me a case of brandy and portwine. This, to treat upwards of two thousand men!'

'I am sure you will manage very well.'

'I shall have no choice but to manage. I am in hourly expectation of supplies. When you arrived I thought perhaps that you had brought me something useful—but it turns out there is nothing in those wagons except tinned beef and ammunition.'

'An army marches on its stomach, remember...'

'As if I could forget.'

If Theo had nothing better to do that afternoon, Hamilton said, he might assist at an operation. It promised to be an interesting

107

study. One of the men, a Private Andrews, had been leaning on his rifle during a lull in target practice—his hand being over the muzzle. The weapon had gone off, and made a great hole in his hand.

'I am pretty sure that the removal of the damaged bones will result in a serviceable limb,' said Hamilton. 'But I need someone to hold him steady. Does the sight of blood trouble you at all?'

Theo said that it did not, and so the injured man was brought in, and his sleeve rolled up to the elbow. He was calm enough until the doctor took up his pliers and hacksaw; then he turned ashen in colour.

'Brace up, man,' said the doctor, not unkindly. 'You shall have a tot of brandy directly.'

Removing the damaged fingers was a simple matter of a pair of good sharp scissors, Hamilton said, demonstrating what he meant; removing the shattered pieces of bone proved a little more laborious. Fortunately, the patient fainted while this was being done.

'I have asked time and again for chloroform to be sent—but do you think they will send it?' said Hamilton angrily. 'There. I have dressed it with oil-silk and tenax—much the best method for preventing gangrene, in my experience. It should result in an excellent stump.'

Gently, he slapped the unconscious man's cheek to bring him round.

'Wake up, there's a good fellow. You will do very nicely. There!' He finished tying up the mutilated limb in a sling. 'Just think how fine your sweetheart will think you, when you next go home on leave.'

'Yes, sir.'

He was no more than a boy, Theo saw. Milk-white under his freckles.

'Off you go,' said Hamilton. 'Tell the sergeant I said you are to be excused anything but light exercise for the next few days... Not that he will be capable of much else,' he murmured to Theo. 'Tell me,' he went on, as he began to gather his instruments together, immersing them, and his bloody hands, in a pail of water. 'Did you ever get around to reading Heine? There is no one quite like him, I find.'

Chapter 9

Laura, December 1879: Rorke's Drift

After Grey Town, the country grew increasingly wild, as the road wound its way towards the Tugela Gorge; passing at times beneath sheer precipices of red sandstone, at others, through verdant tracts of bush, dotted with feathery mimosas, silver trees, and towering clumps of purple aloes. Hour after hour they journeyed on, with never a sight of a living soul. Only the distant barking of a dog, or the glimpse of a cluster of native huts—in shape resembling nothing so much as the beehives in Laura's father's orchard—told of Man's presence in that remote place.

When she had remarked to De Kuiper how empty the land was of people he had shaken his head. 'There are people there all right. You just don't see them.' He threw her a wry look. 'If they wanted to be seen, you would see them, believe me.'

From that point on she could not shake off the sensation of being observed; nor the feeling that, out of sight—just beyond that rock or behind that tree—were human figures, watching and waiting as their little calvacade went by.

On the evening of the second day, they reached the Mooi River Drift; from here, it was but a two-hour journey to the Tugela crossing. It was a manoeuvre which must be done in daylight, De Kuiper said, and so they would go no further that day. They accordingly out-spanned and the fire was lit.

From all around came the sounds of night creatures: the strange mechanical whirring of cicadas and the harsh croak of a nightjar, followed by the bark of a jackal a few miles off. Above, the stars of the Southern Cross scattered their fiery radiance across the dark vault of the heavens.

Emiline Reynolds's voice came softly out of the darkness. 'I shall not be sorry to have seen this—as indeed Theodore must have seen it.'

'Nor I.'

'I have been reading his journal, you know. He seems to have the most tremendous difficulties getting the wagons across the rivers in this part of the country. One can see for oneself how arduous that must have been...'

Laura murmured an assent, conscious that her friend was barely aware of her presence. She seemed to be drifting in thought between the past and the present.

'Such a dear boy,' she murmured a short while later. 'And never the least bit of trouble to me...'

Her voice failed her a moment.

'Forgive me, my dear. I am not quite myself. But it seems to me that the separation between the living and the dead is not as great as many people suppose...'

A figure moved in the darkness beyond the circle of firelight.

'Why, Rejoice,' said Mrs Reynolds. 'Come and sit by me, child. We were talking of my son, whom I hope to meet again before too long.'

The Swedish mission at Rorke's Drift was a collection of low, thatched wooden dwellings in the middle of a bare plain, overlooked by a mountain. This was the Oskarberg: she knew its name from one of Theo's letters. They were greeted by the clergyman— a Reverend Witt—and his curate; the former's wife being absent on a visit to her sister in Howick.

'A shame we did not know exactly when you would arrive,' said the Reverend Witt. 'My Trudi would have wanted to be here, to welcome you.'

Since walking was painful for her, one of his native servants was summoned to carry Mrs Reynolds to the hospital. 'Do not be alarmed, dear lady,' said the Reverend Witt, on seeing her face. 'Johann is as gentle a creature as ever lived.' The hospital, recently rebuilt, was the coolest spot. Perhaps the English lady would be more comfortable on the veranda—and the other lady too? Johann would sleep close by, in case they were frightened—but, in all truth, there was nothing to fear. They were hardly ever troubled by snakes—except a little in the rainy season—and since the war ended, the occasional raids they had suffered on their chicken-coops and vegetable gardens were a thing of the past.

Why, most Zulus were so honest that if you hung your gold watch on a thorn bush and left it there for a week no one would steal it. These people were as gentle as lambs; true followers of the Lord Jesus. If only they could foreswear strong drink and borrowing each other's wives from time to time, they would be as sinless as the angels.

It was late afternoon when they arrived, and by the time they were settled in, and the horses had been watered, darkness had fallen. At supper, Grace was said by Mr Edmundsen, the curate—a taciturn young man whose beardless face was burned a deep red by the sun, so that it seemed as if he were perpetually blushing. The fare was simple—broth and broiled fowl—but offered a welcome change from the meagre rations of the past few days.

Laura took some broth to Mrs Reynolds, in the hope of enticing her to eat, but it proved a futile exercise. She could keep nothing down. It seemed an unkindness to force her; but she was growing weaker by the hour from want of nourishment. The opiates they had with them offered some relief; but these were running low.

After supper, Laura wandered for a while in the little cemetery, where the mounds of greened-over earth offered further evidence of what had happened here a year ago. She stood for a while in the moonlight, which, falling on the white stones, made them gleam like fallen snow. A figure moved in the shadows, and she felt her heart jump. But it was only De Kuiper.

'Paying your respects to the fallen heroes?' he said.

She looked at him sharply, but his face was impassive.

'I felt like some air.' she said. 'It is a beautiful evening, is it not?'

He lit a cigarette. 'It is a clear night, ja.'

They were joined by the Reverend Witt. 'You have found our little churchyard—a charming spot is it not?' he said to Laura. 'And full of memories—not all of them happy ones, alas...'

'You are speaking of last January, are you not?'

'I am,' he replied. 'And since then not a day has passed that I have not thought about it. To witness suffering on such a scale and to have so few resources to alleviate it. We had no medicines, no supplies…' He made a small gesture, indicative of helplessness.

Laura frowned. 'Did so many die, then? I understood that it was no more than a handful.'

'It is true that not so many Englishmen died,' said the Reverend Witt. 'But what of the Zulus? There was not a single family in the country who did not lose a son.'

'The English count only their own dead,' said De Kuiper. 'You do not hear tell of how many the enemy lost—nor of how many of our people died in their war…'

'It was your people who invited the English here,' said the Reverend Witt, with a faint smile.

Next morning, Mrs Reynolds was a little better; but it was De Kuiper's opinion that she was not strong enough to travel. Their plan had been to reach Isandhlwana on the evening of 21st January, in order, Mrs Reynolds said, that they might watch the sun rise next morning, as Theodore would have done on that fateful day a year ago.

It was now 19th January. They would remain at Rorke's Drift for the present. The road was a bad road, even for those parts, De Kuiper said; so that even though the distance was only eight miles, it would take them the best part of a day.

It was strange to be idle after so long a period of activity—the sense of urgency which had possessed them having given way to a kind of lassitude. We are becalmed, thought Laura.

She had offered her services in the kitchen, thinking that two men alone would be glad of some female assistance, but the Reverend Witt raised his hands in feigned horror. 'Joseph would never forgive me if I allowed a foreign young lady into his kitchen. And my wife would never forgive me for upsetting Joseph. He is, as you say, a treasure,' said the Reverend Witt. 'But treasures can also be lost.'

Leaving Mrs Reynolds to rest, Laura sought the shadiest spot she could find, under the spreading branches of a large acacia. She thought she might write some letters—the latest from home requiring a reply; but it was too hot to write. She took up her book, but its tale of a young woman forced to choose between three men did not engage her. After a few pages, she cast it aside.

As she stretched her legs, to relieve a cramp, a trickle of sweat—deliciously cool—ran from the nape of her neck to the base of her spine. From the trunk of the tree, a green and blue lizard regarded her with eyes like tourmalines.

'Miss Brooke...'

She looked up.

'What is it, Rejoice?'

The girl jerked her chin in the direction of the hospital.

'Miss Reynolds...' In her mouth, it sounded like one word: Mizrenol. Her expression was impossible to read.

At once, Laura got to her feet. She found Mrs Reynolds sitting up in bed.

'Why, my dear, you should not have run, in this heat. It is not such an urgent matter as all that... but still, I should like you to know what's what.' She smiled. 'I fear that I am making little sense. But do not be afraid. I have not yet lost my wits.'

The exertion of laughing was evidently painful, for she caught her breath.

'You must not tire yourself,' said Laura, wondering if the other were indeed in her right mind. There was a gaiety in her manner which seemed at odds with the sick-room; and twin spots of colour burned in her pale cheeks.

'I have been thinking how best to order my affairs,' Mrs Reynolds continued. 'I have decided to leave you fifty thousand pounds. I have written to my lawyers to that effect. Frederick's nose will be put out of joint, but then that is Frederick. He and Laetitia and the boys will be substantially provided for...'

'I cannot allow you to do this,' said Laura.

'It is already done. Had Theodore lived, the money would have been no more than his share—and yours.'

She reached beneath the pillow and withdrew a small oil-cloth wrapped volume. It was Theo's journal, which she had carried with her throughout the journey.

'You are to have this, too,' she said. 'I know it will mean more to you than anything else I could give you.'

A little later she said:

'I have so longed to see the place where he lies, but now I do not think that I shall see it.'

113

Emiline Reynolds was silent a while, her gaze fixed on the candle's steady flame.

'You will go there, will you not?' she said at last.

'I will.'

Mrs Reynolds closed her eyes. 'That is what I had hoped.' Her face in the soft light seemed suddenly younger, its lines of strain smoothed out. She smiled. 'Poor child. It has been a strange time for you...'

'I would not have wished it otherwise.'

The other inclined her head, as if to acknowledge that this was no more than she would have expected. Her strength seemed almost exhausted.

It seemed to Laura that she must have fallen asleep, but then she saw that Mrs Reynolds's eyes were open. Her lips moved; the words emerging as no more than a whisper.

'Let the dead bury the dead.' she said. 'I have never known the truth of that sentence till now...'

'You must rest,' said Laura.

'Ah! There will be time enough for that.'

She suffered herself to be made more comfortable, however. As Laura rose from straightening the sheet, Mrs Reynolds took her hand.

'There is a duty to the living also,' she said.

At midnight, Mrs Reynolds sat up in bed. 'Is it you?' she said. 'Is it really you?'

It was not Laura she meant, for her gaze was elsewhere. After this, she did not speak again. Her skin was dry and very hot to the touch. When Laura tried to give her some water, it ran out of the corners of her mouth. She did not seem to be asleep, for her eyes were open. But when spoken to, she did not seem to hear.

A handkerchief, wrung out in what remained of the water, appeared to give her some relief, for she lay quiet for a while; only her hands were restless. A lock of hair which had fallen across her face seemed to trouble her: even when it had been brushed away, her fingers returned to where it had been, twisting invisible strands. At last she slept; or seemed to.

Laura snuffed out the candle, and let her eyes adjust to the dark. Gradually, indistinct forms resolved themselves into a semblance of their daylight selves: the face of the sleeping woman, silvered by the moonlight, resembled that of a carved stone image on a monument; the figure of Rejoice, sitting on a low stool by the door, seemed that of a barbaric goddess.

From outside, came the shriek of some night creature. Then a curious, coughing roar. At the sound of this, Rejoice, who had been immobile as a statue, grew suddenly uneasy. She muttered something in her own tongue, and a figure loomed in the doorway: Johann, the watchman. A whispered exchange followed.

'He says don't be frighten' of the leopard. If he sees it, he will shoot it,' said the girl.

On the veranda it was cooler. The stars nearest to the horizon were larger and brighter than the rest, Laura saw. They were not still, but seemed in constant motion. Until that moment, she had not realized how many colours were to be found there: flashes of blue, green and violet lit up the sky. It was like the kaleidoscope she had had as a child—an endless shifting and reordering of glittering shapes.

She was not aware of having fallen asleep, but the next thing she knew was a touch on her arm. Rejoice said nothing, but her eyes went towards the door. As soon as Laura entered the room, she heard the change in Mrs Reynolds's breathing. Now it was raucous; difficult. What air there was in the room was foul, but when Laura went to open the blinds, a movement from Mrs Reynolds stopped her. Thin fingers clutched at her wrist, and the dreadful sound issuing from Mrs Reynolds's open mouth seemed to fill the room.

They fashioned a coffin out of some of the wood that was left over from rebuilding the hospital; Johann made it, and it was he, helped by Constant and Lucky, who dug the grave. There was still room in the little cemetery, although it had been much in use of late. The grave was as deep as could be made in that stony soil; anything shallower, and there would be the risk of wild animals disturbing the remains.

Rejoice and Mary, Joseph's wife, washed the body, and combed and plaited the scant grey hair. Dressed once more in a clean nightdress, and with her hands crossed on her breast, Mrs Reynolds seemed small as a child; her face, now emptied of expression, a child's smooth mask. When she was ready at last, Laura removed her rings, which were to be returned to her son—slipping these onto her own fingers for safe-keeping. Mrs Reynolds's jet earrings she left in place; the dead should not go naked to their rest.

Between the deceased's cold fingers, she slipped the photograph of Theo the former had brought with her to Africa. Before the coffin lid was closed, she cut off a lock of Mrs Reynolds's hair, to put with the one she had of Theo's. She would weave them together, and wear them in a locket next to her heart.

There were not many at the ceremony: she herself, De Kuiper, and Rejoice were the only mourners, with the Reverend Witt and Mr Edmundsen officiating. When the coffin was lowered into the grave, she thought, Now she, too, is a part of Africa. At a nod from the priest, she bent down and picked up a handful of earth.. It felt friable to the touch—like clay, or ash. It pattered onto the lid with a sound like rain.

As she stepped back, she saw that their number had been had been swelled by others: a line of dark figures stood outside the low wall surrounding the graves. She supposed they must have come from the nearby village, for there were none she recognised. The men were in warrior's regalia, with spears and shields, the ostrich-feather plumes of their headdresses barely stirring in the breathless air. When Johann threw in the first shovelful of earth, a strange high wail rose from the ranks of women. Laura felt her own throat constrict in response, although no sound passed her lips.

The mournful keening rose and fell, growing in volume and power until it seemed to fill the landscape, as if it were an emanation of the hills themselves. It rang in their ears as their party walked back towards the house, where Joseph had set out a cold collation.

It was not until the evening, when Laura was sitting on the veranda composing a letter to Frederick Reynolds, that De Kuiper approached her. She was struggling with a sentence—it is with great regret that I must inform you—and so did not look up at once. His voice broke her train of reflection:

'Will you rest here another day, or do you wish to start for Grey Town tomorrow? If we leave at first light, it will be so much the better...'

She put down her pen.

'Why do you speak of turning back? There are still some miles to go before we reach Isandhlwana, are there not?'

De Kuiper shrugged, not meeting her gaze.

'I thought, now that Mevrouw...'

'You thought wrong. Mevrouw's wish was that we should visit the very spot, and that is what I intend to do...'

'To see with your own eyes.' His tone was dry. 'Of course.'

She picked up the letter she had laid aside, dismissing him with the gesture, as she thought. Still he stood there.

'What is it that you wish to say?' she said at last.

'Just this.' He lowered his voice, as if afraid they might be overheard; although who in that deserted place was there to hear, she could not imagine. 'There is nothing to see. No 'spot', as you call it, to visit. No tomb, to adorn with flowers...'

'I did not ask for your opinion.'

He said nothing.

'Do you suppose,' she went on, 'that I would have come so far, only to turn back, at the last? Even if I had not given my word that I would do so, do you think that any power on earth would prevent me from going to Isandhlwana, whether there is anything to be seen there or no?'

She addressed herself once more to the sheet in front of her. This time, she did not need to look up to know that he had gone. 'It will perhaps be of some small comfort to know,' she wrote, her hand now perfectly steady, 'that your late mother's last request will be fulfilled...'

It was still dark when they set out—with the boys taking turns to lead the way on foot. They were used to it, De Kuiper said, when she protested. She was riding Phaedrus, Mrs Witt's horse, a quiet little roan. The heavy cart and most of its supplies had been left behind; they had no need of it now. They would be gone for a day and a night; on their return, Mr Edmundsen would ride with them as far as Helpmekaar.

De Kuiper, who had spoke no more than a few words to her since their quarrel of the day before, now confined himself to the barest instructions regarding the course they were to follow. She was to keep Lucky and Constant in sight all the time; he himself would be bringing up the rear. If she saw or heard anything untoward, she must cry out at once. If she wished to stop, she must give him fair warning.

They crossed the Drift at its shallowest point, where the broad flat stones made a kind of causeway. From here, they began to climb. The road—little more than a track—was very bad, and for the first few miles, Laura's only concern was to keep her seat; to have taken a tumble would have been painful in more ways than one. But her mount proved familiar with the terrain, rough as it was, and after a while, she felt herself relax.

From all around, came the soft liquid notes of birdsong. Above the dark mass of hills, the sky grew lighter. The air was still cool; she had never felt so alive to its shifts of temperature, and to the varying tones—now black, now grey, now softest purple—of the landscape, soon to be quickened into life by the rising sun. Within a matter of moments, the dark land would be transformed. Jagged shapes of rocks would turn to molten fire, and the sky, like a banner unfurled, would glow scarlet and rose.

In such a landscape, all that was human counted for nothing. This sky, these hills, had existed for aeons before Man, and would continue after he had long ceased to be.

Chapter 10

Rejoice, December 1879: Rorke's Drift

She wept at night, the pale English, when she thought no one could hear her. She was weeping for the old one, now, as well as for her man. In the daytime, she walked around with her eyelids red and her little mouth shut tight. When she spoke it was in a small, cool voice: Yes, Rejoice? Thank you, Rejoice. But her hands trembled in her lap; she squeezed them together, to stop them from trembling. At night she wept—a strange, stifled cry, as if the *Tokoloshe* sat on her chest, choking her with its long fingers. All night long she sighed and muttered, throwing herself from side to side on her narrow bed. It was too low down, that was the trouble. A bed should be higher—raised up on bricks, as Rejoice's own bed was raised—so that no evil spirit could come there.

But they would not be told, these white people.

She had thought, when they first came, that they must be evil spirits themselves, with their horses and guns and their red coats. She had been a child, then. Now she knew that they were men. They could die, too; and they did. The country all around was littered with their white bones. It was not good to leave the dead unburied; which was why the Englishwomen had come. They would gather up the scattered bones—the limbs torn asunder by wild beasts and the skull cast aside like a stone—so that the man they loved was whole again. Then they would build a fire. All night they would sit by it, keeping the dead company. In the morning they would dig a pit for the body, and cover it with stones, to keep the wild dogs away. That was the way it was done.

But now the old one was dead, and the pale English, her daughter, walked around like a ghost in the sun. In the morning, she went to the graveyard and talked to the old one. 'What shall I do?' she asked her. 'What shall I do?'; but the old one, being dead, was silent. At night the English wept and sighed. She had lost her man, and the old woman, too. Others had lost as much as she. More. The whole country was a graveyard. There was not a bush or a stone that did not hide the bones of some brave warrior. She herself had lost four brothers, of the five that were her mother's sons. That was why she, Rejoice, had been sent away, to be trained as a maid at the Christian mission in Durban. It was safe there, her mother had said. The Christians would look after her, even if their god was a fish.

Now she had come back, but it was too late. Her mother did not know her. 'I had a daughter once,' she said, rocking and smiling. 'A beautiful baby girl. But she is dead. They are all dead, my babies.' While Rejoice was away in Durban, her youngest brother, Thankfulness, had gone to join the uNodwengu, although he was not yet fourteen. They were disbanded now, of course, those proud regiments—the uNohenke, the uMcijo, the iNogobamakhosi, the uMbonambi and the rest—all but a few of their warriors dead or maimed. But that did not stop the young hotheads from wanting to join those that remained—'to avenge the blood that was spilt by the red soldiers,' said her brother.

There was no end to it. Nor would there be an end, until all the warriors were dead. Their king, proud Cetshwayo, was already in exile—shut up in an English prison. Soon, he, too, would die, and the Zulu nation would be no more.

If she had the words, she would say to the pale English: *Listen. This is what happened. You are not the only one who has cause to mourn.* She would murmur the words like a spell into the ear of the sleeping woman, as she sighed and moaned. *It was not the intention of our chief to fight,* she would say. *It was the Day of the Dead Moon—an unlucky day for fighting; as indeed it proved to be, for those who were victorious, as much as for the vanquished. But Chief Ntshingwayo had seen the red soldiers leave—a large force the day before; then another party in the morning, drawn out of the camp by our skilful decoys. They were scattered around the hills like grazing goats, leaving the camp with all its treasures—its rocket-guns, its wagons, its sacks of corn—defended only by a few. Our chief took this as a sign that the amadhlozi, the Celestial Ones, had delivered the red soldiers into our hands. So it turned out.*

Thirteen regiments were hidden in the valley behind iThusi Hill when the English scouts came upon them. They fired upon us, and at once warriors from the uMcijo regiment sprang up, and rushed towards them. When the red soldiers saw how many we were, they retreated; but by now there was no choice but to attack. So we formed up in rank, and marched towards the camp. Nothing can stop a Zulu impi on the march, Rejoice would whisper in the ear of the pale English, as she slept. *It can cover forty or fifty miles a day, over stony ground. There are regiments of women, too, and young boys, to carry the warriors' food and sleeping-mats. Twenty-five thousand, all told. A mighty host, to overcome a sleeping lion.*

We pursued the red soldiers until we reached the little hill where the rocket-guns were set up. There was a large party of soldiers with guns—the deadly martinihenry—and many of our warriors were killed. But in the end we overcame the martinihenry, and marched on, shouting 'Usutu!', our battle-cry. Then the Ngobamakosi regiment, which formed the left horn of the buffalo, swept round the south side of the Rocket Hill, outflanking the red soldiers. Many of them took refuge in the donga outside the camp, and fired on us from there. But by that time...

Are you listening? she would murmur, stroking the damp hair back from the forehead of the dreaming woman. *Listen. By that time the Ngobamakosi were circling round so as to shut in the camp on the side nearest the river. Just below that, a number of red soldiers were engaging the Kandampemvu regiment, which was being driven back, with heavy losses—but just then one of the chiefs ran down from the hill and shouted at the warriors to go forward. 'Are you weak women or boys that you allow these red soldiers to frighten you so? For shame! If any one of you thinks he can turn his face away from the enemy he can answer to me. I will kill him with my own hands...' So they went on, with renewed fury, driving the red soldiers back among the tents.*

By now, the noise of fighting and the screams were very loud, and the smoke from the burning camp was so thick you could hardly see your hand before your face. In the middle of the battle, the sun turned black. We could still see it in the sky above our heads, or it would have seemed like the middle of the night. The red soldiers who had not been killed were escaping across the 'neck' towards Jim's House. Many of them were cut off and killed down in the river which flows along the valley; but some got away. There was one induna with a flashing sword, which he waved above his head, so that it seemed to be made of fire. He was the last of the red soldiers to die in battle, although there were some we hunted down afterwards. Their bodies were well-served: the spirits were released by our spears; no witchcraft was allowed to prevail.

Afterwards, she would whisper, brushing the eyelids of the sleeper as lightly as if her hand were a fly alighting there, *afterwards we took what we could carry from the red soldiers' camp. They were all dead, so it did not matter to them anymore. Their horse and oxen were all dead, too, and their tents were burned. That was done to honour the dead: when someone dies, his kraal must be destroyed, or abandoned. Some of our young men found bottles of tywala in the camp, and got very drunk. They also found some black stuff in little bottles which did not look good to drink, and so they poured it on the ground. Others found cans of paraffin oil and drank it, thinking it was tywala. They were sick for many days, and one died. After this we went home to our kraals—all except the Undi and the Udhloko regiments, who had gone to Jim's House, to drive out the red soldiers there. Most of them never returned. They lie buried all around...*

She would put her lips close to the English woman's ear. *All around where you are lying, safe in Jim's House, every stone of which has been washed in their blood. There are no graves for them in your little graveyard. That is only for white people. It was built by Jim himself, and he, dead by his own hand, was the first to be buried here. Afterwards came the red soldiers, and then the old woman, for whom you weep. But you must dry your tears, now,* she would say, as the sky outside the hospital building began to lighten. *The old one is gone, and your tears are of no use to her anymore. You must pluck a handful of leaves from the thorn tree which shades her grave, and carry*

them with you, because that is where her spirit is to be found.
It is not to be found in a stone, and it is not to be found in a
heap of old bones. Nor does the hair you cut from her head and
now wear in a little box on a chain around your neck contain
her spirit.

If she had the words, thought Rejoice, this is what she would
say, because there was no one else to whom she could say it. Her
family were all dead, or gone away; and her mother was wandering in a place where Rejoice could not follow her. Only the old
ones, sitting by the fire knew the story of what had happened on
that day—the Day of the Dead Moon. Soon they would die, too,
and no one would remember the truth of it. Only she would remember.

She wanted to give the story to the English woman, as a gift,
so that she had something to carry home, which would sustain
her through the years before she, too, became old. She would
have liked to tell her all these things, but, as it was, she could only
offer silence. A hand to smooth a feverish brow; a cup of water
to quench a burning thirst; a watchful presence in the night, to
keep the bad spirits at bay.

The old one had been kind to her, and so she was sorry that
she was dead. But she, Rejoice, had known it the moment she laid
eyes on her: she had a look of death. It was there in the yellow-
whiteness of her skin, like the colour of the sky before a storm.
Her eyes, too, had the yellow look that pale eyes get from too
much squinting at the sun. It hurt her to move, the old woman,
although she pretended otherwise. In spite of this, she never
raised her voice, or complained when the comb tugged her hair,
as Rejoice was combing it. 'You're a good girl,' was all she said,
closing her eyes when the pain got too bad.

A good girl. That was not what the lay sisters at the mission
had said. Wilful. Headstrong. Insolent. How she had hated it there!
Once they had locked her in the coal shed all night, to teach her
Christian obedience. She had been on the point of running away
when the English women came. Since they were going to where
she wanted to go, she had decided to take the job. She would stay
with them until they were close to her village; then she would
go.

123

She had not intended to stay with the English and yet she had done so. She told herself that it was for the old one, and yet now that the old one was dead she still lingered on, even though the young one—Miss Brooke—had no need of her. Johann, the fool, had asked her to marry him, but he was too old for her and besides, he had a wife. When she married, it would be to a chief's son, who could afford to give twenty cattle for her. Although who he would pay them to she did not know, with her father and brothers dead, her mother wandering in her mind, and no one left in her village except the old ones.

Chapter 11

Theo, January 1879: Isandhlwana

The invasion had begun. All the feints and delays of the past month since the ultimatum had been issued were, mercifully, at an end. The Zulus will never accept our terms, he had written to his mother a few days before. We have demanded too much. They must surrender everything—or fight. He was not alone in being glad that it had come to this. Do not be afraid for me, he had thought to add. These people know nothing of modern warfare. They cannot hope to prevail. At the Cape, the Gaika and Xhosa rebels had run away, when they had met with superior force.

So, too, the Zulus would run away.

Before dawn on 11th January, they crossed the Buffalo River. There was a ground mist and it was very cold; they shivered as they descended to the drift. Heavy rainfall had turned the river into a torrent. As he stepped into the water, he felt his horse prance sideways in protest; he urged her forward, but the current was almost too strong, and by the time they reached the middle of the river, it was as much as he could do to keep them both from being swept away. But he gained the bank at last. Others were not so lucky. As he patted the frightened animal's flank, murmuring words of encouragement, he heard a shout from higher up the drift, where the river ran strongest.

A group of natives, belonging to Hamilton-Browne's contingent, had tried to cross on foot, linking arms to avoid being carried off their feet by the fast-flowing water. One had lost his balance, however, and had gone under, dragging his fellows down with him. Hearing the commotion, Hayes—who had already reached the bank—turned his horse's head and plunged back into the river; but by the time he reached them, it was already too late.

How many had been lost, no one could say for certain, as only

125

a rough head-count had ever been done. 'Better for the black bastards to drown that to blow one another's heads off—a saving on ammunition, too,' joked Coleman; the Basuto being notoriously bad shots, who had so far accounted for more of their own side than they had Zulus. Still, it was distressing to see the poor devils suffer such a fate.

After the disaster of losing the Africans, they ferried the men over on ponts: a laborious, but safer, procedure. It was evening before they finished the crossing—by which time the earlier arrivals had already pitched camp. Now it stood, stretched out in a line as far as the eye could see, along the bank of the river. The order was given for the men to fall out for dinner. It was the usual fare: bully beef and biscuit, washed down with a cup of muddy coffee.

Afterwards, he smoked a pipe, and settled down to writing letters. 'Nights are cold, but the days are broiling hot here,' he wrote to Laura, 'but far better than the infernal rain, which as you know from my last has plagued us this past month.'

Tomorrow we start at daybreak for Sihayo's kraal. His sons are the cause of all this mischief , as they have behaved in a very ungallant way towards two of their wives. The said ladies having run away & taken refuge in Natal, they were then pursued & dragged back to Zululand, where I am afraid to say they were summarily killed...

He did not repeat the joke that had been doing the rounds of the mess-hall, about the ease with which divorce could be obtained in Zululand: a handful of large stones would suffice. 'Shut the bitches up good and proper,' said Coleman. 'Seems to me these niggers have got things the right way about...'

So we are to arrest these gentlemen, & bring them to trial...

Not that it would come to that, he suspected. The Zulus were not known for surrendering without a hard fight—and, after months of anticipating this moment, the redcoats were in the mood to give it to them...

Early next morning they set out along the track, which led from the camp to the hilltop stronghold. It was a fine, hot day; the mist had burnt off by the time the reached the Batshe valley, and they were all in good spirits—Lord C most of all. Below the kopje, a herd of cattle was grazing: the strange, humpbacked beasts so prized in this country.These were captured without difficulty—auguring well for the campaign ahead, remarked Lord C.

At once the Zulus opened fire, killing two of the native auxiliaries, and wounding two dozen more. But they did not prevail for long, and within a few minutes, the caves had been cleared. Colonel Degacher led the assault on the kraal ;when they reached the summit of the hill where it was situated, there was no one to be found, except for three old women and a girl who had been left behind. Lord C ordered the kraal to be burnt. It made a fine sight: black smoke rising like a funeral pyre, against an azure sky.

'Well, we have seen some action at last,' wrote Theo to Laura.

Sihayo's Kraal is burnt, & one of his sons killed. So Ld C is well content; & our party covered with glory. This is as well, for the rest of our time has been spent in making roads—not an easy or pleasant task in this country, with the men in a bad temper (for this is usually a job for the Engineers, you know) & the sun beating down on the back of one's neck, & the flies a never-ending plague—but it must be done, if we are to advance further...

With the ground still soft after the rains, there could be no thought of reaching Ulundi before the month was up.They must advance by degrees, that much was plain. Another camp would have to be found, which better commanded the country. It was Major Clery who chose it, Hallam told him. He had said 'This will do,' although Mansel of the NMP—who knew the country well, of course—had been dubious.

'He did not like the way the hill looms over it all,' Hallam explained. 'Open ground would have been a better choice, in his opinion. I must say, I'm inclined to agree with Mansel; but you know how the good Major likes to have the last word.'

Theo had not been part of the reconnaissance party—his

platoon having been given the unwelcome task of road-building. It was gruelling work; he fell onto his cot each night like a dead man. The best time was the hour before sleep, when he lay in his tent with the flap open, looking up at the sky. The stars here were extraordinary; he never tired of gazing at them.

Those eight days passed in a kind of dream—waking at first light to the tremulous flutings of birds—flocks of *witte ogie*, so light they barely caused the grass-stalks on which they perched to bend; swallows; finches; a strange black bird with a rust-red breast—this ethereal music overlaid with earthier sounds. The groaning and stamping of the oxen, waiting for their fodder to be brought; the grumbling of the men, turned out of their tents to face another day.

If there was time, he would slip down to the river, to splash cold water on his face and breast, the beads of it drying within moments on his sleep-warmed skin. He'd drink his coffee while he was dressing. There was no time to be lost if they were to make the most of the day—every hour worked before noon being worth two thereafter. His servant would be waiting with his horse. With luck, they'd manage another mile today.

Yesterday he'd had one man down with sunstroke; another with a poisoned foot. The men were surly, resenting the added burden of the tools, the relentless toiling in the blazing sun, while their comrades had it easy, roaming the country in search of the enemy—which had so far failed to show itself, beyond one bewildered old man and a couple of young girls herding goats.

Secretly, Theo was in sympathy with O'Rourke and Jones, the two most vociferous complainants. Had O'Rourke wished to spend his days wielding a pick and shovel, he could have done so in comfort in his own precious home, he said with some asperity—although precious was not the epithet he used. Jones—a watchmaker by trade—had merely raised his blistered hands in ironic confirmation of O'Rourke's remark.

Their route was towards the new camp, ten miles from where they lay at present: it was a fine spot, Hallam said. A broad plain, in the shadow of a mountain, from the top of which you could see for miles around.

'The weather continues fine & hot,' Theo wrote to Laura.

We have been hard at it these past few days, preparing the road. Tomorrow we set out for our new camp, at Isandhlwana Hill. This afternoon Hallam and Marlowe and I rode out a little way towards it. On the way back we shot a brace of guinea fowl for supper, so you can imagine how pleased we were! This is a very fine country, with rolling hills & spacious grasslands, dotted with thorn-trees, & great rocky cliffs looming over all. How I wish you were here, sweetest love, to see it—but, alas, that cannot be.

In the strange, dead calm of those days, it was easy to forget the purpose for which they had come. Only now and again—in moments of idleness, or before falling asleep at night—did thoughts of what might, or might not, lie before them rise to trouble him. The truth was, he did not know—any more than his commanding officers knew—precisely what they were 'in for'; although there were murmurs around the camp that a force of up to 30,000 Zulus was, even now, assembling in the hills. This was an exaggeration of course; and even if there were that number—which he doubted—they could never match the firepower of the British army. Although he had seen for himself at Sihayo's Kraal the kind of resistance their warriors could muster. It had been a tough, eight-hour fight, but at the end, they—the British—had emerged victorious. Which was as it would be again. Theirs was simply the best army in the world. They had the best equipment, the best officers and the best-disciplined fighting force. No band of half-naked savages could hope to beat that.

On 20th January the column set out: a slowly moving, heavily laden line of ox-wagons, horses and men. Riding at the head of his company, Theo was put in mind of a picture he had once seen: 'Hannibal Crossing the Alps'—although there were no elephants to be seen. But such an unwieldy progress, with so many stops and starts, and so much heaving and cursing and shouting, as the men in charge of the teams urged on their beasts, and such a smell of horseflesh and leather, and a dazzle of polished brass and steel, seemed worthy of a Roman—or Carthaginian—army.

He amused himself with the thought for a while, hearing in

the clank and clash of arms and accoutrements, the rumbling of wheels and the drumming of hooves, the ghostly tread of ancient legions, traversing a foreign land. By the time the sun was fully up, every man was drenched in sweat. The flies grew more and more troublesome: a pestilential cloud, forever descending and being beaten off, and descending again.

It was late afternoon by the time they were set up, in a long line that ran in front of the hill, facing South-East. In front was the broad valley of which Hallam had spoken; on either side, ridges of hills. It was, as the latter had said, a fine site: well protected by the mountain. The whole extent of the camp was about eight-hundred yards, with most of the wagons scattered about the ridge, to the rear of the camp.

Dinner was an almost festive affair. A mood of satisfaction—that they were making progress at last—was in the air. After the day's exertions, officers and men alike were tired, and most turned in early, Theo amongst them. Weeks of living in the open air had hardened him: he was no longer the callow youth of his Cape Town days.

Other things, apart from exposure to sun and weather, had brought this change about, he was well aware.

He opened his journal. He had written nothing for over a week. I cannot stop thinking of her, he read, with some disgust. She has usurped the place that rightfully belongs to another...An image of Pretty's brown breasts, with their dark nipples, flashed across his mind. The scented tangle of her hair.

He could not suppress a groan.

'What's the matter?' said Hallam. 'Belly-ache, is it?' He examined the thick brown residue at the bottom of his tin mug with an expression of distaste. 'This filthy muck is enough to give any man the runs.'

Theo murmured in agreement, although his pain was not in fact of the corporeal kind, but something worse: an ache in the heart; an ague of the mind. He wrote:

I pray that my transgressions will be forgiven. I have wronged too many of those dear to me—my sweet Laura most of all—through my lascivious acts. And yet it did not

130

seem like wickedness when we were together, Pretty and
I. At our last meeting, did I not call her my Wife in the sight
of Heaven? My God forgive me for that falsehood, though
it was said in earnest at the time...

He could not recall that occasion without a shudder. It had nearly
proved his undoing, in more ways than one. She had come to the
barracks—a thing she had never done before; nor were they permitted visits, especially not from such a one as she. Had any of
his superior officers got wind of it, there would have been a fearful row. Fortunately Hallam was the only one of his comrades in
the room, when Theo's man had brought the message.

'Young person to see you, sir,' Williams had said, with a meaning look. 'Says as how it's urgent.'

Hallam had raised an eyebrow, but when the girl came in, he
left them alone without a word.

Theo had felt his face grow hot with the shame of it, knowing
his friend's views on the subject of 'light' women. 'It is no exaggeration to say that the common soldier's addiction to whores
undermines all our efforts to discipline him. If he cared as much
for his weapon as for the "weapon" between his legs, we should
have the best fighting force in Christendom...'

Now here was Theo, no better than the 'common soldier' at
his most weak and foolish, *tête à tête* with his coloured mistress.

He had been packing his boxes; throughout their interview,
he clasped the book he had been about to add to the pile: Scott's
Ivanhoe, he recalled. A man torn between two women—the fair
and the dark.

She had been crying, he saw. He hadn't had the heart to be
angry with her.

'You are leaving,' was all she said. He remembered the look
of her dark eyes, with their reddened whites.

He could say nothing.

'It is true, then?' Her voice shook slightly.

From outside came a volley of shouted commands, and a stam-
pede of hurrying feet.

'You knew how things stood,' he managed at last to reply.

'Yes.' After her moment of weakness, she withdrew into

dignified aloofness. 'There is something you must know,' she said.

'If my Laura had an inkling of this, it would break her heart,' he wrote. 'I could never be so cruel to one so dear...' And yet how well did he know her, this pale and serious young woman he had promised to marry? He had poured out his heart to her in his letters, it was true—but what did he know of her heart? Everything he had written was a lie: a smokescreen, to conceal a shameful truth.

How it would disgust her, if she knew—she, who placed such a high value upon plain speaking! He would not be able to look her in the face, that much was certain. He had traduced the promises he had made; he was unworthy of her.

As for his mother—what she would say if the truth were known was too painful to contemplate. His mother, who had written of her pride in him... *my precious boy*... why, it would kill her if she knew what he had become. Her fine, bright son given over to filthy desires.

This time, his groan was silent; but when he opened his eyes, Hallam was looking at him oddly.

'Touch of the sun, old chap? You ought to turn in early,' he said. 'Busy day tomorrow, chasing the Zulus about the country. That's if we can find any of the blighters,' he added with a laugh.

Next day he awoke at first light to the smell of hot coffee prepared by the ever-reliable Williams, and a basinful of hot water in which to wash. He had given up shaving after Grey Town—most of them had—and now sported a beard several shades darker than his hair, which was now bleached almost white.

Burnt by its three months' exposure to sun and wind, his face was now as dark as a coolie's, he thought, catching sight of himself in the scrap of looking glass which hung on a nail in the tent, and in which he now checked that his tunic was properly fastened. No one at home would know him now.

A fleeting image of Laura, in her blue dress, flitted across his mind. Her eyes full of tears, as they had been that last time ; although she had been trying her utmost not to cry...

He pushed the thought away. 'How things will turn out for us remains to be seen,' he had written last night in his journal. 'God grant that we come at last to a happy conclusion.' He had not been thinking solely of the enterprise in hand; although that, too, had yet to be resolved. Whether he could look his betrothed in the face again after everything else that had passed was also in question. He felt soiled; stained not only by the physical fact of his amorous adventure, but by the betrayal of faith it constituted.

Certainly, if he had ever deserved Laura's love, he had forfeited that privilege now.

The camp was already stirring as he left the tent, although it was not yet five. The peremptory commands of the sergeants as they made their rounds were underscored by the muffled cursing of the men. Fires were being lit in the camp's field kitchen, where the cooks were busy setting up for breakfast. The clanging of metal utensils against cooking pots could be heard above the murmur of two thousand-odd voices; the whinnying of horses and the lowing of the tethered oxen on the far side of the sea of tents a muted counterpoint to this human babble.

The latrines were at a distance of twenty yards from the edge of the camp. At this time of day, the stench from the 'long-drops' was not too bad; by noon it would be unspeakable. Pulling down his breeches, he crouched at the edge of the pit, feeling his bowels loosen and smelling the sweetish stink of his own shit rising. There was still a scattering of pale stars above the line of hills.

From where he squatted, it seemed as if the white lines of tents covered the whole surface of the plain—an area of level ground between the kopje and the crag. This—the rocky eminence of Isandhlwana itself—rose to a height of four hundred feet above the camp, dwarfing the cone-shaped tents with its massive bulk. A crouching lion, said some; a sphinx, said others, pointing out the resemblance between this fancied monster and the emblem worn on the regiment's cap-badges—an omen, surely?—although no one could be sure of what.

He wiped himself on the remnants of a two-month-old Times; a sacrifice, but he had read the thing from cover to cover, as indeed had every officer in his section. All its news was of Afghanistan; there seemed little interest in what was going on in Natal. Not to put too fine a point on it, Sir Bartle Frere's vainglorious little war was nothing but an embarrassment to the British government. The 'ultimatum'—refusal to comply with which had been the ostensible reason for going to war—had been a joke. By insisting not only that the Zulus should disband their army, but that they should cede authority over all civil matters to the British, Frere had been asking the impossible—and he knew it.

'He expects the Zulus—as warlike a bunch of fellows as ever lived—to lay down their arms,' said Hallam one evening, as they smoked their cigars. 'To emasculate themselves, in a word. This of course they will not do. The whole thing is nothing but a trumped-up excuse. Frere will have his war, whether Disraeli wishes it or no. Unfortunately, we are the poor devils who must see it through...'

Buttoning his fly, Theo gazed once more at the mountain: a sphinx, yes—especially from its eastern aspect. From the west, its shape reminded him more of a fortress. A dark tower, rearing high above the plain, like the outpost of some ancient, alien power.

'*What in the middle but the Tower itself? The Dark Tower— blind as the fool's heart,*' he murmured softly.

The sun was almost up. It would be another fine hot day. As he retraced his steps, he caught a whiff of frying bacon—that would be the Colonel's breakfast being got ready. Old Glyn was a Tartar when it came to his rations. Back at the tent, Hallam was eating a dish of porridge, and shouting for Clarke to bring his boots.

'Confound the man. Here we are, getting our marching orders at last, and half my kit still dirty...'

'Why, are we moving?' said Theo, surprised at this information, for the camp had not been struck.

'I am, dear chap,' replied Hallam. 'Expeditionary force. His Lordship's orders. Zulu raiding party sighted in the Isipezi region; we're to flush 'em out.'

'Save some of them for us, won't you?'

'Will do, old chap—if they let me,' said his friend with a grin. 'Clarke! Look sharp with those boots! I haven't got all day...'

It was a fine sight seeing them all go off together: the noble leader and his entourage first, on their handsome mounts, whose coats had been polished until they shone, and whose stirrups, bits and spurs sparkled like gold in the morning sun. It seemed a picture out of an old book, thought Theo—of knights-at-arms on prancing steeds, setting forth to do battle. Following the officers, the ranks of men in scarlet tunics were as well-drilled as clockwork soldiers.

Watching them wheel about in flawless formation, he felt his heart swell. What was it Hallam had said? The Flower of England. Light flashed on polished brass buttons, and gleaming harness; orders were shouted; fife and drum began to play; and the column began to move off. Bringing up the rear were the ox-carts, loaded with provisions and ammunition. Theo caught Hallam's eye, and raised a hand in greeting; but the latter, already caught up in the seriousness of his role, made no reply beyond a blink of recognition.

Then he was gone.

Already the advance guard was lost to view in a haze of white dust. Above the distant hills towards which they were proceeding, the sky was the pure unclouded blue of midsummer. Even though the sun had been up no more than an hour, it was warm; by mid-day it would be like a furnace. Sighing, Theo returned to his section of the camp, where those men not detailed to water the horses were falling out for breakfast.

He made a brief visit to the horses' lines to check on Albion, who had been off his feed for a day or two. Having given orders that the animal was to be give a hot mash, with linseed oil, to settle him, Theo returned to his tent. He had some requisition orders to write—a tedious but necessary task. If he finished with any time to spare, he would update his journal with an account of the morning's muster. Hallam would laugh to hear himself described as a knight from the days of King Arthur—but that was what, in that moment, he and his comrades had appeared to be.

> *O, what can ail thee, knight-at-arms,*
> *Alone and palely loitering?*
> *The sedge is withered from the lake*
> *And no birds sing...*

Smiling to himself at the notion of Hallam with plumed helmet and lance, Theo turned his attention to more mundane matters.

No one who did not have inside knowledge of it, he thought—as he began to compose a list of tools broken, tools lost, and tools required to continue the job—could have any idea of how tedious the army could be. It was nothing but waiting for things to happen: routine, punctuated by monotony.

At dawn on 22nd January Theo was awoken by the stamping of horses' hooves. Then came the hurried tread of feet. Six hundred of their number—a third of the column—were to join Major Dartnell's force in the Hlzakazi Hills. The enemy had been sighted in the area by scouts the previous day. If they would not stand and fight, they must be hunted out, Lord C had said at dinner the night before, to general applause.

Smiling, he had raised a bumper of champagne, and had given them: 'The twenty-fourth.'

'The twenty-fourth!' they had roared, and in that moment, looking at the flushed and gleaming faces around the table, Theo had felt a lifting of the heart: these were his comrades—as close, if not closer, to him than brothers.

Now he watched them go—an army of shadows, slipping away before it was light like houseless souls returning to the realm of the dead.

All around, the camp was stirring. He knew he was not alone in feeling disconsolate at being left 'out of it'. To have been riding through the hills in the cool of the morning seemed eminently preferable to remaining here in camp, with nothing to look forward to but the certainty of roasting alive on the griddle of this scorching plain.

Returning to his tent, he took his journal from its oilskin bag, although there was barely enough light to see by. He read over the entries for the past few days. What gloomy stuff it was. He had been dwelling too much upon the state of his soul, and not enough upon the matter in hand, which was winning a war.

On an impulse, he tore out the offending pages and screwed them into a ball. What was done, was done. There was no help for it.

4.30 a m: The grey hour before dawn; sky very black, with

a few stars. Our tents gleaming white in the half-light; a gleam of fires here & there. For all our numbers, we are so small in the face of this vast landscape. The hill like a slumbering giant—a beast, which might shake us from its coat on rising, like a dog ridding itself of a troublesome burr...

In the margin, he drew a sketch of the mountain, trying to fix its distinctive shape. It was a poor enough scribble; he was not good at drawing. He must have dozed for a few minutes, because the next thing he knew was that he was no longer alone. He felt a brief clutch of alarm, before he recognised the visitor.

'Davy.'

'Sorry, sir.' The boy was anxious to please, as ever. He'd signed up only the week before they'd embarked for Cape Town. It was his first taste of war. 'Thought as you'd like some coffee, sir.'

'That's good of you,' said Theo. From the boy's tremulous tone, he knew there was something more.

'Cartwright said,' Davy went on, pouring the coffee with an unsteady hand, 'as there's hordes of Kaffirs... sorry, Zulus, sir... in the hills above the camp, waiting to come down...'

'Did he indeed?' Theo took the steaming pannikin with gratitude, although the taste would not match the expectation aroused by the smell.

'Yes, sir.'

'Tell Cartwright that Lord Chelmsford has gone out this very morning to hunt down the Zulus in those hills. He would not have done so if he had thought that they were going to attack the camp, now would he?'

'I suppose not, sir.'

'There you are, then.'

Still the boy seemed uneasy—and it was no wonder, with all the rumours that were flying about the camp. It was all the fault of this infernal waiting. It made the men nervous as kittens. Theo yawned hugely to conceal his own agitated state.

'If you've nothing to do, you can clean those boots of mine.'

'Yes, sir.'

'And then fetch me some hot water, would you? I feel like having a shave this morning.'

The feel of the razor was good against his skin, stripping away the thick fuzz that had accumulated there. When he was done, he wiped off the surplus foam with the shirt he had just taken off. One advantage of bivouacking close to a river—however muddy the stream—was the greater frequency with which one could change one's linen.

It wasn't until he was buttoning up the fresh shirt that he noticed a spot of blood on the front. Damnation. He must have nicked himself. Frowning, he considered whether or not to change. If there was one thing that drove the Old Man wild, it was an officer turning up on parade in a soiled shirt. As he was deliberating, he heard a commotion from the far side of the camp.

Sticking his head out to see what the matter was, Theo saw that two of the scouts had returned. He was not near enough to hear what was said, but one of them flung himself from his horse with what seemed unnecessary haste, and, leaving the sweating animal in the care of one of the men, made his way with all speed in the direction of Colonel Pulleine's tent. His companion remained seated upon his mount, as if in readiness for some precipitate action, although all around the business of the camp went on as usual.

Others had heard the shouting, and emerged from their tents at the same time. One of these was Coghill, who had dragged himself from his bed with difficulty, having twisted his knee the previous day chasing after chickens in a burnt-out kraal.

'What's all the fuss?' he said.

'I was just going to find out.'

'No doubt it's a false alarm,' said Coghill.

'No doubt. How's the knee?' Theo thought to enquire.

Coghill winced. 'Sore, confound it! Just my infernal luck to be laid up today, of all days. I'd have been off with the rest of 'em, chasing Zulus, otherwise.'

'Never mind,' laughed Theo. 'We might have a crack at them yet.'

And it was with a pleasurable sense that something might, after all, be about to happen that he reached the bell-tent, from within which could be heard the rise and fall of the commanding officer's voice. 'Well don't just stand there, man,' he heard

Pulleine say. 'God damn your eyes. Get to it!' Moments later, the scout Theo had seen earlier hurried out.

'Sorry, sir. Didn't see you there...'

'No harm done,' said Theo. 'What's the news?'

The other stared at him for a moment before replying.

'Zulus. Thousands of them,' he said in a low voice. He waved an arm in the direction from which they had come. 'Hidden in the valley. Whitelaw and I went up over the hill. And there they were.' His voice shook slightly. 'I tell you, there are thousands. Three or four thousand, I'd say. The place is black with them. You'd think it was a swarm of bees.' He began to laugh. 'A bloody swarm of bees...'

Theo frowned. 'Which direction did you say this was?'

'Over there,' the man insisted, pointing north-east—a direction opposite to the one the column had taken a few hours earlier. Either he was mistaken, in the agitation of the moment, or the information on which they had been acting was at fault; and this could hardly be.

'Any idea of the speed of the advance?'

Again the man laughed.

'You've seen how they can run,' he said. 'Like a bloody express train.'

Returning to his tent, Theo ran into Smith-Dorrien.

'Have you heard anything? Are we to fight?' Theo asked him, but the other merely shrugged.

'I haven't the least idea, old boy.'

He had had just ridden up from Rorke's Drift, he said. His orders were to return with the empty wagons and collect the stores that had been left behind.

'I shouldn't mind a spot of breakfast, if there's any going,' he said. 'And some fodder for poor old Dolly...' As he spoke, there was the sound of rifle fire to the north of the camp. 'I say!' He bared his long white teeth in a delighted grin. 'It sounds as if things are getting warmer.'

'All of us are impatient to get on with it,' Theo wrote in his journal.

And it may be that we will have our chance at last! Zulus

139

sighted to N.E. around 8.30 am. Estimated to be 3,000 to 4,000 strong: a goodly number, if true. Speed of advance hard to judge, but reckoned to be about six miles per hour. In which case, the *'Assyrian'* might well descend *'like the wolf on the fold'* within two hours...

And there it was: the order to 'turn out'. He closed the book; further thoughts would have to wait. His blue patrol coat had been brushed and hung up ready for him by the efficient Davy. He put it on, and took his sword from the rack. His revolver had been cleaned and loaded; he picked it up, and weighed it a moment in his hand. It took so very little to kill a man, he thought: crooking a finger could do it. He put the gun back in its holster and strapped the bandolier across his body. All that remained to put on was his cap.

He glanced at his watch: a little after nine. He wondered idly whether Pretty was awake yet—yawning and stretching her thin brown arms above her head, as she sprawled in the tousled sheets they once shared, before rising, a naked Naiad, to admire her reflection in the looking-glass with its border of sea-shells.

He did not think of Laura.

'C' Company was drawn up with the others in front of the camp, with the native levies bringing up the rear. It was already hot; it would be hotter before the day was out. He was glad of his light cap—so much more comfortable that the weightier helmet—and of the absence of his beard; the feel of the sun on his fresh-shaved skin was delightful. Sitting there, astride his quiet horse, he felt the strangest sense of elation. There was, he supposed, a satisfaction to be derived from the state of being perfectly ready—which it seemed they were. Let what would happen, happen.

On either side of him, as far as the eye could see, stretched the lines of horses and men: broad bands of scarlet and blue, with their bright white helmets. Except for the mechanical whisking of horses' tails and the occasional toss of a horse's head as the flies grew troublesome, the silence was absolute. The ranks of infantry standing at ease, the cavalry drawn up in their turn, appeared like a single body: an organism, governed not by the desires of its separate parts but according to the will of its central authority. This, for the present, was Pulleine; and for the present, all was harmony.

Above the bleached grass of the plain rose the distant hills; above the hills, the sky. Theo's eye followed the trajectory of a bird, high up in that blue empyrean. He amused himself by speculating what its view might be of that great scorched valley, on which the orderly lines of tents would seem, from that height, no larger than white stones, thrown down in a child's game of 'Fives'...

Far off, he saw what appeared to be a puff of smoke. Firing, he thought—although there was no accompanying report. The smoke became a cloud; a whirlwind of dust, advancing along the road that led from Rorke's Drift and resolving itself at last into a company of men on horseback. Colonel Durnford was at their head, in his brigand's garb: a crimson bandana wound, turban-like, about the brim of his wide-awake hat.

'Now we're in for some fun,' murmured a voice, but when Theo turned to see who had spoken, the faces of his men afforded no clue. Durnford and his company dismounted; the former with his aides-de-camp making his way towards Pulleine's tent. He had not gone ten paces when something arrested his attention. Out of the corner of his eye, Theo saw him point towards the ridge.

As if conjured up by the very gesture, a party of Zulus came into view. It was not possible to make out their number from that distance. For a long moment, the two enemy forces regarded each other; then, as if made shy by the encounter, the impi retreated out of sight. Durnford seemed gratified at this, and continued on his way towards the tent.

Then for a long while nothing happened. The sun rose higher in the sky, which seemed like a great blue bowl upended above the plain, whose monotonous stretches of whitened grass and stones seemed to shimmer in the sultry air. Raised voices came from the bell-tent, from which, presently, the two officers were seen to emerge.

It was too far off to hear what the dispute—if such it were— had been about; but, in any case, as the senior of the two,

141

Durnford now assumed command. There was not a man in the regiment who would not have followed him to Hell and back, should he have required it. When he asked for volunteers to join him in 'chasing up the enemy', the air was a sea of upraised hands.

'Well done, my boys,' said the Colonel. 'But you know that I cannot take all of you. Some must stay and guard the camp, along with Colonel Pulleine. For it would not do if the camp were to fall into enemy hands, now would it?' He said this last as if it were a great joke. The men roared accordingly. When the company rode off, with their turbaned leader at its head, those that were left behind could not but feel a keen pang of disappointment.

When Durnford's force was no more than a scarlet blot upon the hillside, Colonel Pulleine emerged at last from the tent where, like Achilles, he had been sequestered. His disgruntled air, as he gave the command for the men to fall out for dinner, was not improved by the downward droop of his long moustache.

So far the day had been nothing but rumour—no sooner scotched than supplanted by further rumour.

'What's happening, Sir?' Theo ventured to ask his superior officer, when that gentleman ambled along the lines towards him on his bay, Tamburlaine. 'Are we in for some fighting at last?'

Captain Essex pulled a doubtful face.

'Hard to say,' he replied. 'In my view, this might all be a storm in a teacup. Or the blighters might attack at nightfall. In any case,' he went on, 'there isn't much advantage to be gained from waiting around here. You may tell your men to stand down their weapons, Lieutenant Reynolds. Better if they get a bit of dinner inside them, than stand about here all day in the broiling sun...'

Dismissing his platoon, with orders to remain on hand if they were needed, Theo made his way towards the officers' mess. Here, he found a handful of his fellows: O'Riordan—a Catholic, whose dark, saturnine cast of features seemed that of an earlier time, of arcane ritual and Jesuitical intrigue. Now he tore into a heel of stale bread, as if his life depended upon it. Shaw, who had been at Sandhurst the year before Theo, was a ruddy-faced, affable fellow, fond of cards and girls. He nodded at Theo as the latter helped himself to a plateful of the salty beef stew to which he, like the rest of them, had become all too accustomed these past few weeks. 'Beastly, ain't it, this waiting around?' he said.

Glover, who had joined them with other officers of the 90th at Pietermaritzburg, stirred his food around with a listless air. In the one conversation Theo had had with him, he had confessed to a fondness for painting in watercolour. He had tried and tried to 'catch' the mountain in whose shadow they now sat, but it had proved elusive, he said. 'The trouble is, it will keep changing its shape,' he'd said, with a wry look. Now he caught Theo's eye, and gave a slight smile, expressive of nothing more than weariness, perhaps.

Marlowe was attempting to rally young Parr, who was sweating profusely, doubtless as a result of the recent bout of fever that had laid him low. 'Come now,' the older man said. 'Don't tell me you aren't raring to enter the fray? Think how fine one of those Zulu war-shields will look upon your wall, when you and Maisie...'

'Madeleine.'

'Madeleine, then. When you and she are married and have your children clustered all about you, you can point to the shield and say...'

'Don't talk cock,' said Coleman, his mouth full of food. 'There's blood on your shirt, man,' he said, as Theo sat down opposite him. 'Call yourself an officer, and you can't even muster a clean shirt? I call it a damned disgrace.'

'Pay no attention to the miserable cur,' said Marlowe, with a wink at Theo. 'His piles are giving him grief...'

'I'll give you grief, you little shit,' was the snarled response. 'You may depend on me for that.'

'Now then, gentlemen,' protested the gentle Glover, a clergyman's son. 'Let us not quarrel amongst ourselves. Surely we should be directing our venom at the enemy, not at one another?'

'As for you,' said Coleman, 'You can bloody fuck yourself...'

'What a bear it is,' said Marlowe. 'But at least, with Coleman, one knows where one stands. There's no side to Coleman...'

'What's that you're muttering?' said Coleman.

'Nothing, my dear chap, nothing. Rumour has it,' continued Marlowe sotto voce, 'that our friend's ill temper is on account of some bad news received from home—to wit, that the inestimable Mrs C has finally come to her senses and...'

His words were cut short by the sound of rifle fire, close at hand.

'Good God!' The colour drained from Marlowe's face. O'Riordan crossed himself.

A moment later, all of them were on their feet, frantically buttoning tunics and reaching for their swords.

Outside, was a scene utterly different from the one they had left behind, so short a time before. Now, instead of the orderly rows of men eating their dinner, was pandemonium, with cooking pots overturned, fires being stamped out, and plates and utensils hastily abandoned, as men seized their rifles and hurried to their posts. Officers scrambled up onto their mounts, shouting orders into the confused throng.

'What has happened?' Theo shouted, seeing that one of these was Melvill, the Colonel's Adjutant.

'Major Russell is killed, and the battery taken,' was the reply. 'Our orders are to form up in lines to the right of the slope. Captain Younghusband's company is to take the left side. They are almost upon us—look!'

And indeed what had been nothing but the whitened grass of an empty plain was now a dark mass of warriors. Where there had been bare hills was now a torrent of oncoming bodies, so many they could not be numbered. For an instant, Theo felt as if his eyes must deceive him. He blinked—but there it was: grass blades had turned into soldiers, like the dragon's teeth.

'Black devils,' said Coleman, with a kind of awe. 'Look at them. The bloody black devils...'

After that, there was no more leisure for talk: the only words that followed were those of command. Lines were formed across the front of the camp, and the order to fire given. At once, the dark lines of advancing bodies fell down into the grass—only to rise up once more, as the rifles were being reloaded.

It was like the waves of a black sea, Theo thought; an optical trick, in which white gave way to black which gave way in turn to white.

All around, the air was filled with the screams of horses. A pall

144

of smoke lay over the ground, so that the landscape appeared like that of some strange and terrifying dream. Again, the dark waves rose up from the grass; again, they fell, as if cut down. Rise and fall and rise and fall...

A good many had, it seemed, fallen to rise no more—black bodies blossoming red, as their ranks drew within range of the guns. Now they were closer, it was possible to make out details: white shield or brown; the leather apron they wore across their privates; the iron head-ring that denoted a married man...

How they could run. It seemed they had no fear of death at all. Rise and fall and fall and rise. It was appalling to see how fast they came on.

Chapter 12

Laura, January 1880: Isandhlwana

From the summit of one of the range of hills across which they had been travelling since daybreak, they beheld the plain, and the mountain beyond it. It was now broad daylight, and a haze hung over the scene, so that its contours were hard to make out. A shifting landscape it seemed at this distance, whose exact relationships were impossible to determine. A hill, which seems close by, might lie five miles away, Theo had written, describing just this phenomenon. 'What seems unbroken ground might be undermined by ditches, in which an enemy might lie concealed. It is, in short, a treacherous place...'

She had sat up until late last night reading the journal. Its observations seemed to her to be that mixture of the quotidian and the profound which reflects that of life itself. His letters had been more considered, both as to content and to style. Realising the implications of this, she had been prepared for harder truths than had been revealed by the latter. But there was nothing untoward. Only a few pages torn out, towards the end...

'There,' said De Kuiper. 'That is Isandhlwana.'

Even if he had not spoken, she would have known it. The mountain's leonine shape was quite distinctive. Seeing it now was like coming face to face with the Sphinx in the Egyptian desert: it was both instantly recognisable, and utterly strange—a monument, she thought, keeping guard over the bodies of those that lay there.

Such poetic fancies vanished within minutes of reaching the place. It was nothing but a charnel-house; a midden, strewn with rubbish of every description. Bones and skulls of oxen, sardine tins, broken glass, and what she saw with a shiver must be remnants of clothing, lay scattered about—as did old boots, the nails falling out of the rotting soles, now shrivelled and deformed by rain and heat; belt buckles, and cap badges.

She stooped to pick one up, wondering at the chance that had brought it here—a banal object now transformed into a relic—before letting it fall again. Amongst twisted ends of old straps and harness, the splintered remains of ammunition boxes were strewn; spent cartridges lay about in profusion, with other debris: tent pegs, scraps of rope, a broken spear, and here and there amidst the rest, a fragment of what she supposed must be human bone.

When she had pictured herself, all those months ago, arriving at this place, it had been as the culmination of a pilgrimage. If she had hoped for anything at all, it was that there would be something—she knew not what—to signify an end. Instead, there was nothing but this great emptiness: these bare brown hills, this desolation.

De Kuiper was right. It had been a meaningless adventure. She was foolish to have thought it could be otherwise. All that was left of the young man she had known—of all those young men, in all their energy and grace—was this sad trash. A heap of bones; a belt buckle; a scrap of torn paper. *My dear old girl, Hoping this finds you as it leaves me...* Angrily, she brushed away a tear. To weep seemed an insult to the dead, whom tears could not bring back.

Raising her eyes at last from the littered ground, she saw the mountain, dark against the sky. In spite of the heat of the day, it cast a cold shadow over the plain. This, then, was the emblem of all that she had come for. If nothing else, she could say that she had climbed to the very top, and had, perhaps, in so doing, set her feet in the footsteps of the one she had lost.

The ground was stony and the going difficult; she slipped and stumbled at every other step—the plain with its yellow grass giving way, as she climbed the hill, to tumbled rocks, interspersed with thorny shrubs, the earth baked dry in between. The sun blazed down. It was almost noon—the hottest time of day at the hottest time of the year.

So he and his companions must have sweltered and scorched.

Flies buzzed around her eyes, greedy for a taste of the salt liquid that collected there. Her skin burned with the fiery rash that had afflicted her since they left Grey Town. Yet she paid it no heed, intent as she was on reaching the summit. From that eminence, she was convinced, she would be able to see the field in its entirety—to see it, perhaps, as he had seen it.

From there, everything that had been obscure would become clear at last.

Her dress caught on the scrubby thorn bushes; her boots were caked with dust. She stumbled and almost fell; recovering herself just in time. Above her, the enormous sky burned with a fierce white light. Sweat trickled down her back, soaking her under the arms and around the waist; it puddled under her collar and beneath the brim of her hat. Her boots were chafing, but she no longer felt the pain. Her head was aching, but she no longer heeded it.

Overhead, in the hot white sky, two black birds wheeled, their harsh shrieking cries the only sound in that desolate place. She paused to catch her breath. Below lay the battlefield, and the site of the former camp, dotted with the cairns of white stones marking the spot where soldiers had died. There were many of these—she gave up counting after fifty.

One of them would have been for Theo, but there was no way of telling which one; nor indeed how many others were interred beneath each cairn; perhaps as many as thirty, De Kuiper had said. All higgledy-piggledy, with one man's remains mixed up with those of his comrade—or his enemy.

In the partial shade afforded by one such mound, the horses cropped the grass, watched over by one of the boys—she thought it must be Constant, but it was hard to tell at this distance. The glare was intense, striking off the burnished surfaces of rocks with almost palpable force. Her mouth was dry.

She wished now that she had thought to bring her water-bottle. De Kuiper would have some; but she had left him some way back along the path, saying that she preferred to go on alone.

'As you wish,' he had said, with a shrug, seeing that there was no persuading her otherwise. 'Only take care you don't break an ankle.' Sitting himself down in the shade of the overhanging rock to smoke a cigarette, while he waited for her to return from fulfilling her uncertain quest.

After she had been climbing for another quarter of an hour or so, she reached the summit; from here, she could see right across the plain. Its tracts of dry grass were the colour of sand. A veritable wasteland, with nothing but low brown hills, and deep scars that marked the presence of dry water-courses, to break the monotony.

To the north, beyond the line of little hills, the horizon disappeared in a haze of heat. It was here that something—a movement, barely discernible at this distance—caught her eye. It seemed no more than a flicker; a dark spot across the vision. She blinked, and it was gone.

She turned her attention to the task in hand. At the apex of the mountain, where she stood, the ground flattened out, to form a shallow depression between the rocks. Here she began to dig, scraping at the hard red earth with her nails, until they were broken and dirty.

When the hole was deep enough, she took the ring she had taken from the dead woman's hand off her own finger, and dropped it in. It glinted at her, gold against red, as she took a handful of earth, and covered it up.

Let someone find it, if they would, a hundred years from now. They might wonder at the inscription: *Amor Vincit Omnia, A.D. MDCCCLII*—or at the stroke of chance which had brought it here.

She stood up, brushing the earth from her hands. It was time to go down. De Kuiper would be wondering what had become of her. But as she turned to begin the descent, she swept her gaze once more across the landscape. The dark spot of a few moments before had become a wavering shape; as she watched, this assumed a more definite form—which was that of a horse and rider. A strange enough sight, in this lonely place.

Descending proved more fraught with risk than climbing up the mountain had been. With every other step, her feet threatened to slide from under her on the loose stones, and it was difficult not to break into a run, so precipitous was the slope. The sensation induced by this, of not being quite in control, unnerved her.

Suddenly, she wanted very much to be away from this place. Its silence and brooding melancholy seemed to weigh on her spirits like lead. She would say to De Kuiper that they should start back, as soon as they had breakfasted.

He must have got tired of waiting, for he was not where she had left him. But as she neared the bottom of the hill, she caught sight of him once more. He was standing in the middle of the plain. With him was another man, dressed, as he was dressed, in the rough clothes of a farmer. As she approached, she could hear their voices, conversing in Dutch.

They broke off, as she drew near.

'Ah, Miss Brooke,' said De Kuiper. 'Do not be alarmed. This man means us no harm.'

If he said anything more, she did not hear it, for her gaze was fixed upon the stranger's face. Which was not, in fact, that of a stranger. Changed as he was, she would have known him anywhere.

She went to speak, but no sound came out.

It was he who broke the silence.

'By God, Lollie. I had not thought to find you here.'

Chapter 13

Theo, January 1880: Isandhlwana

For as long as he lived, he would not forget the way she looked in that moment—the shock of seeing him turning her white to the lips, as if she were the ghost, not he. Shock turning, in an instant, to wondering joy, like that of a child waking from a long, dark dream. Tears filled her eyes.

'But—you are dead. You are dead!' she cried.

'I am dead—as far as the world is concerned. I died, on this day, a year ago.'

'What are you saying? You are here. You are safe!' Tears ran down her face, unchecked. She seized his hands in hers, and kissed them. 'O, it is too wonderful,' she said.

'My darling girl.'

'What is it, man?' the Dutchman said, in his barbarous tongue. 'What have you said to her, that she should weep so?'

He ignored the interruption, thinking only of the woman who stood before him. He drew her to him, and, for a moment, she let herself be comforted.

'Don't cry, little Lollie.' he murmured, stroking her hair. 'I cannot bear it...'

The sound of her pet-name unleashed a fresh storm of tears.

'O, why did you not write?' she cried. 'All these months, we thought you dead, and now...'

'I could not write,' he said. 'For I am dead, remember?'

She stiffened in his arms, and drew back a little, the better to see his face.

'I don't understand you,' she said.

'My country, too, believes me dead. A hero,' he added, with a smile that only pointed up the absurdity of the word. 'But, as you see, I am alive. And by no means a hero.'

She was silent a moment, considering this.

'But how...?' she began; then broke off, a troubled look clouding her face.

'How did I escape?' he finished for her.

She nodded.

'Come,' he said. 'Let us walk into the shade, and I will tell you how I escaped. Tell him,' he added, indicating the Dutchman, 'that you wish to speak to me alone.'

She made a sign to the other that he should leave them.

Glowering, De Kuiper withdrew a few paces, to where the horses cropped the grass in the shadow of the mountain. The sun was now directly overhead.

It was precisely the time of day when, a year ago, all that he had held dear had been destroyed in one brutal hour.

When the onslaught came, it was not as he had envisaged it, in all his imaginings of this moment. Nor had the skirmishes in which he had taken part prepared him for what was to follow. Then he had been one of a superior force—in numbers as well as skill-at-arms; the enemy's spears no match in open country for the lethal accuracy of the Martini-Henry rifle.

Now that superiority was reversed. They were so many. Seeing the first columns appear over the brow of the hill had been a feeling like no other. He'd felt his stomach muscles clench; his bowels turn to water. He'd drawn a deep breath. The 'Assyrian' indeed. The sound of their battle-cry was enough to stop the heart. On they came, chanting and drumming their spears against their shields. A swarm of bees, flowing down over the lion's mane. The air was thick with them: rank upon rank—inexorable. A molten darkness, closing in—like a tide encroaching on the shore; like Death itself.

Already the scarlet ranks were being overwhelmed. He could only watch, appalled. Round after round was fired into the advancing horde, and still they came, their naked bodies gleaming like polished jet. Who would have thought flesh could withstand bullets with such ease? Perhaps it was witchcraft; he could not say.

He had a confused recollection of firing his gun, and of the gun jamming, as the barrel got too hot. He had killed two or three by then, he guessed, although it was impossible to tell. However many one killed there were always more to take their place. They were not afraid of the guns, it seemed, although they had seen their comrades cut in two by the bullets. They flung themselves upon the bayonet's end as if embracing a lover.

When his gun would not fire he knew it was all up with him. The man he had been about to kill was almost upon him. For what seemed a long moment they grappled together. He could smell the other's sweat; see his eyes widen and his nostrils flare in the fury of the struggle. Then, with what seemed a superhuman effort, he jabbed and felt the blade go in. Hot blood spurted out. He felt the body go limp, and with a cry of disgust, flung the heavy carcass off him.

His impressions of that time—it was not long, perhaps no more than an hour—were feverish: at once as rapid as gunfire and as slow as nightmare. Bodies exploding in air, in a red mist of blood and bone. Screams of horses, and men, in their death agony. The smell of sweat, and shit, and fresh spilled blood. Men fighting hand to hand, like figures on a Greek frieze. Black warriors against red soldiers. Spears against guns. Who would have thought the former could ever have prevailed?

There had been a point—he could not have said precisely when, but it could not have been long after the sun was at its zenith—when he knew that all was lost. The ammunition they had on them had run out, and they had had to smash the boxes to get more—but even that was not enough for them to overcome such a host. At last, 'The Retire' had been sounded, and they fell back towards the camp, their lines in disarray.

There was no order to it at all; they might have been a bunch of frightened schoolgirls, for all the discipline they showed. In amongst the tents, what little order there had been broke down; it was every man for himself.

He had been among the lucky ones to have got himself a horse—his beloved Albion had been his saviour that day. The rest—more than a thousand men and officers—had been cut down where they stood. The air was thick with smoke, so that it seemed as black as night. From all around came the screaming of animals; oxen, horses and men. All around lay the dead and dying;

the air resounded with their groans.

One man's head was split open, as neatly as if done with an axe. Another had been hit between the eyes, the bullet carrying away the back of his head, leaving his face perfect, except for the small round hole—as if it were a mask.

He saw his sergeant, O'Rourke, with a stump of bone where an arm should be—the rest carried off by the explosion of his over-heated gun; Marlowe, with his belly ripped open and his guts tumbling out upon the ground in a glistening string. Worst of all was the sight of Coleman, with his lower jaw torn away: its bristling red beard a handsome prize for the warrior who had slain him.

He did not know how he had made it through that slaughter-house, but he had done so, leaving the groans of the dying and the foul stench of burning and of human ordure behind.

He had got down as far as the river. The cliff was steep, and his horse stumbled more than once, so that he had been lucky to avoid a broken neck. On the way he had passed others, also part of that blind and desperate flight. He saw Smith-Dorrien, struggling with his horse at the bottom of the ravine. Coghill shouted something at him, but did not stop.

He did not see what became of either of them.

Their mutilated faces were the worst thing. He saw them still, in his dreams. The lower jaw had been ripped away in some instances; in others it was the upper lip which had been torn off. In either case, it was an obscenity: a nightmare vision of bared teeth and exposed tongues, which, once seen, could never be erased from the mind's eye. It was on account of their beards, he had learned since—it was Corrie who told him. Ag, ja. That is their way. They are a Godless people...

He had stared at her in disbelief when she said it, but afterwards, he saw it must be so. For them, it was a trophy, he supposed: a proof of valour. To carry away such a relic was to show that one had vanquished, not a beardless boy, but a full-grown man: a worthy adversary.

Remembering his own clean-shaven state that day, he wondered if it had been that which saved him. Although they had not spared the boys, either. He thought of young Davy, who had no beard or moustache worth speaking of, let alone worth stealing—and yet it had not saved him from a terrible death, speared through the throat with such force that the blade had stuck fast in the ground, so that he drowned in his own blood.

The bodies too had been ripped apart—evisceration of the enemy after death being another Zulu custom, Corrie said, to allow the dead man's spirit to escape, so that he would refrain from extracting vengeance on his murderer; but though horrible enough, it could not compare with the horror of destroying a face.

It was as well, he thought, that no one who loved them could see what had befallen the corpses of these men—how swiftly they had been reduced from living, breathing beings to stinking lumps of flesh and shattered bone.

As to his own loved ones—he did not permit himself to think too often of them. The realisation that they believed him dead had been a gradual one; but having become a ghost, he did not see how he, in all conscience, could return.

He had given his coat to Wickham, although it was plain that he was done for, poor fellow. 'I'm cold,' he had said. His teeth had chattered as if he were suffering from frostbite. He supposed that Wickham might have been taken for him. Once the Zulus had been at him, how would anyone have been able to tell them apart?

In the months since that dreadful day, he had returned to the place several times—the first time being the worst. It was at nightfall, because the risks of being seen were too great. Corrie had tried her utmost to dissuade him, but he had been adamant. He had to go. It was barely two months since it happened, and the country all around was still dangerous.

Where they were—he and Corrie—you would never have known it, though. It was so quiet you would have thought it at the ends of the earth.

How long he had travelled that night he had no way of telling. All he knew was that he could not stop. He would go as far as he could go, before hunger and thirst and loss of blood overcame him. It was Corrie who found him: half-starved and delirious, in the cave above the waterfall, that was close to her farm. She had found his horse running free in the ravine, she told him. Where there was a horse, you would generally find a man.

Chapter 14

Laura, January 1880: Isandhlwana

When he had finished speaking, she was silent, turning over in her mind all that he had said. As if the telling of it had exhausted him, he stood with his head bowed, his eyes on the mess of broken things that lay at their feet. Even though he had grown thinner and browner, with hair and beard that were longer than she recalled, this was the same man she had known two years before.

Yet between that man and this lay a gulf that could not be bridged. It was as if he had left his old self on that distant shore, with all its hopes and dreams of what life would bring. The man who now looked back at her had no further use for dreams. He had seen all that life could offer, and sickened of it.

'How you must despise me,' he said, as if he half-guessed her thought.

She shook her head. 'No.'

He smiled. 'You are kind. But you need not spare my feelings. There is nothing you could say to me that could be worse than the things I have said to myself...'

'You have nothing to reproach yourself with,' she said.

'Ah! If I could believe that!'

'You must believe it.'

But even she sounded doubtful.

'If only you had written,' she went on, with a kind of despair. 'To let us know, at least, that you were alive...'

He almost laughed at this. 'How could I have written?'

Still she persisted:

'Just a word or two. A sign. You do not know what a difference it would have made...'

He was silent a moment. 'Forgive me,' he said at last.

'There is nothing to forgive,' she said. 'But...' She broke off. 'Oh why did you not write?' she cried. 'It would have meant so much to her...'

He stared at her, his face gone grey. 'Of whom do you speak?'

'I was speaking of your mother,' she said in a low tone.

'What of her? Have you news of her?'

She lowered her gaze, but he had seen what was written there.

'What is it? Has something happened?' He seized her wrist.

For a long moment, they stood face to face.

'I am sorry,' she said softly. 'I would have given anything not to have been the bearer of such news...'

'Tell me.' His grip on her wrist tightened.

'She is dead,' said Laura. 'Two days ago. At Rorke's Drift.'

He looked at her with what seemed a kind of terror—as if, she thought afterwards, her words were a judgement on him. 'She died here? In Africa?'

'She was not well when she came. She had not been well for a long time...'

'Ah, yes.' He seemed abstracted for a moment. 'Yes, yes. That is true. She was not well. But... in Africa?' he said again, as if the fact of it were too much to comprehend. 'At Rorke's Drift, you say?'

'Yes.'

Tears started into his eyes. Roughly, he brushed them away with the back of his hand. 'This is the worst of all,' he said. 'That you should know the truth about me is bad enough. But that she...' His voice failed.

Laura was silent.

'What I don't understand,' he said. 'Is why was she here?'

'For the same reason I am here,' she said. 'We came for you.'

'I would to God that you had not!' he cried. 'I would live it all again—even the worst of it—if only to have prevented that.'

'She wanted to come,' said Laura. 'It was her dearest wish to see the place, knowing her own time was short...'

'And believing me dead,' he finished, with a terrible smile.

'You do not understand. She was glad to come. Her last words were of you...'

At that, he could no longer restrain his tears. 'Poor Mama. She should have had a better son.'

Around them, the deserted plain stretched still and bare in the implacable light of the late afternoon sun. There was no sound but the wind rattling the dry thorn twigs, and far off, a bird crying.

Theo seemed, in his abstracted mood, to have forgotten her existence. When she spoke, he gave a start, as if recalled to himself.

'What will you do?'

He stared at her a moment. 'There is nothing for me to do. I must live the best I can, with what is left to me of life. There can be no going back, that much is certain.'

'Is there no possibility at all of a pardon?' she said.

'Not for me.'

'But if you were to give yourself up to the authorities...' she said. 'Surely there must be some hope of an appeal to a higher power?'

A faint smile flitted across his face. 'The penalty for desertion is death,' he said. 'What grounds could there be for an appeal? I have betrayed my country.'

'I don't believe that.'

'It is true, nonetheless. My only recourse is to remain what you see—a living ghost. A pariah. Exiled from the place that bore me, and from those I held dear...'

'You must remain in Africa, then?'

'I have no choice.' Again, the grim little smile touched his lips. 'Or rather, I do have a choice. A coward's death, or a living death.'

'It is too terrible,' she said.

His expression softened. 'Don't weep, little Lollie. I don't deserve your pity.'

She took his hand, and drew it to her breast. 'I know you would never do an ignoble thing.'

'Don't say that,' he said. 'It is too much for me to bear.'

Whilst they had been speaking, De Kuiper had withdrawn a little way; now he drew nearer.

'One minute more,' she told him.

'I will fetch the horses,' De Kuiper said.

'Must you go?' said Theo. The words were barely more than a whisper. 'We have had so little time...'

'We must, if we are to reach Rorke's Drift before nightfall...'

'Rorke's Drift. That fatal place,' he murmured. 'Is it really there that she lies?'

'In the little churchyard, yes.'

'Ah, what I would not give to see that spot!'

Both were silent a while. Then he burst out once more:

'You must not go! I cannot bear to lose you so soon, having found you again...'

'I will return,' she said.

At once his face cleared. 'Yes. But not here.' His gaze took in the empty plain, over which the dark tower of the mountain silently brooded. 'Not here, to this accursed place...'

He turned back towards De Kuiper, whose presence until that moment he had not acknowledged, and said a few words to him in halting Afrikaans, to which De Kuiper replied.

'He knows the farm where I am staying,' Theo said. 'He will bring you there tomorrow, if you will come.'

'I will come.'

The moment of parting was upon them. He took a step towards her. To have clasped him to her breast would have required the barest effort—and yet she did not. Seeing in his face both his recognition of her holding-back, and his acceptance of it.

Afterwards, she was to remember the way his eyes had looked, and the slight smile that had played about his lips. He watched as she walked over to where De Kuiper was waiting. When she had mounted her horse, he raised his hand in farewell.

He seemed in no hurry to leave himself—although when they were gone, he would be alone, on that darkening plain.

'Until tomorrow,' he said.

Chapter 15

Rejoice: January 1880, Rorke's Drift

It was dark by the time they got back, Miss Brooke and the *baas* and the boys—these last two full of all that they had to tell. But she paid them no attention, foolish pair. All her concern was for Miss Brooke. She, too, was burning with news: 'Rejoice, something remarkable has happened. I hardly know how to tell you...'

She was walking up and down as she spoke, as if she had forgotten how to be still. She would not eat anything. She was not hungry at all, she said. 'O Rejoice—you believe in ghosts, do you not?' she said, her eyes as bright as stars in her thin white face. 'Now tell me—do you believe that a man can come back from the dead?'

Rejoice was about to say that she had seen it happen more than once. There had been a man in her village who had died from snake-bite. Then the *sangoma* touched him with his rod and he was alive again. A woman had lain for three days without moving or speaking—bewitched by her husband's lover, it was said. The *sangoma* said, Get up, my sister, and she had done so, although a moment before she had been yellow and stiff as a corpse...

But Miss Brooke was now talking about her God, who had died and been buried and rose up again. Rejoice had heard about that God before, from the sisters at the Christian mission. He was called Je-sus. He had a sweet kind face as smooth as a girl's, and long hair that curled to his shoulders. When he opened his robe, you saw his heart, like a glowing coal, through a hole in the middle of his chest. Je-sus could make the dead rise up, too. He knew how to cast out devils. That was also something the *sangoma* could do—but Rejoice said nothing of this to Miss Brooke. She would not have listened in any case, burning as she was with the desire to see her Resurrected One; her dead love that was dead no longer.

'Tomorrow,' she said to Rejoice. 'Tomorrow I will be with him.'

That night, the *Tokoloshe* must have visited Miss Brooke again, for she muttered in her sleep, and ground her teeth, and would not be still, even though Rejoice stroked her forehead with a cool cloth, and murmured Go to sleep now—the way she did when her brothers were small, and had the fever. Once she cried, piteously, 'Do not leave me!'—even though Rejoice was there beside her. And Rejoice promised she would not leave, for as long as Miss Brooke had need of her.

In the morning, Miss Brooke was pale and silent. She ate nothing, but only drank a little water. When Rejoice said to the *baas* that her mistress was not well, and was in no fit state to travel, he only laughed, in that way that white men did when they were angry. 'You tell her, *meisie*. She doesn't listen to me.' The *baas* was angry, because he was in love with Miss Brooke, and all she cared about was the man who had died and come back. Being in love made you angry a lot of the time, Rejoice had observed—although she herself had never been in love; nor did she want to be. It was a kind of sickness, she thought. Only the strongest witchcraft—or death itself—could cure you.

She told Miss Brooke: *You must not go. You are ill. You must rest, or you will surely die. Stay here awhile, until you are well. If your dead man who has risen from the grave, your Je-sus, loves you enough, he will wait for you. Tomorrow, when you are better, then you can go…*

But if Miss Brooke heard Rejoice's words, she paid them no attention, smiling in that way she had, as if she were thinking of something else entirely. 'Don't you see?' she said. 'It is our destiny to be together, he and I. Why else would he have come back to me? It is meant to be…'

Then she rode away, on the red horse that belonged to the Reverend's wife, with the *baas* on his own horse beside her.

'Don't you wish you were coming, too?' said one of the boys—the elder, and more foolish—as he made ready to follow. He patted the place in front of him on the saddle. 'There is room here for a nice girl…'

'Then you had better find her,' said Rejoice—which made the other one, the younger, laugh so much he almost fell off his horse.

'*Kom*,' shouted the *baas* in an angry voice—so there was no time for anything more to be said.

Not that it would have made any difference if Rejoice had gone with them. What was going to happen, would happen, whether she was there to see it or not.

No matter if you called it God, or destiny, or witchcraft, there was a force which shaped people's lives, and which it was impossible to resist. If you threw down a handful of pebbles, some would land with the black face uppermost, some the white. Only the *sangoma* knew what it meant; but that there was a meaning, was not in doubt. Useless to try and change it, once the spell was cast.

Chapter 16

Theo, January 1880: Blood River

Corrie had said to him it would come to no good. She had begged him not to go, but he had paid her no heed. It was a cursed place, she said: nothing to find there but ghosts. She had been right, of course—what else was it but the ghost of his own life that had had been there to meet him, wearing a face he knew all too well; a look which reproached him for what was lost, and for the man he had been?

To the naked eye, she was not so very terrible, his ghost—such a pale, small thing, in her straw hat and dust-streaked petticoats. And yet, in that moment, when she turned her wondering gaze on him, and he saw in her eyes the reflection of all they had once meant to each other, she seemed an avenging Fury. At that moment, he would have given anything to have seen another of his ghosts in her place: poor tortured Davy, with his bloody smile; Wickham, shuddering with cold in the blazing noon; or any of those nameless ones with ruined faces that gibbered at the periphery of his waking thoughts and pursued him in sleep—anyone, in fact, but this slight, prim girl, who merely looked at him, and told him what he was.

Seeing her standing there, amongst the rocks and the yellow grass that grew up through the bones of his fallen comrades, had almost stopped his heart.

Yet, at the same time, it had not been a surprise to see her; it was as if he had been expecting it. Returning to the scene of the crime in order to face the tribunal of the dead—was that not what his journey had been, and was she not the best prosecuting counsel they could have had? In her they rose up, those tongue-less multitudes, silenced as they were by bullet and spear and by the choking desert earth, and confronted him with his sins.

Not that she had said very much at all; although what she said had been enough to undo him forever.

It was the look in her eyes he couldn't bear: the look that told him, as plain as if she had spoken, what she thought of him, and what he had done to her. A look of sadness restrained; one might have said, a wounded look—if such a word had not suggested too much in the way of self-pity.

Had there been the slightest vestige of this—of the feeling that she considered her own suffering as of more account than his—it would not have caused him such anguish. But it was the feeling that she held something back—that, even now, she was trying to spare him—which he could not bear.

In dreams it was now his mother's face that he saw. Her gentle smile, with its underlying pain. He cursed himself for the grief he must have caused her. She had died not knowing that the cause of all her grief still lived, not ten miles from where she had breathed her last.

The cause of all her grief: that was all he had been, or now would ever be. Laura had thought it, too; he had seen it in her eyes. That look—swiftly checked—of mingled pity and horror. She knew what his neglect had done, to herself and to his mother. She had witnessed, as he had not, the gradual wearing-down of his mother's spirit.

Surely there was no being on earth as accursed as he: a man who had killed his mother, and yet still lived?

My curse upon you all the *sangoma* had said, with his dying breath. This, surely, was his: to have outlived his comrades, and to know the horror of that survival.

Laura could never love him now—that much was certain. Although in that first instant, in the aftershock of seeing her there, the thought had flashed across his mind: She is here, and everything can be as it was before.

But in the very moment of thinking it, he had known it to be impossible. Her presence was the only true thing; all the rest was a lie. She shrank from him as it was; how much more would she recoil when she knew the facts of what he had done? His betrayal—for that, in plain English, was what it amounted to—of all that he should have held most dear. His country (even now, he could not stop the tears rising in his throat at the word); his comrades; and his family—all these had been cast aside, in the act of running away.

Coward. That was the name for him. While others had fought and died in the cause of honour, he had thought only of saving his own skin. The punishment for that was death; he had avoided it so far because he had not been found.

Except that she had found him. He was no longer a ghost, but a living man—risen up from the grave, like Lazarus. Would she give him away? He imagined not; that was not her way. Condemning a man for such a fault would seem to her a kind of arrogance.

Would she choose exile with him? He could hardly expect it. To be a pariah in a strange land, with not even the comfort of her own people to turn to, would be too much to ask of anyone. A living death. No, he must accept his fate as his alone. The time when he and she might have been together had long since passed.

Instead, he had Corrie, who had taken him in, and sheltered him—an act of mercy or an act of need, he knew not. They had each other; that was all. As to Pretty... but he could not bring himself to think of her. Another of his betrayals. It seemed that everything he touched had turned to dust.

He is crossing a vast white plain. The sun beats down. There is no shelter. His boots chafe. His horse went lame some time ago, and he is now on foot, advancing towards the mountains, which seem to get no nearer, although he has been walking, it seems, for hours. All he knows is that he cannot turn back. Of his destination he is less certain. Around him, the world has been reduced to just this forward momentum; this dull, inexorable trudging towards a horizon which never varies.

Small sounds attend his passage: his footsteps (halting a little, now, since one heel was rubbed raw of its skin) snap the stalks of the dead grass. Insects whine about his eyes and ears. Every time he brushes them away, they return. His mouth is dry. All he can do is go on, putting one foot after another.

Raising his eyes at last from this steady plod, plod, plod, he sees that the hills—once so distant—have come closer, so that they seem, almost, to have surrounded him. The sky—once so bright—has darkened. The sun is setting. Soon, night will fall.

It is then that he sees it (fool that he is, to have come so far, and yet not to have known the place): the mountain, rising before him. Against the sunset's bloody rays, its squat dark shape is unmistakable—a fiery beacon, drawing him closer. In that moment, he sees that he is not alone. Along the hillsides, stark against the flaming sky, stand those who have gone before him—his comrades, whose names are a roll-call of all that he has lost.

At once his heart, so heavy all this time, feels light. He takes a step forward, raising his hand, in greeting or valediction.

Chapter 17

Laura, January 1880: Blood River

De Kuiper knew the place—it was across the Bloedrivier. One of the homesteads built here forty years before, at the end of the great trek that had brought his people to the Promised Land. This last had been said without irony, but he had glanced sideways at her as he spoke, as if to see what she made of it.

'Where did your people come from?' Laura asked, although she was not in the least bit interested in the reply. Her heart was beating so fast that it felt as if it might fly out of her breast.

'The Cape,' said De Kuiper. 'Before we were driven away.' Again, he threw her a look. 'By the English. Your people.'

She was at a loss as to how to reply; then she saw that he was laughing at her.

They rode on in silence for a while, the sun getting higher in the sky. As they neared the river, the country grew more verdant, with rolling meadows and small white farms set amongst groves of blue gums. It was a pretty scene, but Laura was blind to its charms. She had slept badly, and it was as much as she could do to keep her mind on the road ahead. Her thoughts would fly off so. More than once, De Kuiper was obliged to put out a hand to steady her, as they crossed a patch of uneven ground. If it had not been for his vigilance, she would certainly be lying at the bottom of a ditch with her neck broken.

All the events of the previous day filled her mind like the remnants of a troubling dream. Was she waking or sleeping? Even now, she could not tell.

The moment when she had first seen him—a black shape against the sun—was when it had begun, this strange dark dream in which she was caught up. She had not been able to make out his face at first, so dazzling was the light, but she had known him at once. When he spoke it had been both the most natural thing

167

in the world and the most appalling. Dead men do not speak. He must be a ghost, then. But if he were a ghost, why did he not vanish as soon as approached—and why was his hand as warm and solid as her own?

Only his eyes, she saw now (seeing them again in her mind's eye) had a deadness to them. She shivered, in spite of the heat, and De Kuiper looked at her, frowning.

'Do you have fever?'

Her head was aching, but that was no more than the sun. 'I am quite well.' The words like little chips of glass. Quite well. Quite well. Qui twell. She shook her head to dislodge them. She would not be ill. She would not.

'Drink.'

A water-bottle was thrust in front of her face. She drank gratefully—greedily—although the water tasted brackish.

'Three miles. Maybe four,' he said.

She nodded, to show that she understood. Soon she would see him. Soon.

It was midday before they found the place—a low white house in the Dutch style, set back from the road at the end of a narrow track. The gate at the entrance to this was half off its hinges, so that the boy had to drag it to one side to let them pass. The fields on either side were overgrown with weeds. Nearer the house, the earth was blackened, as if by fire, with green shoots already showing through the black. The farm buildings had a neglected air, their shutters unpainted and their walls patched with mould.

No one appeared at De Kuiper's call, but a dog barked forlornly within the house.

De Kuiper frowned. 'I was sure this was the place. A mile beyond the crossroads. There is no other it could be.'

The pain in Laura's head had now settled into a steady drumming, like fingers beating a tattoo upon a table. She opened her mouth to reply, but at that moment her attention was caught by a slight movement, just out of the range of vision.

A woman holding a gun stepped out of the shadows at the side of the house. 'Come closer,' she said, 'and I will kill you.'

De Kuiper answered her in Afrikaans.

She did not at once lower the gun. 'What do you want?'

He spoke to her again, and this time she put down the gun. She was no more than a girl, Laura saw—younger than Bessie, perhaps. She listened, frowning, to what De Kuiper had to say. Her reply was terse.

'He is not here, your friend,' De Kuiper said, translating this for Laura. 'He went away, early this morning.'

'Did he say when he would return?' Her words seemed to her to have a hollow sound. Return. Re-turn.

Once more, De Kuiper addressed the girl. She replied, this time at greater length.

'She says he is afraid that the English soldiers will find him. They will kill him, if they do. And so this place is no longer safe for him.'

'Tell her,' said Laura, 'that we intend no harm to Lieutenant Reynolds.' It was an effort to form the words. 'Ask her,' she went on, 'if she knows where Lieutenant Reynolds has gone.'

As De Kuiper was speaking, Laura was conscious of the girl's eyes fixed upon her. Their expression was not friendly. Nor was there any softening of tone in her reply.

'There is a cave a few miles from here,' said De Kuiper, when the girl had finished speaking. 'She will take us there, if one of the boys will mind the farm until we return.'

'Is she alone here, then?'

'Her father is dead, and her brothers have gone away to join the police.' De Kuiper shrugged. 'Many farms have been abandoned because of the war.'

Lucky was left on guard, while the girl, Cornelia, took the remaining horse. Before they set off, she glanced at Laura, and said something to De Kuiper, who shook his head.

'She asks if you and Lieutenant Reynolds are married.'

'Tell her we are not.'

'I have done so.'

The track was the red of old iron, or a dried wound; it lay across grassland, an immense waste of yellow stalks, that rustled dryly as they passed. There was no other sound except the ceaseless buzzing of the flies. Brushing them away was futile; they only returned. The horses suffered the most: around each long-lashed eye, a jewelled crust of insects gathered thickly.

After a mile or so, the track ran out, and signs of human occupation—a roofless barn; a broken axle—were no longer to be seen. Now they followed what was no more than faint traces of a previous passage: trampled grass-stalks, and once, caught on the wicked spikes of a thorn-tree, a scrap of fibre torn from a coat, perhaps. Ahead was nothing but the vast plain, pathless as the sea, with the grey line of hills beyond it.

The sun beat down; Laura could feel its heat on the back of her neck. If only she could see him once more, everything would be all right.

She remembered the first time. She had been sent on some errand by her father; she could not now remember what. As she had approached the house, there had been a barking of dogs. She had hung back, contemplating flight. But then the door had opened, and a face—his—looked out. *I thought I saw you hovering there. Don't be afraid. They won't bite...*

She had stammered out her message, unable to look at him. But that face, glimpsed in no more than a startled heartbeat, fixed itself indelibly in her mind's eye.

The ground grew steeper as they drew nearer to the escarpment. Here, there was no grass, but only stones and stunted bushes. The rocks were the same dull red as the earth. Split, they showed a seam of glittering grey. She had never seen so desolate a landscape.

We are to go to Africa.
When must you leave?
In a month.
That is not long.
No. Oh Lollie, don't you see? It is a great chance for me.
When I return we will be married. What do you say?

De Kuiper was saying something, but she had not heard a word. She followed the direction of his pointing finger and saw, in the shadow of the hill, the riderless horse.

Of what followed she had only the most imperfect recollection.

170

Fragments, merely, remained. At some point they must have left the horses behind, with the boy; although she could not recall having done so. There had been the climb up to the cave; then what they had found there. The girl had gone on ahead—perhaps to give warning of their approach. The moment before she screamed she—Laura—had known the worst of it.

Although nothing could have prepared her for the horror.

The smell was the first thing—the heat of the day having acted upon the freshly-spilt blood, of which there was a great deal. The place was spattered with it. Painted, had been her thought; as if the cave were a room, to be thus distempered. The walls had received the full force of it, when the gun went off. Taking with it half a man's head. For in fact half of what had once been there (she saw, with the same dreamy fascination) still remained, recognizable as his head, his face—albeit in profile. The rest gone to red pulp: a raw mess, in which nothing remained that was human.

The body was the third thing (after the smell, the redness). Sprawled like a child's in sleep. Yet no child ever slept with such utter abandon. Sounds. These were the last thing she noticed, although they had been going on all the time. The buzzing of the flies. The high, shrill keening of the girl. Yet around it all—around the thing that lay there, appallingly still—was silence. Or rather, a roaring absence, like the deafness following an explosion.

There was silence, and there was darkness. The darkness was strange, because it was still broad daylight, surely? She thought for a moment she must have been struck blind. But no—it was only that her face was covered with a thick, wet cloth, that kept out the light. It had a smell of damp wool. She would have removed it from her face, but her arms were held fast by the bedclothes. She was in bed, then—that much was certain.

She must have stirred, or made some sound—for a chair scraped, and she felt someone bending over her. The cloth was taken off her face; the sudden access of light was blinding, and she closed her eyes. Low voices conferred; she could not make out what they were saying. Then someone said her name—it sounded foreign; strange. She wanted to reply—to ask, 'What is this place, and why am I lying here?' But her lips refused to form the syllables. Her tongue felt thick in her mouth. All that emerged were formless sounds, like those of a young child, or an animal.

A cup was put to her lips, but the effort of raising her head to drink was too great, and the water ran down her chin, and onto her chest. She would have liked to wipe it away, but her hands were useless: swollen lumps of flesh, it seemed. Her head, too, had swelled to enormous size. It lolled on the pillow like a baby's on its feeble stalk. Light. It was light as a soap bubble. If they had not tied her down, she would float away, into the hot bright air.

A voice told her she must sleep; but that was impossible. With all these people here, talking at the tops of their voices, how could anybody sleep? Such a babble of voices, in every language under the sun; it was quite deafening. All those words, words, words, echoing in her ears with a sound like thunder. And yet there had been a silence. A darkness, too. If she could find it— that still, dark place—she knew she would be able to rest.

She is walking across a wide, white plain. Overhead, is a white sky, as empty as the plain. In front is the mountain: a dark shape against the light. If she could just reach it, she would find what it was that she had come to find...

When she opened her eyes at last, it was dark in the room. This was a new kind of darkness: soft blue, instead of red. Someone was sitting on a chair beside the bed. When she looked to see who it was, the other returned her stare: a long look, in which there was no pity. She moved her lips, and this time, instead of mumbled sounds, words formed themselves:

'What has happened?'

A pause ensued, during which the girl, whose name she could not recall, appeared to consider. 'Do you not remember?' she said at length, in her strange, harsh accent. Her eyelids were swollen, as if from weeping, and as she spoke, she clenched her fists in her lap. 'Ask him.' The words were flung out, like a challenge.

In the doorway stood De Kuiper, wiping the earth from his hands. There was blood on his shirt. She saw that he was about to speak—but there was no need, for she remembered everything.

They left at first light for Helpmekaar, where Lucky and Constant were to meet them with the wagon. De Kuiper had thought it best under the circumstances; although he would have preferred it otherwise. But she had been too sick—to have made the journey back to Rorke's Drift that night would have killed her, De Kuiper said. At Helpmekaar, there were doctors, and medicine. Better for her to rest there until she was well. It need not delay them more than a few days.

To what had happened the day before—was it really only that?—he made no reference. It was as if the horror of it could not be spoken of.

She waited until he had finished saddling the horses.

'Show me the place,' she said.

In the little graveyard behind the house there was a mound of freshly turned earth. All the last names on the wooden crosses surrounding it were the same; his alone would be different. An Englishman's grave.

For a few moments she stood there, thinking of nothing. My heart is a stone, she thought. There was no sound but the dry desert wind, blowing the red dust around, and the stamping of the horses.

She was too weak to get up upon Phoebus unaided, and had to rely on De Kuiper to lift her into the saddle. He had already taken leave of Cornelia Venter. The girl made no word or gesture of farewell, but stood watching them go, the dog at her feet. Until that moment, Laura had never felt with such intensity the force of another's hatred.

They had gone only a few miles when she felt a sharp spasm run through her, and she was obliged to dismount, almost falling to the ground in her haste. She barely had time to hoist her skirts before her bowels gave way; what came out was a stinking liquid, which spattered the dry earth. Again, the pain racked her body, calling forth a groan. But when De Kuiper moved to help her, she shouted at him to leave her alone. Only when it felt as if there could be nothing left to come out of her, did she rise, trembling, and call for water.

De Kuiper had proved to be a competent nurse: neither too

173

forward with offers of assistance, nor dilatory in providing what was needed. He had held the cup for her while she drank, and had kicked dust over the foulness on the ground. He had lifted her onto her horse, although she was too weak to do more than merely hold on. De Kuiper had walked in front, for the rest of the day's journey, leading both her horse and his own.

Later, he had sat by her while she wept and muttered in her sleep. She awoke, just before dawn, to see him crouched on a rock, a short way off, the coal of his cigarette glowing and fading in the soft blue air of early morning.

When she began to weep, she could not stop—an ugly sound; raw, as if torn from her throat; her body racked with sobs. He is dead, she cried. Nothing she had done had come to any good. She had found him and her finding him had killed him, it was as plain as day. She had driven him from his refuge, a hunted animal, and harried him to his death. It was as sure as if she had been the one to pull the trigger. Had she never seen him, never set foot in this cursed land, he would be alive; dead to her, still—but alive.

Only her cursed insistence on seeing the quest to its end had brought this about.

Poor man—how he must have suffered to see her. And she, remorseless to the last, had forced him to hear the terrible news she had borne with her. Forced him to share her guilt and her grief at that earlier death. It was as if, seeing him already laid low, she had scourged him with whips. After that, what else was left for him but death? In that refuge, at least, he would be safe from pursuit.

Shivering with fever—she could not stop trembling. Her eyes gone wide black pupils opening up to a world beyond this.

He takes the gun and makes himself ready to receive it... Like a lover; opening himself to what must come. Such an intimate invasion; surrendering to death. His lips parting to take it in, the cold metal pressing against his teeth... Steadying himself. For this is not some rash act but a calculated thing. Releasing the safety-catch... (How could he not, at that sound, regret his decision?) Click. The moment of no return.

O the stars the stars. How coldly they glitter in all that darkness.

Of the journey to Helpmekaar she had little recollection. An impression of a shadowless plain stretching in all directions, of intense heat and tormenting thirst, was all she knew. De Kuiper's voice in her ear, urging her on across that stony desert, followed by merciful intervals of darkness and oblivion, all that remained.

To open her eyes, after one of these blank interludes, and find herself lying in a camp-bed, shaded by a canvas roof, rather than on the hard ground, surprised her for no more than an instant. She had been ill; that much was certain.

She raised herself up, to get a better sense of her situation, and was immediately overcome with faintness. She lay still for a minute. Something was different. When she sat up once more, she realised what it was. Her light-headedness was not, then, merely the after-effect of fever.

Her involuntary exclamation brought De Kuiper to the door of the tent.

'You are awake,' he said.

'Yes. My hair...' Her hands described an absence; a soft weight that was no longer there.

'It was necessary to cut it.'

'I see.'

'The doctor ordered it,' he said.

'It is of no consequence. It was only the surprise of it, that is all.' She reached for her shawl. 'I suppose this is Helpmekaar. Have we been here long?'

'Three days.'

'I am sorry to have been the cause of such a delay. But I am quite well now.' Again, her hands sought the shorn hair at the nape of her neck. 'This will, at least, make dressing less arduous,' she said.

What she wanted most of all was to wash. She was still wearing the undergarments in which she had travelled, and was aware, suddenly, that she stank of sweat and sickness.

'Would you send Rejoice to me? I think I might need her today.'

'Rejoice is not here.'

He was obliged to explain, since she recalled little of the

events of the past few days. The only thing she recalled was the thing she would have preferred to forget.

'Something must have happened,' she said.

'So it seems,' said De Kuiper. 'I will tell the doctor that you are awake.'

'You are a fortunate young lady,' said the doctor, with a smile. 'If our taciturn friend'—she realised he meant De Kuiper—'had been any less prompt about bringing you here, I would not have given that'—he snapped his fingers—'for your chances.'

He took a meditative pull on his cigar. 'I am sorry about your hair. But it is quite a rule with me, in cases of enteric fever. To cut the hair, I mean. I find that it can make all the difference in bringing down the patient's temperature—as indeed, it appears to have done with you...'

'Please do not concern yourself,' said Laura. 'I am grateful for all that you have done.'

He waved away her thanks. They said nothing more for a while. It was evening; the sun having gone down an hour before. They sat by the fire, in front of the doctor's tent. Before them, dimly visible through the encroaching gloom, was the tin-roofed hospital building, and the line of tents in front of it—all that remained of a camp which had once held two thousand men.

De Kuiper had set out some hours earlier; it was his expected return, with the errant wagon, which delayed their repast: a simple affair, the doctor said, of soup and a broiled fowl. He had persuaded Laura to take a pre-prandial brandy; he himself was more of a whisky man, although both had their uses, medicinally.

The effect of the brandy, coming as it did on an empty stomach, was to increase the feeling of unreality by which Laura had been possessed all day. At that moment, she felt she could have said anything to anyone, and it would not matter.

'Do you believe,' she said. 'That one can die of a broken heart?'

He considered the question.

'Certainly.' he said at last. 'Only—' He threw her a glance. 'It is those who survive that one is inclined to fear for more.'

176

Chapter 18

Rejoice, January 1880: Rorke's Drift

She had known there was something wrong even before she saw them return—both on horseback, which had not been so before. The boy, Lucky, riding the small red mare which belonged to the Reverend's wife; the other, Constant, very pleased with himself to be riding a great white horse he could barely control, so that it kept dancing sideways, and showing the whites of its eyes. A bad horse, was her first thought. Not ill-natured, but broken in spirit. The smallest sound could make it tremble—a door slamming, or a pot being dropped in the yard.

She thought it must have been badly treated; but when she said as much to Constant, he denied it. It was skittish because it was an English horse, he said. Basuto horses were much quieter, everyone knew that. It had belonged to the English soldier, who was now dead. It had been a bad death, he added in a low voice, his eyes looking fearfully around. He for one had been glad to get away from the place. He would say nothing more than this, but it was enough.

The English woman was sick; that was why they had returned alone. She was with the *baas*; he it was who had sent them, to fetch the wagon. (How his chest had swelled when he said that, foolish boy!) They were to take the wagon and the supplies and go back to Helpmekaar, where the *baas* and the English were waiting. Then they would return to Maritzburg. He was to have a horse of his own, the *baas* had said. With the money he had earned on this trip, he would be able to get married. There were already four cows in his father's *kraal* which belonged to him; with the money, he could buy six more...

So he babbled on, poor fool, casting love-lorn looks in her direction. But if Johann was too old for her, this one was much too young. She wanted a man for a husband, not a smooth-faced boy.

But she let him talk, besotted youth, whilst they loaded up the wagon—he and Lucky manhandling the sacks of meal, and what was left of the tinned salt-beef, together with the fresh vegetables and bread that the Reverend and his wife could spare them. Mrs Otto was a plain-faced thing, with her pink skin and pale hair like dry grass in little plaits around her head, but she had been kind enough to Rejoice. When she had been shown the place in the graveyard where the old woman lay she had turned to Rejoice with such a sorrowful expression in her big blue eyes that it had made Rejoice feel sad just to look at her. '*Ag*! Poor thing!' she had cried, clasping her hands to her breast, an it had seemed as if her pity was as much for Rejoice as for the old one, who was, in any case, no longer in need of pity.

As Rejoice was packing up the old woman's clothes and those that the English, her daughter, had left, Mrs Otto had appeared in the doorway, wringing her large red hands. '*Ag*! If I had been here!' she sighed, as if her presence might somehow have stopped the old woman from dying. 'May I help you?' she said presently, in a different tone, before starting to fold the garments which yet remained to go in the box. So startled had Rejoice been at this, that she almost dropped the pair of boots she was holding.

Then she remembered: this was the wife of the Reverend Otto. She was certainly as strange as he; and he was like no other white man she had met. For it was his custom, every morning after he had finished praying, to strip to the waist and dig for an hour in the vegetable patch with Johann and the other men. 'We are all God's servants,' he said. 'Black or white, He sees no distinction between us.' Once, he had taken Rejoice aside and spoken earnestly to her of Bishop Colenso. Did she know that the bishop's name amongst her people was *Sobantu*, meaning Father of His People? Bishop Colenso was a good man. He had been against the war; although he had not been able to prevent it. If he—instead of that warmongering Englishman, Frere—had been listened to in the first instance, a great many deaths might have been avoided. 'But we must not give up hope, you and I,' said the Reverend Otto, as if his hopes and Rejoice's could ever be the same.

Now, after many tears from Mrs Otto, and angry looks from

Johann, because Rejoice would not agree to marry him, they were on their way—the wagon piled high with the provisions and the boxes of clothes and spare ammunition they needed for the journey back to Durban. Not that she, Rejoice, intended to go all the way to Durban. That was a terrible place. They had boxed her ears and called her a Godless savage.

She took her seat as usual among the boxes, but Constant said she must sit on the bench up front, like the English ladies did—because she was a lady, wasn't she, with her fine clothes and the airs she gave herself? She had paid him no attention, foolish youth; but after a while she went and sat next to Lucky, and shooed away the flies with a horse-hair whisk.

When Constant saw them sitting together, he was angry, and said how was it that she preferred a boy to a man? But she took no notice of his jealous words. She liked Lucky: he reminded her a little of her brother.

As they jogged along, he told her about his family and the village where he was born. It was all gone now: the *kraal* had been burnt when the great king passed through with his armies. By this he meant the Zulu king, of course; he himself was Basuto. Their people had been enemies for a long time. In spite of this, he seemed to bear her no ill will. His mother was alive, he told her; and his sisters, too. When he was a rich man, he would return and build them all a house. Afterwards, he would do nothing but sit in the doorway and smoke his pipe.

The sun was high in the sky when they stopped to rest, near a deserted *kraal*. Six huts stood around a stone cattle-pen—the same pattern as in her own village. All the huts were empty, and all the food had been taken away. Around was nothing but the thick grass, and a plantation of mealies that grew as tall as a man. She was uneasy, but Constant only laughed, calling her a frightened little girl. There was nothing to be afraid of while he had his gun. They would not be expected at Helpmekaar until sunset; they had plenty of time, he said.

Lucky unyoked the oxen and set them to graze, and then he and Rejoice looked for sticks to build a fire. He was in high spirits, chattering away about the fine house he would build—finer than any of these poor huts—and about the cattle he would have,

179

when he was rich. All the while, she was afraid, although she could not have said why. It was as if somebody watched them from close by; she could feel that gaze boring into the back of her neck. But when she looked, there was no one. Nothing but the wind, stirring the long grass. Nothing but the white horse, swishing its tail.

But still those eyes... it was as if a fly crawled slowly over her skin. With a shudder, she brushed it away. But there was no fly. Sweat ran down her face, pooling at the corners of her mouth with a taste like tears. When they returned to the kraal, Constant lay stretched out in the shade, with his hat over his eyes. So she made a fire, and boiled water to make tea, the way the English had shown her. It had a bitter taste, but she liked the bitterness. It gave her strength. Then she made mealie porridge, and when they had eaten it, Lucky curled himself up in his cloak and went to sleep.

She must have slept, too—she could not say for how long. Perhaps an hour, perhaps only a few minutes. When she opened her eyes, she knew at once that something was different. The sun was still high in the sky and the grass still waved and the white horse still twitched its tail—but they were no longer alone. Tall figures had stepped out of the grass and now blocked out the sky.

Before she could cry out, one of them, a warrior wearing the head-ring of an *induna*, stepped forward, and, in one easy movement, cut Lucky's throat from ear to ear. His blood gushed out, and fell onto the dry earth with a sound like rain. Constant took longer to die. He was shouting that they must let him go; they could take it all—the cattle, the bags of meal—he wanted none of it. They could have the woman, too. Him they killed with a spear through the eye, bursting the eyeball. His scream seemed to go on for a long time. When he was quiet at last they turned to her. They had already overturned the wagon and driven off the white horse. It was the oxen they wanted.

She prepared herself for death. She knew that other things might happen to her before, and she prepared herself for this, also. Even so, it was difficult not to cry out when one of the men kicked her legs from under her so that she fell on the ground. When he threw himself down upon her, it knocked the breath from her body. She saw his eyes, glaring into hers like those of a maddened ox. She felt hot blood on her face, which she though must be her own.

But then the man rolled off her with a grunt of pain, blood—not hers, after all—streaming from a gash in his head. The *induna* stood over him, a heavy wooden club in his hand. 'Get up, you fool,' he said. 'Leave the girl alone. Can't you see she is one of ours?'

When she had enough breath to speak, she thanked him. 'Where is your village?' he asked her, and when she had told him, he said, 'You had better go there, my sister.' 'Yes, my lord,' she replied, thinking it best not to say that there was nothing left there for her now.

Had things been different, the *induna* was the kind of man she should have married: tall, and handsome, with a warrior's mien.

After they had gone, she sat for a while in the dust. Then she took the spade from under the wagon, which now lay on its side, and began to dig, just outside the ring of houses, where the dead were laid. It was not good that Lucky and Constant should lie un-buried, for the wild dogs to eat. But when her hands were raw and bleeding she threw the spade away. The ground was much too hard. It would take her until nightfall just to dig a single grave.

Instead she covered Lucky's face with her shawl. Constant she could not bring herself to touch: he had soiled himself, and the flies were already at work upon him. All around were the English woman's clothes, scattered on the ground, from the boxes which had broken open. She picked up as many of these she could hold, and, with the bundle in her arms, set off along the road to Help-mekaar.

She was not sure how far she walked that day; or even if she were going in the right direction. Her only thought was to walk for as far as she could, and see where it brought her to. If she reached a village, they might take her in. Or they might drive her away—she had no way of telling. But she would not die for a few days yet. She was strong, and she had water to drink and mealie porridge to eat—which had been all she had been able to save from the wreck of the wagon. The *induna* and his men had taken

181

the rest—all but the tinned beef, which was no use to anybody.

Just before sunset on the second day, she saw the horse and its rider coming towards her—a black shape against the red sky. It was the *baas*. 'What has happened, *meisie*?' he said. She told him that Constant and Lucky were dead, and that the soldiers had taken the oxen. 'Do you mean the English soldiers?' he wanted to know, and she said no, she meant her own people. He had looked at her, frowning. 'There is blood on your face,' he said. 'Did they hurt you, *meisie*?' She told him no; and that it was not her blood. 'That is good, he said. He helped her up onto his horse and climbed up behind her. 'Your mistress is waiting for us at Helpmekaar,' he said. 'She was sick, but now she is well again. We leave for Grey Town tomorrow.' She said nothing, and after a while he spoke again. 'I am sorry about Constant and Lucky,' he said. 'They were good boys. They did not deserve to die. When we reach Grey Town, the English soldiers will hunt down those who did this. They will punish them severely. The English are merciless towards those who attack their own.'

When they got to Helpmekaar, the English woman, Miss Brooke, was waiting. Because of her sickness, she had grown thinner and older. When she saw Rejoice, she did not speak at first. All she did was to hold her at arm's length and stare at her, with the tears running down her face, so that her cheeks grew quite red and ugly. Even the sight of the clothes that Rejoice had brought did not seem to make her happy, although the dress she had on was torn in several places, and so dirty that you could no longer see what colour it had been.

After she had finished crying, Miss Brooke wanted to know if Rejoice had suffered any hurts to her body, or if the men who killed Lucky and Constant had harmed her in any other way. She meant had they forced her. When Rejoice said that they had not, Miss Brooke seemed as if she did not believe her. Would Rejoice allow the doctor to look at her, she said. He was a good doctor. But Rejoice had never willingly let any man touch her body; and there was no reason why the doctor should touch her now. She was not sick.

If anyone needed the doctor, in Rejoice's opinion, it was Miss

Brooke herself. Her sickness was gone, it was true; but anyone could see that she was broken inside. Maybe the *Tokoloshe* had stolen her spirit away, so that nothing looked out from behind her eyes but a dead thing. Maybe she had spent too long with the dead, so that she had become like them. Rejoice could not tell for sure. At night, she no longer cried out in her sleep; but her lips moved silently, as if she whispered secrets. In the morning, she would stare at nothing with her big pale eyes, while Rejoice combed her hair. It was ugly hair—flat, like dead grass. Now that it was cut short, it made her look like a boy—if a boy could wear a dress.

They had been travelling for two days, and Miss Brooke had hardly said a word. The sun was at its hottest, now, and she did not even remember to ask for water when she was thirsty. If Rejoice had not reminded her, she would have died long before now. Sometimes it seemed to Rejoice as if she wanted to die. Then she could be with the old woman, and with the man she loved, who had been dead, and then alive again, and was now dead once more. If Rejoice had said what was in her heart she would have told her, *They are gone. That is all there is to say.* Lucky was gone, too, with his quick smile; and Constant, who had loved her. It was not good to think too much about such things.

As the sun was going down on the third day, they came to a farm. It was a poor, broken-down place. There was only an old man and his wife to look after it. They were thin and white-haired, and so shrivelled up in their black clothes that Rejoice thought it would not be long before they, too, must die. Their son had been killed fighting the Zulus. Now there was no one to tend the fields. If *Meinheer* and *Mevrouw* wanted to stay, they were welcome to Wilhelm's old room, they said. The girl could sleep in the barn. There was plenty of straw. When Miss Brooke was told what they had said, she was angry. Her face, that had been so pale, was patched with red.

'She will not sleep in the barn. She is not an animal,' she said.

'There is only one bed,' said the *baas*, with a shrug. 'You and she can share it. I will sleep in the barn.'

But in the end, it did not happen like that. What happened was this: after they had eaten the meal—salted pork and boiled mealies—which Rejoice had cooked, because the maid who belonged to the old people had run away, Miss Brooke went into the room where they were to sleep, and closed the door. Then the *baas* went out to the barn to see to the horses. She, Rejoice, washed up all the dishes and knives and spoons and dried them and put them away. '*Dankie, meisie,*' said the old woman, and then she, too, went to bed. The old man took the dog outside to do its business and then brought it back and tied it to the doorpost. He was the last to go to bed, except Rejoice.

When she went in, Miss Brooke was lying on the bed, with her arms by her sides and her eyes wide open. Rejoice helped her to take off her dress, and her boots, because she had forgotten to do so, and then she washed Miss Brooke's face and hands as if she had been a child. After she had taken off her own clothes, she lay down. The bed was a wide one, made of dark wood. She had slept on one like it, at the Christian mission; although the mattress had not been as soft as this one.

In the middle of the night, Rejoice woke to find that the moon was shining on her face. The bed beside her was empty. Nor was the English woman to be found elsewhere in the room. Her shawl was gone, too. If the *Tokoloshe* had taken her, she would have had no need of her shawl.

Rejoice went outside, slipping past the old dog that was asleep by the door. She had not gone far from the house when she heard a sound, coming from the direction of the barn: a kind of cry. At first, she thought it was an animal, stirring in its sleep— but then she heard it again, and knew it was a human cry. She waited for a few moments longer, until she was certain that the cries she heard were not those of someone in pain. Then she returned to the house, and got into bed, and closed her eyes.

Some time before morning, she heard the door creak, and the mattress give beneath the English woman's weight as she got into bed. In the morning, Rejoice said nothing, and Miss Brooke said nothing to her. Outside, the *baas* was already saddling up the horses. He whistled softly to himself as he did so.

Chapter 19

Laura, February 1880: Kranskloof

She dared not close her eyes, because if she did so, she saw his face. It was as she had seen it that last time—one half being recognisable as his; the other not. If she closed her eyes, even in daylight, that image flashed upon her inner eye. The dear curves of his cheek and chin on one side; red eyeless flesh on the other...

Those eyes, which would see no more, had once gazed upon her with love. That hand, which had wrought such damage, had touched her cheek in parting only hours before. Until tomorrow... Had he known, even then, what he meant to do—or had the madness of despair overtaken him without warning?

'Until tomorrow,' he'd said. Perhaps he had known that there could be no 'tomorrow' for them. If he had offered her the choice between sharing his exile, and returning to the life she had left behind, how would she have answered? Even now, she did not know. He had spared her the decision, that much was certain...

She lay, her eyes wide open, listening to the gentle breathing of the girl who lay beside her, the soft contours of whose face she could make out quite plainly in the moonlight. Her mind was in that state of preternatural wakefulness in which everything seemed sharp and clear—like figures in a magic-lantern show.

Here, against a painted desert and a painted sky, was the Hero, in his soldier's scarlet—here the Heroine, in blue. Here, too, was the Villain, his face half-hidden by his cloak. She knew him from somewhere—but where?

Now he was coming towards her. She wanted to scream, but could not. Then he let his cloak fall, and she saw his face—that terrible face—and woke with a start...

She rose from the bed, and took her shawl and went out. It was not like sleeping and it was not like waking, either. The moon had made everything as bright as day, so that she could see quite plainly. She crossed the yard towards the barn and pushed open the door into hay-scented darkness.

'Who's there?' he said.

The moonlight falling through the open door must have wakened him; or perhaps he had not been asleep.

She said nothing but stood there, in that cold white glare, letting him see her.

'Close the door,' he said.

She did so.

In the dark, it was easier. They did not speak. She felt him touch her face. When she drew his head to her breast he made a small sound in his throat. The feeling of his body upon hers was astonishing: such strength, such heat. She bit her lips as he came into her, so as not to cry out from the shock of it. But as he began to move, she could not restrain her cries. Afterwards, there were tears on her face, and he kissed them away.

She must have slept, then; for the next thing she knew, he was shaking her gently. 'You must go,' he murmured in her ear. The sky was getting light, as she crossed the yard. In another hour or so, they would have to be on their way. When she got into bed the girl was lying curled up on her side, as she had been before. She closed her eyes, and when she opened them again it was broad daylight, and the girl was coming in with a jug of hot water and a basin.

Laura washed her face and hands, then stripped off her shift and began to soap her breasts and armpits. Still the girl stood there.

'I can manage, thank you,' said Laura. She could feel the soreness between her legs; the smell of him was there, as she bent to wash. 'Perhaps *Mevrouw* would like some help with breakfast...'

The girl nodded. Then she reached out, and pulled something—a wisp of straw—from Laura's hair.

She saw herself as if from a distance: a figure in a landscape. Hot sun on the back of her neck; her skin burning. Her dress stuck to her legs; its bodice clung damply to her body. Prickly heat bloomed on the insides of her legs, on her throat, on the undersides of her breasts. She no longer paid it any attention. She

considered her sunburnt arms, her hands—once white as lilies—
now burnt brown, and blistered as a working woman's hands.
Her body, moving with the horse's rhythm, was lean and strong.

If it were not for the inconvenience of having breasts, she
could have passed as a boy, especially since her hair had been cut.
She preferred the way it felt—the absence of weight on the back
of her neck—to the way it had been before.

They reached the Drift before noon. The river was low, and it was
an easy crossing. By the time they had got over, the sun was high
in the sky, and De Kuiper said that they should rest for an hour
or so, until it was cooler. In another day, if they made good time,
they would be in Grey Town, he said.

To what had passed between them the night before, he made
no allusion, either by look or word, for which Laura was grateful.
It was as if it had never happened—or rather, as if what had happened belonged to another realm, one of darkness and silence,
which bore no relation to that of waking life.

Only when they were, briefly, alone together—Rejoice having
gone in search of firewood—did he speak at last. He had been
standing there, in the shade of the thorn-tree beneath which they
had set up their camp; saying nothing, merely looking at her.

'There is something you must know,' he said. For a moment,
it seemed as if he might be about to break their pact of silence,
and to speak of things that were better left unsaid. But in the end
it was not of their relation to one another that he spoke, but of
something else. 'I have a wife, in Pietermaritzburg.' He could not
meet her gaze. 'And children.'

'Ah,' she said. She felt as cold as ice, despite the noonday heat.
'I am sorry.'

'There is no need. What happened was not of your making.'

'Even so, it was wrong... what we did. May God forgive us.'

'I do not wish to speak of it.'

He was silent a moment. His face, half-obscured by the broadbrimmed hat, was unreadable, the eyes in shadow. 'There is one
thing more,' he said. He took something—a sheet of paper, folded
in two—from inside his jacket, and gave it to her. 'It was in his
pocket,' he said. 'I did not read it. I saw only that it was meant for

you.'

And indeed, her name was written on the outside, in the hand which had become as familiar to her as her own.

'Thank you,' she said, turning aside to read what was written there in private.

De Kuiper stood there a moment longer, as if there was something more he might have said. Then he seemed to recollect himself, and, drawing the pouch from his pocket, began to roll a cigarette.

'My dearest girl,' she read. At the sight of that familiar hand, she could not stop the tears coming to her eyes, so that she could not see for a moment. Afterwards she wished that she could have remained blind for a while longer—if not forever—so as not to have been able to read what was there.

I write these words in the knowledge that, when you read them, I shall deserve your pity even less than before; any claim to your affection I forfeited long ago. Were that affection to turn to abhorrence when you have read what I have to say, would be no more than my due. If there were not another in the case, I would have let 'the rest' be 'silence'—which is all I must dare to hope for in this world and the next.

But you see, you are not the only one to have been hurt by my actions. When I left Cape Town, I left behind not only what vestiges of pride and self-respect remained to me, after a year in that infernal city, but more tangible evidence of my fall. There is a woman by the name of Pretty (I know of no other) whom I left with child. I need hardly say that she is not a virtuous woman—if you were not the only one in this Godforsaken place with the power to help me, I would have cut off my right arm rather than bring you into any relation with such a one as she.

But the child... I cannot help but feel that the child deserves a better fate, than the one which has been foisted upon it, by its unhappy mother's degraded condition of life and its father's profligacy. It is for this reason that I turn to you, in my extremity.

I will not insult you further by asking you to forgive me. All I ask (and I know it to be no light thing) is that you seek out the mother of my child. When I saw her last in Cape Town, she was living in the Malay quarter, which is called Bo-Kaap. When my estate is settled, at some date beyond my death (how strange it is to write these words!) you will find that I have settled what money I have on you, my intended bride. If you would not regard it as a mockery of all that we once were to one another, I would ask that some of that amount be used to educate my child— whether son or daughter, I do not know.

To write thus to one who has been (and remains) so dear to me, has been hard. What follows after will be easy by comparison.

Your

Theo

The sun was setting as they came within sight of Fort Napier, and the sky was blood-red above the dark line of hills. In an hour— perhaps less, if they quickened their pace—they would be back in the bosom of civilisation, or at least what passed for civilisation here.

It was strange, thought Laura, to be travelling this road again. Only a few short weeks had passed since she and her companions had set out from this place, on a journey whose outcome had seemed, even then, to be far from certain. The more she thought about it, the more their enterprise seemed like an act of wanton folly, as a result of which she—to speak only of herself— had lost all that was dearest to her in the world.

Emiline Reynolds's death had deprived her of a second mother—one who had loved her without reserve. The pain of it was very hard to bear. She was only glad that her dear friend had been spared what she herself had had to endure since.

She understood how it was that some went mad with grief. Perhaps she had been mad for a while; she could not say. If the shock of Theo's death had brought her close to madness, it was— perversely, perhaps—his last injunction to her that had restored her to something like sanity. 'Seek out the mother of my child,' he had said, in that sad letter—the last of all the letters which were now all that remained of their love.

A cruel irony, one might think, that the last communication she should have received concerned not his feelings for her, but his love for another woman. For that it *was* love which had made him risk everything, to save her and the child she had borne him, Laura had no doubt. It was strange that this, which might have been a source of bitterness, was not. If Theo had killed himself because he could not live with dishonour, then this—the saving of woman and child—arose from the same impulse.

It did not occur to Laura to blame him for his betrayal of her. What would have been the use of that? Whatever sins he had committed, he had paid a heavy price for. If further atonement was required, that was for God, not man, to decide.

She herself had no right to judge anyone. Her sin and his had, after all, been the same. Although hers, she saw, had been as much an act of self-abnegation as desire. A way of cancelling all that had been; of obliterating joyful memories, as well as those unbearable to think of.

Captain Austen was to escort the two women as far as Durban. Fortunately, he proved an undemanding companion, preferring to while away the heavy hours between sunset and going to bed with the laying out of endless games of Patience. This was a relief, as Laura could not have borne much conversation. She had not even the excuse of keeping up her journal to exempt her from being sociable, having given up writing in that volume some weeks before.

Once, tired of her own thoughts, she had taken it up again, and glanced idly through its pages, whose narrative seemed now to belong to another life. The woman who had written these descriptions of people and places and the woman who now read over them, were one and the same—and yet, how far apart! She barely recognised the phrases as her own; they seemed the artless prattling of a child.

Only the last entry had anything of truth about it;

'She is gone—last night, about four o' clock. I do not know

that I shall have the strength to carry on without her.'

The rest was blank pages. Well, let them remain so. There was nothing she could add that could better express the bleakness that was in her heart.

In Durban, she sought out Major Hallam. His lodgings were in an obscure street, in a part of town which, if it had ever been fashionable, was not fashionable now. In fact, confided Mrs Tremayne, with a genteel shudder, one could scarcely call it respectable. If Miss Brooke had a message she wished conveyed, why, the boy could take it...

The street in question did not strike Laura as so very bad. She wished that the same could have been said for Major Hallam, whose appearance, since their last encounter, had altered for the worse.

'You will forgive me if I do not get up,' he said, as the servant, a slender young man in a white turban, announced her. 'Thank you, Rashid. You will notice that we are in India here,' the Major added, motioning Laura to sit down. And indeed, the house, with its silk hangings and low divans covered with bright cushions, and its pervasive smell of incense, might have been an outpost of the subcontinent—not that she had ever been there.

'I am sorry to find you ill,' she said. 'I would not have troubled you if I had known...'

The Major politely waved this away. 'It is nothing, I assure you.' His face gave the lie to this: it had the look of a death's-head. 'A touch of malaria. All too common in this region, I am afraid.'

She was silent a moment, wondering how best to frame her question.

'Tell me why you have come,' he said, with his queer twisted smile. 'For I do not flatter myself it can be for a glimpse of my handsome face.'

She met his gaze without flinching.

'There was a girl,' she said. 'In Cape Town. Theo... that is, Lieutenant Reynolds and she had a child...'

She saw from his expression that he knew something of this already.

'Go on,' he said.

'It was Lieutenant Reynolds's last wish that the child should be found. If there is anything that you can tell me which might help towards that end, I would be grateful.'

'How did you learn of this?'

'From Theo himself. In a letter...'

'My God,' he said, in a low voice. 'That must have been a cruel blow.'

'It has not been the worst.'

He looked at her steadily, as if seeing her for the first time.

'You must not judge him too harshly,' he said. 'He was a young man, and young men often behave foolishly. I told him as much at the time.' He smiled. 'Of course he did not like it...Ah, here is Rashid with our tea.'

The ensuing minutes were taken up with the business of pouring out, and handing round cups, so that Laura wondered if perhaps she would leave the Major's house no wiser than when she entered it. But then he set down his cup.

'I saw the young woman but once,' he said. 'But I will tell you all I can...'

They had not been in Cape Town more than a few days when she heard her name called, as she was walking down the street. It was Septimus Doyle, looking, if anything, more dishevelled than ever. His hair was longer than at their last meeting, and he had grown very brown.

'But this is wonderful,' he said. 'I was just thinking of you.'

She realised, with a flicker of self-reproach, that she had not thought of him in a long while. Although there had been a time, not long after their first meeting, when he had seldom been out of her thoughts... But all that was past.

He seemed in an excitable mood, talking very fast about a great many things. He had been to the diamond mines in the Transvaal, he said. There were diamonds as big as eggs for the taking. Men hauled them up by the bucketful. Fortunes were being made, and lost, every day.

While he spoke, waving his hands around with his customary animation, she cast about for reasons to get away. The fact was, they had been back almost a week and she was no nearer finding the girl and her child. She had asked at the hotel, and had received only blank looks. The porter said he would ask around—but nothing had come of it so far. At the barracks, it had been a similar story. There were a lot of girls in the city, the sergeant on duty had said, looking a little askance at her. Pretty. He would vouch for the fact that some of them were pretty; although they were not the sort he would want to introduce to his mother, if she took his meaning.

Now, as she half-listened to Septimus Doyle's tales of his travels, it struck her that here at last was the solution to her troubles. He was a journalist, was he not? What else did journalists do except discover information to which others were not privy?

'There is a favour I would ask,' she said, cutting across an account of what a man named Rhodes had said to a man named Barnato. 'But it may be that it is too difficult...'

It was plain that she had piqued his interest. As she explained further, she saw his customary expression of sleepy amusement sharpen into alertness.

I do not know if I will be able to help you,' he said, when she had finished. 'But I can promise you that I will do my utmost.'

'I have every confidence in you,' she said.

'Indeed!' he cried, throwing her a whimsical look. 'Then perhaps I have cause to hope...'

Chapter 20

Septimus, April 1880: Cape Town

Since his return from Kimberley six weeks before, he had been working up a series, entitled 'Scenes from the Diamond Fields', which was to feature in next month's issue. This would be surrounded by decorative frieze featuring various 'types' mentioned in the article: a group of bearded prospectors, with picks and shovels; a native worker, stripped to the waist; an overseer with *sjambok* and whip; a boy, leading a heavily laden mule. On the facing page would be a larger illustration, 'got up' by the newspaper's chief engraver from the sketches Septimus had supplied, of the 'Big Hole' itself: that vast pit, thirty acres wide and five hundred feet deep, into which so many descended each day, as if into the mouth of Hell.

Such comparisons Septimus kept to himself, however. It had been with the greatest of difficulty that he had obtained permission to visit the mine and its new proprietor. It would not do to draw too obvious a parallel, even in jest, between Kimberley and the infernal regions; nor between Mr Cecil Rhodes and the Prince of Darkness.

'Imagine the crater of an extinct volcano,' he therefore wrote, 'with sides like precipices—or a vast spider's web, rather'.

For from the top of the crater, thousands of wires lead down to the various 'claims'—wires along which the diggers, as they extract the diamondiferous earth, send it up to the surface for sorting. At one end of each wire, in this enormous cat's cradle, is a bucket, which is hauled up from the depths of each shaft by means of a horse 'whin'. Beneath slowly turning wheels that resemble nothing so much as cogs in a giant's pocket-watch, the patient beasts walk endlessly round in circles, their efforts reinforcing those of their human counterparts.

For below—far, far below—in the depths of the pit, is what seems at first glance to be a swarming ant-heap. On closer inspection, it becomes apparent that the ants running hither and thither are men, intent on carrying away the riches of the earth with the assiduity of the insects they so resemble. Observing this tireless industry, one might almost be witnessing the building of some wondrous edifice of antiquity- the Pyramids, say, or the Roman Forum—so nearly do the excavations resemble the foundations of an ancient city...

He did not imagine that Mr Rhodes—who was reputed to be something of a classical scholar—would mind the implied comparison to the pharoahs, or to the imperial emperors.

The first surprise, when at last he had been ushered into the great man's presence, was how young Rhodes was: scarcely older than he was himself. But then Rhodes had been a mere boy of seventeen when he had first come to South Africa. The stories were already the stuff of legend: of how he had been a sickly youth, with a weak heart, sent to recuperate in the warmer climate of Natal after his doctor had said he would not live beyond twenty-one; of the trip he had made by ox-cart across the veldt to the diamond fields, armed only with a pick and shovel and a set of the Greek classics, with which he had been preparing for his entrance examination at Oxford.

Even so, it was hard to reconcile this slight, diffident man with the ruthless Tartar he was said to be in his business dealings.

He seemed rather at a loss as to why Septimus was there at all.

'You have seen the mine, I take it?'

'I have, sir. A most interesting experience.'

'You are an American.' An expression of perplexity crossed Rhodes's long, mild face. 'I was not told I would be speaking to the American press.'

'No, sir. That is, I represent a British newspaper.'

'Indeed. And what do you make of Kimberley, Mr...'

'Doyle, sir.'

'That is an Irish name, is it not? I am an admirer of your Mr Parnell.'

'Indeed,' said Septimus.

Had the great entrepreneur been aware of how little interest he had in Parnell, or Biggar, or O'Connell—or any of that argumentative Republican crew—he might have thrown him out on his ear. But Septimus had not travelled six thousand miles, risking all manner of perils from shipwreck to sunstroke, just to go home again.

So he composed his features into an expression suggestive of regret that they had not more leisure to devote to the finer points of Home Rule, and tried again.

'Kimberley strikes me as a fascinating study,' he said. 'At once modern and primitive...'

Rhodes emitted a bark of laughter. 'Do you think so?'

'To observe, as I did earlier today, a line of black men hauling a truck loaded with diamonds, was to be transported to Ancient Egypt, with its hordes of half-naked slaves that built the pyramids...'

Rhodes frowned. 'These are not slaves, Mr Doyle. They earn a wage which is far beyond anything they could hope to earn elsewhere.'

'Of course. I meant only...'

'You have seen the native compounds, I suppose?'

'Yes.'

This had been the final stop on Septimus's tour, after the mine itself, and the giant washing machines, and the 'pulsator', which shook out the diamonds from the dross, and the sorting-room, where the stones were picked out by hand.

Apart from all this, and from the huts where the white men were quartered, was a large square patch of ground, surrounded by a wire fence, and covered over by wire netting. It was here, in lines of galvanised iron huts, that the native workers were obliged to spend their hours of rest, locked in, once their shifts were over, until daybreak brought release.

'You would not call the conditions there inhumane?'

'No.'

If the loss of liberty were not, in itself, a form of inhumanity, Septimus thought, but did not say.

Rhodes seemed to have read something of the sort in his expression, for he said sternly, 'The searching-room is a necessary precaution against theft. The men do not object to it.' A wintry smile flickered across the mine owner's sallow face. 'We are not barbarians, Mr Doyle. But human nature is human nature, is it not?'

Septimus made a sound indicative of agreement, although in truth he had been revolted by the crude pragmatism of the searching-room, where native workers wishing to leave the company's service must submit to a week's solitary confinement and daily doses of purgative, in order, as the overseer who had shown him around had said, 'to flush out the stones from their nasty hiding-place.'

This was another story that he could not tell. But time was ticking away, and he still had not asked about the rumoured takeover. He tried a bold approach: 'They say that, within the next twelvemonth, you will become the major shareholder in the De Beers Mining Company...'

'They say that, do they?' murmured Rhodes, affecting a sudden interest in his fingertips.

'You will be the richest man in South Africa, it is said.'

'Is it now?' Rhodes smiled. 'I seem to have caused quite a stir. My advice, for what it is worth, is to believe only half of what you read, and less of what you are told.'

Septimus understood that he was being dismissed.

'Even had I the wealth of Croesus,' said Rhodes in a meditative tone, 'it would scarce be enough to do all the things I have in mind to do.'

'What things?' asked Septimus, with a sensation of clutching at straws.

'Why, to build an empire the like of which has not been seen since the days of your pharaohs, Mr Doyle. America, for all its 'know-how', cannot do it. It must be done in Africa. And I am the man to do it. There!' Rhodes laughed. 'That is your story.'

Septimus rose.

'Wait.' From a drawer in the desk in front of him, the plutocrat took out a handful of diamonds. Some were dull as river pebbles; others, cut into faceted shapes, glittered like fallen stars. 'Do you have a wife, Mr Doyle?'

Septimus shook his head.

'An Intended, then? Ah. I see from your face that you do.' From the heap upon the desk, Rhodes selected one of the brilliant stones. 'Give her this, with my compliments. Women like such things, I am told.'

It was hard to dislike a man who had just given one such a gift; although there was, Septimus judged, no calculation in the gesture. What, after all, did Rhodes care for his opinion, good or otherwise? It was all one to him.

Septimus took his leave, with the diamond in his pocket. He had the distinct impression that even before he left the room, Rhodes had forgotten his existence. A strange man, he thought, for whom wealth was only a means to an end: a fantastic dream of empire, beside which even those of the ancients could not compare.

He had not thought to see her again, and yet here she was as large as life, hurrying down Long Street as if there were not a moment to be lost. He had always admired that about her: the air she had of having things to do. Of being up to doing them, too. It was more than one could say for a lot of women. But then, Laura Brooke wasn't just any woman. What she had undertaken would have taxed the strength of many men, let alone that of a mere girl. She was extraordinary. He guessed he had known it from the first.

Now here she was, walking into his life again, as she had into his thoughts these past six months and more.

'Miss Brooke! Hi! Laura! Say, wait a minute, can't you?'

'Mr Doyle.' She waited, while he caught his breath.

He mopped his brow. 'I said to myself, "It cannot be. She is in Natal." Yet here you are.' He could not stop the grin spreading across his face.

'Here I am,' she echoed.

'May I walk with you?' She made no objection, and so he fell into step beside her. 'Well, this is a piece of luck,' he said. 'How are you? And what did you make of Natal? A strange, wild country, is it not?'

'I suppose it is,' she said.

In the face of her silence, he grew garrulous. He could not resist trying to impress her a little with his tales of the diamond
fields. And she had seemed interested enough at first.

Only when she interrupted him, had he realised that she had
not been listening.

'There is a favour I would ask.'

He had thought little of it at that moment; it was only later
that he understood what she wanted of him. At the time, all he
could think of was how fortunate it was, that he had an excuse
to see her again.

'How long do you stay in Cape Town?' he had asked; then
wished that he had not.

'We leave for England at the end of the month.'

'That is very soon.'

'Yes.' Her smile was rueful. 'I am afraid that I must get back.
We still have packing to do, and...'

'How is Mrs Reynolds?' he asked, to detain her a little.

The smile vanished. 'Of course. You do not know,' she said.

As she spoke, he was conscious of an emotion at odds with
those which might have been thought proper to hearing news
of another's death; although he had liked the old lady and, indeed,
felt regret at her passing. His feeling of relief—of gladness, almost—was not in fact to do with her death, but was only the sensation one feels at the confirmation of a suspicion. On seeing
Laura Brooke a few moments before he had thought, She is
changed. But how? Now he knew the reason for that alteration.

'I am heartily sorry for your loss,' he said. 'If there is anything
that I can do...'

'There is not,' she said. 'But thank you.'

They parted a few minutes later. As she was turning away, he
noticed that something else was different.

'Your hair...' he said, before he could stop himself.

She did not seem to mind the impertinence.

'Yes,' she said with a slight smile. 'I cannot think how I ever
bore the weight of it.'

All through the rest of that day, he could think of nothing else but seeing her again.

The street in question was in a poor quarter of the town, near the harbour. It was not a place where a respectable woman should venture and he told her so.

Before he had finished speaking, she held up her hand. 'I know what kind of place it is. That is why I should like you to accompany us. Rejoice and I,' she added, as if his questioning look could have been related to the latter rather than the former statement.

He saw that it was useless to try and dissuade her. 'If you are with us, there will be nothing to fear,' was all she said. From any other woman, it would have sounded like coquetry; from her, it was merely a statement of fact.

So it was that they climbed the steep street, with its rows of low, mean dwellings, until they came to the house she was looking for, and of which he had heard tell. From the outside, it was no different from all the others. He climbed the steps to the narrow door and knocked; after a few moments, a face looked out. He stated his purpose. The face disappeared and, after another interval, the man returned.

'She is gone. I do not know where,' he said, with a shrug, not even bothering to disguise the lie.

Septimus repeated his request, allowing the other to glimpse the money he was holding. This time, albeit with a show of reluctance, the man opened the door.

Until now, the two women had remained below in the street; now they made as if to follow. Their way was barred by the old man, whose muttered imprecations grew increasingly loud. Neither paid him the slightest attention.

'Come, Rejoice,' said Laura Brooke.

He had never thought her more wonderful than in that moment.

The door of the room was ajar. He was the first to enter. What struck him at once was the smell: a cloying stench of sickness and stale female flesh, overlaid with a sickly-sweet smell of incense.

As his sight adjusted to the dimness, he made out the figure that was lying on the bed. It was a woman—although you would never have guessed it. Eyes that had grown too large stared out of a face that already seemed that of a cadaver. A terrible recognition flared in those dark orbs a moment; then died.

'You are not the one,' the woman said. Her voice was a harsh whisper. 'He said he would come. But he does not come. He lied to me.'

It was clear to him that she was raving; also, that she had not many days to live. Women of her kind did not last long; it was a despicable trade.

He turned to block the sight of her from the two women behind him, but they were too quick for him, paying no attention when he objected that this place was not fit for them. Within moments, both had made themselves at home—opening the window a crack to let in air, straightening the disordered sheets, plumping pillows and fetching water for the poor patient, as if these minor courtesies could hold at bay the horror that was to come.

When all was to her satisfaction, Laura Brooke knelt down by the bedside, and took the dying woman's hand between her own. 'He did not lie to you,' she said softly. 'He is dead. I have come in his place.'

The woman on the bed said nothing, but her eyes showed that she understood.

For a few moments, no one spoke; the only sounds being the invalid's harsh-drawn breath, and the flapping of the blind, as the breeze from the open window stirred it.

He was struck by the tableau they made, the three women: one dark, one fair, and one whose youth and bloom was gone, so that she seemed a grotesque travesty of womanhood. It seemed a subject for Gericault; he had seen such things in Paris, when he was there. Pitiful, but with a kind of nobility...

'Where is the child?' said Laura Brooke.

At this, the woman gave a start, but made no reply.

'He sent me to find the child,' the Englishwoman went on. 'It was his last wish that I should do so.'

'She is dead,' was the whispered response. 'You are too late.'

Laura bowed her head. An interval elapsed, during which

sounds from the street—a barking dog, a crying infant—penetrated the silence. Perhaps they had been going on all along, but he had not heard them.

At length, Laura Brooke rose, and stood looking down at the emaciated frame, whose contours beneath the sheet already seemed those of a corpse.

'I am sorry that your daughter is dead,' she said. 'I had hoped to be of help to her—and to you.' She took some money from her purse, and placed it on the table. 'There is nothing to be done here,' she said in an undertone to the maid.

The two women turned to go.

'Wait.' The word was barely audible. With what seemed a supreme effort of will, the creature stretched out a skeletal hand. 'You must go to Amina's house,' she said. 'It is there you will find her.'

The large dark eyes had filled with tears, so that they seemed still larger than before. For an instant, the face was beautiful. 'My precious jewel. My darling one. Take care of her,' she said.

'I will treat her as if she were my own,' said Laura Brooke.

At the house of the Malay woman, they found the child: a well-grown girl, not two years old, with her mother's dark complexion. The eyes with which she regarded the world—a calm unblinking gaze that seemed to Septimus at that moment to belong to someone much older—were pale blue in colour. Exquisite, he thought.

There was some discussion—haggling was a more accurate word—before the transaction was made; although its outcome was never in doubt. When they left, the maid, Rejoice, was carrying the little girl in her arms.

As they crossed the street, Septimus offered Laura his arm. It pleased him that she did not withdraw her hand, for the remainder of their walk back to the hotel.

'If you'll permit me to say so, it's a great responsibility you've taken on,' he said.

'I hope I shall be equal to it.'

'Of course, it may be different in England,' he went on, conscious that he was treading on dangerous ground, 'but in my own country, a child like that—a half-caste child, I mean—would not

202

be welcome everywhere...'

He felt her stiffen slightly.

'Are you saying that you disapprove of what I have done?'

There was a coldness in her voice he had not heard before.

'Why, not a bit of it. Don't get me wrong. I only meant to warn you it won't be easy...'

'I never thought it would be. Please don't think me ungrateful,' she added, in a softer tone. 'Without your help I could have accomplished nothing.'

He made a deprecatory gesture. 'I did very little.'

'On the contrary. If you had not led us to that poor woman when you did...' Her voice faltered. 'It would have been too late, and we might never have known what had become of the child. For that reason alone, I am eternally in your debt...'

'If only that were true!'

She gave no sign of having understood him.

'You have been so kind. I hope we shall meet again before I leave Cape Town,' she said, as they came within sight of the hotel.

'You may depend on it,' he said, pressing her hand.

Chapter 21

Rejoice, April 1880: Cape Town

She did not like the city. It was too loud, and it smelt bad. The houses had sharp edges, instead of being round, the way houses should be. There were many sick people in the streets. The first time she saw someone lying by the roadside—a girl of about her own age—she had wanted to help her. The girl's face and clothes were all covered with dust from the horses and carts that were going past all the time, but nobody stopped to help the poor girl, or even seemed to notice. 'What is wrong, my sister?' she had said, but the girl had only looked at her with eyes that seemed to see nothing. She, Rejoice, had gone to fetch water, to wash the dust from the girl's face, and to cool her parched lips, but when she returned, the girl was gone.

Then Rejoice had been angry, and said to herself that she would run away. This was not a place that she wanted to be. It was too far away from everything she knew, and from the people that knew her name. There, you would not leave a young girl to die all alone, with not even a rag to cover her head or some tea made out of sweet-smelling *buchu* to take away her pain. Even if you could not stop Death you could at least take away its sting. She, Rejoice, knew about such things because her mother had taught her, in the days before Rejoice had been sent away to live with the Christians and her mother had gone mad. So: there was a kind of *buchu* you took for sleeping sickness and a kind you took for a sore throat. A kind to cure a bleeding womb, and a kind to cure nightmares. One kind you planted near the house, to keep away witchcraft and lightning, and another you hung like a charm around a baby's neck, so that he would grow up strong. There was a kind you boiled into a tea, which would take away pain in the body or in the heart. She had given some to the old woman when the pain was very bad, and it had calmed her a little.

But there were some sicknesses which even the strongest *buchu* could not cure. Miss Brooke's was one such. Something inside her had broken, and could never be made whole again.

Now that she was no longer searching for her man, because her man was dead, she searched for another. This was a girl; her name was Pretty. Since they had come to the city, that was all they had done. Searching high and low for a girl neither had ever seen. It was hard, in a place as big as this, that had so many people in it, to find one whose face you did not know. Everywhere they went it was the same: they asked for the girl, but no one knew her; or, if they knew her, they could not say where she was to be found. It was as if she did not exist; perhaps she did not, except in Miss Brooke's dreams. Miss Brooke herself did not know. 'Sometimes it feels as if we are chasing a phantom,' she said. 'Does it not seem like that to you, Rejoice?' A phantom was her word for a ghost, or an evil spirit. Rejoice said that she did not know. But Miss Brooke was not listening to her, in any case. 'I seem to have spent my life chasing one phantom or another,' she said, with a sigh. 'And yet I cannot rest until I have done what was asked of me.'

So they went on, up one street and down another, repeating the girl's name at every house they came to, it seemed. 'Have you seen a girl called Pretty? A coloured girl, about twenty years old...' Always the answers were the same: a blank look; a shake of the head; a muttered denial. Only once did a man seem to recognise the name. But it was no use, either. 'I do not know where she is,' he said, with a shrug that said he cared even less. 'I have not seen her in a long time.'

After this, Miss Brooke became more determined still to find her phantom. 'I know that she is somewhere in the city,' she said. 'All I have to do is find out where.' This was not as easy as she made it sound. Had their search been in Rejoice's own country, they could have found the girl in a day. There, no one could stay hidden for very long. Even if you were to run to the edge of the furthest plain, or climb to the top of the highest mountain, someone would be watching. In a land with so few people in it, you could not become lost, the way you could in a crowded place. Although even here, as it turned out, you could not remain unknown forever.

They had been no more than five days in the city when they met the American. They had been walking down another long street where nobody had seen the girl when a man shouted out Miss Brooke's name. This was the American, although Rejoice did not know that then. He seemed very happy to see Miss Brooke, smiling all the time and gazing at her as if she had fallen out of the sky. He did not smile so much when they went to the house where Pretty was. Here they found her, soon to become a phantom, and Rejoice thought that Miss Brooke would be content at last.

But there was still one more she had to find—not a phantom, this time, but the little one. When Rejoice saw the child, she knew at once why it was that she had come to the city. The child looked at her with its eyes like the sky and held out its arms to her and she picked her up and that was all there was to it. And Miss Brooke said, 'She will stay with us from now on, Rejoice'—as if there could ever have been any other end to the story.

The woman who had taken the phantom's child—a fat, slovenly thing in a black dress shaped like a sack—looked as if she might have had something to say about that; but when Miss Brooke showed her the money, she forgot that she meant to object, and fixed her greedy gaze upon it.

'One can guess only too well what would have been the child's eventual fate,' Miss Brooke said to the American, who said nothing in reply, but only shook his head. By this time, Rejoice had the child—Theodora, said Miss Brooke—held fast in her arms. She did not cry, the little one, when she was taken away; even when the clothes were taken off her, so that she could be washed, she made no objection. Only when Rejoice was obliged to put her down, to ease the ache in her arms, because she was not yet used to carrying her all day long, did the child cry. She was a strong child, and soon learned to climb up on Rejoice's back, where she could ride, safely wrapped in a shawl, while Rejoice did her work.

Seeing them so much together, people thought that Rejoice must be the child's mother, and Rejoice allowed them to do so—even though the child did not much resemble her, with that pale skin and those strange light eyes. Only when Miss Brooke was there, was there a different story. Theodora—Dora, as she soon became—was to be Miss Brooke's daughter, Miss Brooke said. Although how anyone could ever mistake them for mother and daughter, Rejoice did not know. But it pleased Miss Brooke to say it. As long as Rejoice was the one who took care of Dora, it did not matter to her whose child Dora was said to be. Hers were the arms that Dora came to, and the back she clambered upon. The first word she said was 'Mama', and it was not to Miss Brooke that she said it.

If Miss Brooke believed that she had found a daughter, at the end of all her searching, then who was Rejoice to tell her otherwise?

They were going away very soon, Miss Brooke said to Rejoice—to the country where Miss Brooke was born, and where the red soldiers came from. They would have to sail for many days and nights, as the country was very far. It was further than Durban was from Cape Town, and that had taken three days by ship. It was further than the furthest, she, Rejoice, could imagine; so far, said Miss Brooke, that they could never come back.

Rejoice said nothing, but only nodded—for what would have been the use of saying to Miss Brooke that near or far was all one to her? Where Dora was, there she would be. That was all there was to say. When she had set out that day from her village for the Christian mission, she had known in her heart of hearts that she would not return. After that first leave-taking, all the rest would be easy.

Chapter 22

Laura, April 1880: Cape Town

Now that the child was found, there was nothing more to do; and so Laura did nothing, surrendering herself to the strange mood of lassitude which seemed to have overtaken her in recent days. Perhaps it was no more than weariness—the result of weeks and months when sleep had been, at best, a fugitive commodity. Her illness, too, had drained her of strength, as it had blighted her looks; not that she cared much for that.

Since Rejoice had taken charge of the child, there was little, in fact, for her to do, but sit and reflect on everything that had passed since she left England. The thought of resuming her life there was strange. She could hardly imagine it now. Incredible to think that, in a month, she would be sitting in her old place at the far end of the table, pouring out tea for her father and sisters; although of course it would just be Violet, now, since Bessie—Mrs Havelock as she was now—would be installed in her own home.

It occurred to her that it could not be long until Bessie's confinement. How odd to think that, within the year, she and Bessie would both be mothers... Granted, hers was a somewhat unorthodox kind of maternity... But that she would love the child as her own was not in doubt.

And, if not for a quirk of fate, Dora might indeed have been hers. She wished more than anything in the world that it could have been so. Strange that in all their letters and conversations, she and Theo had never talked of having a child. It had been taken for granted, she supposed, by the very fact of their being betrothed. Like so much else, it had been understood, not spoken.

It struck her then, as she sat idly turning over the pile of letters in her lap, that on most of the important matters of life, she and Theo had been silent. They had not spoken of the possibility of having children; nor of child-bearing itself; nor of the act which gave rise to child-bearing. To have done so—at least where the last of these was concerned—would have been shocking; unthinkable. She wondered now why that should have been so; and why she had never questioned it.

They had spoken of love, it was true—but only of love in its less corporeal manifestations. She could not help feeling that there was something wrong with this: to speak of love as if it concerned only a meeting of minds. An intellectual sympathy—had that been all there was between them after all?

She thought of that night in the garden, a month before he went away. They had wandered out after dinner, talking of inconsequential things. She recalled the heavy sweetness of the night-scented flowers, rising on the humid air. A feeling of breathlessness, as she realised he was going to kiss her. It hadn't been like the other kisses—a gentle brushing of lips. This had been urgent; almost violent. Her mouth, next morning, had been tender and slightly swollen.

Half-swooning with her own as yet undefined desires, she'd felt his heart pounding madly against her. His hands were on her hips, pulling her to him. For a few moments, as they stood pressed together, she'd felt his excitement—the awful blind striving of his aroused flesh—until with a groan of what sounded like despair, he'd pulled away. 'My God. Lollie. This is too much for me to bear.'

He'd fumbled—hands shaking a little—for his cigarettes. The two of them had stood, awkwardly apart, until he was master of himself again. 'What a beast I am,' he had muttered, half to himself, it seemed. She had wanted to reassure him, but she had not known what to say.

After that time, he was more guarded with her, she saw. It was as if he could no longer trust himself to 'behave'. She had to smile at the absurdity of the expression. As if the flesh were an unruly child, to be subdued.

Not that he had ever expressed himself to her in any such way; he had acted, in fact, as if nothing at all had happened. Which it had not. Except that there was now a great Unspoken between them—which was everything that had to do with the love of the body. For them, the act of love would forever be an act of darkness; its mysteries cloaked in shame and silence...

Another's image—one she had tried, and failed, to erase from her consciousness—now offered itself. She had clasped that body in her arms; had felt its muscular heat; its hard flesh pressed against her; pushing into her...

This, then, was what the silence concealed. This clasping, this heat, this pressure, this intrusion.

Even now, she could hardly believe what she had done. 'May God forgive us,' he had said. She herself neither sought, nor expected, such forgiveness.

So Theo had gone away, and his letters had come, in his stead. Page after page of descriptions of places he had been, and people he had met. Discussions of books he had read and thoughts he had had. Some of it melancholy; most of it gay—as if by keeping up the spirits of those at home, he might keep his own spirits from sinking.

Phrases leap out at her from the carelessly shuffled pages:

Well, here we are in Durban, and a more pestilential place it would be harder to imagine. It could not be hotter, dearest girl, than if this were Hades itself. How I long for a cool hand—O, such a pretty hand!—to smooth my brow, and the touch of a pair of soft lips—but alas, I must long in vain...

Sweet words, that had once made her weep; now her eyes remained dry. Had he meant any of the loving things he had written—or was it all a show, to conceal the absence of any real feeling? She could not say. All she knew was that sitting down to write prettily of cool hands and soft lips to one woman, after sweating through the act of darkness with another, was behaviour unworthy of the man she had known. Perhaps, after all, she had not known him.

She put away the letters, when she heard the voices on the stairs: Rejoice's low cajoling accents and the musical prattling of the little one.

'Look at this big girl!' cried Rejoice, as the infant toddled in. 'This big girl has eaten a nice ripe mango for her tea!'

'She had better not get a taste for mangoes,' Laura replied with a smile. 'For there will be none, where we are going.'

And as the child put up its face to be kissed, she felt, as she had done more and more since the little creature had come to live with them, that lightening of the spirits which only such contact could bring.

If all else was dust and ashes, this was gold.

Chapter 23

Septimus, April 1880: Cape Town

In the event, it was a few days before he saw her again—his own affairs having proved unexpectedly pressing. The day after his little adventure with Laura Brooke, he had received a cable from McClintock, instructing him to conclude his business in Cape Town with the greatest despatch, and make his way to Kabul, where, as McClintock put it, things were 'growing very warm indeed'.

So he'd got his posting to Afghanistan at last. The elation he might have felt at this longed-for development was less than it might have been. The knowledge that, in gaining one prize, he might have to give up another, was a torment to him.

If he were to speak, it must be soon, for she would be leaving in a week. There could be no further prevarication—he must tell her what was in his heart.

'Dear Miss Brooke,' he wrote.

—or may I call you Laura? It seems to me that our relations of late have been such that I might do so without appearing 'fresh', as we Americans say. But let that pass...What I have to say to you has nothing to do with matters of form, and everything to do with matters of the heart.

Simply: I love you and want you to be my wife.

There! It is abruptly said—but I was never one for mincing words, where my emotions are concerned. You will laugh, I am sure (I can almost see the quizzical expression upon your face). You will say, 'But he is a journalist—what else does he do all day but mince, chop—and indeed, fricassee—the English language? How then should he find himself so much at a loss, where a simple matter of 'yes' or 'no' is at stake?'

For that is what it comes down to, I guess: my fate, in your hands. Your answer—one word, no more—will decide everything.

Forgive me if I sound excitable, or strange. I have not slept these past nights, for thinking of what might (or might not) be.

But that is for you to determine.

I am at the above address until Sunday week. After that, I am bound for India, and thence to Kabul.

I guess I should have said more about my prospects, and about the kind of life I would be able to offer you, were you to accept my poor proposal... But that is for another conversation; you are not, I dare to hope, a woman for whom considerations of wealth or 'position' count for much.

I mean, that you will take me as I am—or not, as the case may be.

I remain,

Your very faithful servant,

P. Septimus Doyle

Turning down Adderley Street, on his way to the hotel, he heard his name called. From the window of the hansom that just then pulled up at the kerb, a white arm, in a satin glove, was extended. An elegant head in a plumed hat appeared. A veil was lifted. 'It is you. Why, you are quite a stranger, these days!' said Cora De Villiers. 'I heard you were in town. But you have not been to see me.'

He made some excuse—a poor one, to judge from her expression.

'Never mind that.' She cut short his muttered apology. 'I am glad to have met you at last, for I have a great deal to tell you.' She opened the carriage door, and patted the seat beside her. 'Come.' Seeing his hesitation, she said, with a dangerous glint in her eye that he knew well. 'Surely you are not frightened of being seen with me? Is my reputation then so bad?'

He had no choice but to comply with her wish; although he

would have given anything not to be sitting there, on display as Cora De Villiers's latest boy, for all the world to see. Idling away the time with his former mistress—which would once, not so long ago, have struck him as delightful—now filled him with a mixture of impatience and ennui.

She must have divined something of his mood, for her expression grew sullen. No sooner had he taken his seat, than she flung the window up with a disgruntled air, and rapped on the roof of the cab to tell the driver to go on.

'Well,' she said, throwing him a penetrating glance from her black eyes. 'You are quite the 'masher', these days. Africa evidently becomes you. Although I must say, it has not improved your manners. You have not troubled to enquire after my health, I notice. But it is of no consequence.'

Here Mrs De Villiers leant towards him with a confidential air. He could smell her violet-scented breath; see the slight softening and puckering of the skin beneath her jaw. 'I have some news that might be of interest to you, however.' She smiled—the smile of one who delights in cruelty—and at once he knew of whom she was about to speak.

'I wonder,' Mrs De Villiers said, 'if you are aware of what has become of your particular favourite—the inestimable Laura Brooke? She is in Cape Town, you know—but I am afraid you will find her dreadfully altered. Why, my dear, she has cut off all her hair! As for her face, it is grown quite coarse and brown.'

'I have seen Miss Brooke,' he managed to interject. 'I thought she was looking remarkably fine.'

'Did you indeed? Well, there is no accounting for tastes, I suppose. Did you know that your wonderful Miss Brooke has acquired a child? Some half-caste brat. Ada Vermeulen saw them out together in the Botanical Gardens. Your Laura Brooke, and her black maid (for she has got herself a maid at last). Walking around as cool as you please, with the child between 'em...'

Once unleashed, her spite had no limits. He wondered how he could ever have thought her beautiful.

'Ada assumed, as one would, that the child must be the maid's (although why one would bring one's maid's child to a public park I cannot imagine). She was quite taken with the infant (Ada can be an awful fool). Was it Polly's (or Sally's or Dolly's) she wanted to know. To which your Miss Brooke said no. 'This is my daughter,' she said. Can you believe that? 'My daughter.' The woman must have lost her wits. Not that she isn't 'cute enough, when she wants to be, from what I've heard...'

They had reached the junction with Strand Street at last. Septimus shouted to the driver to stop. He would hear no more of this. But as he went to get out, Mrs De Villiers delivered her parting shot: 'They say she is to have half Emiline Reynolds's fortune, sly little thing. How she managed it is anybody's guess. The son will have something to say about that! But then, she always was a 'deep' one, your Miss Brooke.'

When he reached the hotel, the concierge was unable to say whether Miss Brooke was at home, or not. 'They go out, they come in,' she said, with a shrug. Septimus hesitated a moment. He had intended to leave the letter at the desk; but the idea that, through some misadventure—or wilful intransigence on the part of this fat slattern—it might fail to reach its destination, gave him pause. He would, at least, deliver the note into her maid's keeping, he decided.

'Can you at least tell me where Miss Brooke's rooms are to be found?'

'Second floor,' was the grudging reply. 'Third door on the left.'

With beating heart, he climbed the stairs. If there was no one in, he would slide the letter under the door... He rang the bell, and waited, suddenly overcome with foolish nerves. A minute—two—went by, and he began to feel a kind of relief, mingled with disappointment that he was not, after all, to see her.

As he went to draw the letter from his pocket, the door opened.

'Why, Mr Doyle!' Her face was flushed. 'I thought I heard the bell, but then I thought, 'no one knows we are here'...'

'Except me.'

'Except you, of course. Do please come in. Although I am afraid we are at sixes and sevens here...'

She was in the throes of packing, it transpired. The maid, Rejoice, had taken the child for a walk—'So that I can get on,' said

Laura Brooke, with a smile. 'Because she will get into all the boxes, you know, as children do.'

He thought that she looked no more than a child herself, with her face covered in smuts, and her shorn hair starting to curl.

'What a fright I am,' she murmured, wiping her hands on her brown Holland wrapper. She swept a pile of newspapers off a chair onto the floor. 'Won't you sit down?' she said. 'I could ring for some tea. Would you care for tea?'

He replied that he would not.

'What I have to say won't take long,' he said. 'I ask only that you hear me out.'

Her silence gave him leave to continue. He drew a breath.

'I have loved you from the moment I saw you,' he said.

'Mr Doyle...'

'Please. Let me speak. I don't ask for more than that.'

She lifted her chin in a gesture of assent.

'I know that there's little chance you could care for me.'

Her face was expressionless. He might have been talking of the weather.

'But if you ever felt that you could find it in your heart to do so...'

'I do not think that that will ever be the case,' she said, with a look that softened the harshness of the words. 'I am sorry if I have ever given you cause to suppose otherwise.'

He saw that she was not as perfectly in command of herself as she had appeared to be. 'I hope you will not think me cruel,' she said, in a voice that trembled slightly. 'I have liked you too well for that.'

She must have seen the sudden flaring of hope in his eyes, for she said quickly, 'I shall never marry. I do not think that it is my destiny to do so.'

'You say that now,' he protested, 'But in a year or so, you might reconsider...'

She shook her head. 'I shall never marry,' she said again. 'And there is the child to think of now...'

'Oh, if that's all that's holding you back,' he said, with the feeling of clutching at straws, 'you know it makes no difference to me. I mean that I'd be happy to...' His gesture, intended to convey his willingness to embrace whatever she might ask of him, seemed rather one of helplessness.

'You are very good,' she said softly. 'But my answer is still the same.'

'Very well.' His sensations were as if he had suffered a physical blow: he felt winded, and on the verge of unmanly tears.

'I am sorry,' she said again. 'I hope, at least, we will meet in London...'

'I will not be going back to London,' he said, realising it was true. 'I am summoned to Afghanistan, to report on the fighting there. War, you know, being rather my 'game'.' He gave a mirthless grimace. 'After that, I don't know. I may perhaps go back to America. For there is nothing in England for me now,' he could not resist adding.

'I hope, whatever happens, you will still think of me as your friend,' she said in a low voice.

'As to that,' he said bitterly, 'it is really too soon to say.' He saw her flinch, and was glad. 'There's one more thing,' he added. 'Give me your hand.' From an inside pocket he withdrew the diamond, and dropped it into her open palm. 'I'd hoped you might wear it as a ring,' he said. 'Now... I can't say. You must do with it as you like.'

'I cannot accept this.' She gazed at the stone, almost with horror, it seemed.

'It's yours. I don't want it. Come,' he said, with an attempt at levity. 'You've refused my heart. At least accept this poor substitute.'

Returning to his lodgings, he sat for a long time looking at the fire. He had several invitations for that evening, but felt a curious disinclination to take up any of them. Outside the window, the sky darkened and the lamps were lit—and still he sat, as if turned to stone. In his mind, he went over what had passed between them. 'I shall never marry,' she had said. With what an air of bleakness she had spoken! It was as if she had seen her Fate written, and was resigned to it.

He drew the letter from his pocket, and read it through, wincing a little at some of its more facetious phrases. What a vain fool he had been, to suppose that he could ever have made her happy... With a sound that was more like a sob than a laugh, he threw the letter into the grate. The fire, which had been moribund, flared up at this introduction of fresh fuel, and was soon blazing merrily.

He watched, as first the edges of the paper caught; then the middle, until the whole was a sheet of flame, against which his words, ill-chosen and futile though they had turned out to be, enjoyed a brief incandescence.

my fate, in your hands...

When nothing was left but ashes, he rose and began, mechanically, to dress.

Chapter 24

Laura, May 1880: Table Bay

Rejoice had gone below, to start unpacking; although Laura had urged her to remain on deck. In less than an hour, they would set sail. This might be her last sight of her native land. But when she said as much to the girl, Rejoice had merely shrugged. This was not her country, she said. She had left her country a long time ago.

As she walked away, the child, Dora, began to weep—soundlessly at first; then becoming louder. In the days since her removal from her foster-mother's house, she had become very attached to Rejoice. Now she seemed reluctant to be parted from her. Of Laura she was more wary.

But she suffered herself to be lifted, and allowed Laura to dry her eyes. Then, her brief access of grief ending as quickly as it had begun, she put her two middle fingers into her mouth, and gazed with every appearance of interest at the big ships being pointed out to her.

With her large blue eyes and brown skin she was quite beautiful, Laura thought. She seemed also to have inherited—although from which of her parents it was impossible to say for certain—a quick intelligence, and an amiable disposition. Added to which advantages was the fact that she would never be poor.

With the child in her arms, Laura stood at the rail, looking back over the bay, towards the city. Above its low white buildings, rose the great fortress of the mountain, an impenetrable wall between all that was the past, and whatever the future would bring. That morning there had been blood on the sheet when she woke; the relief she had felt had been tempered by a feeling which could only be described as disappointment.

Now she would never know what it was to bear a child of her own.

An image of Jacob De Kuiper's face, the last time she had seen it, flitted across her mind. It had been at Pietermaritzburg, a month ago, when he had delivered her into Major Austen's care. They had not shaken hands, but he had looked at her as he made his halting farewell: a long look, which said everything that there was to say.

She felt no remorse about the episode. It seemed to belong to another life—one she had left behind, as a serpent sheds its skin. Whatever impulse had compelled her to seek him out that night—whether from a need to be comforted, or from some more questionable desire—had now been satisfied. She would not succumb to such weakness again.

Towards Septimus Doyle her feelings were more ambivalent. She had liked him—more than liked him, if truth were told. What faults he had were only those that all men had. If circumstances had been different, they might well have married—but they were not. He had said that he loved her, but he did not know her. Had he known how dead she was to every human feeling, he would have recoiled in horror.

The light was beautiful—clear and golden, with the sun about to set. The gentlest of breezes rippled the surface of the water. On the quayside, people had gathered: some out of idle curiosity, or a simple delight in seeing a ship cast anchor; others because they were taking leave of someone on board. She thought she saw the American amongst them—although it was too far away for her to be sure. She waved her hand, in case it was him, and encouraged the child to do the same. No answering wave came back; and when she looked again, the figure had gone.

Lightning Source UK Ltd.
Milton Keynes UK
10 May 2010

153997UK00001B/6/P